Running

on Empty

L. B. Simmons

Running on Empty

Copyright © 2012 by L. B. Simmons

Cover by Okay Creations (www.okaycreations.net)
Edited by Jennifer Roberts-Hall
Formatting by JT Formatting

ISBN-13: 978-1481901901
IBSN-10: 1481901907

For My Beautiful Daughters –

My darling girls,
As with everything I do, there is always a lesson. Even when I write. But just in case you miss it, I'll give you the shortened version. Life is too precious and too short to safeguard yourself from hurt. Be willing to experience all life has to offer. To weather the ups and downs as you face them. Take the good with the bad. Because no matter the *collar roaster* ride life hands to you, you should hold on tight and enjoy the ride. Make the most of it. It's the only way to ensure you have no regrets.
Remember your stories.
Remember your childhood.
And remember that I will always love you and you will always be my babies. Even when you're *fifty* years old.

CHAPTER ONE

"What the *hell*?" I mutter to myself, eyeing my reflection. I scoot closer to the mirror, practically sitting on the counter, and inch my way forward to get a better look at what exactly is going on with my hair. My dark brown hair is damp, falling in wavy layers to my shoulders. This is normal. What's not normal is this one little area that's just not cooperating. I tug at the one inch section of my long hair that will not lie down. It's just sticking up, straight in the air, mocking me. Pulling on it, I notice that there's a thick white film covering the entire section. And it's sticky. *Great.*

I wipe my fingers on my old fluffy pink bathrobe and continue examining my hair in the mirror. This is *not* right. I know I just put a new product in my hair, but it's supposed to make it soft and shiny like the gorgeous model on the commercial, not stick up like a ten year old boy with a cow lick. I grab the nearest brush, *My Little Pony – of course*, and attempt to tame this bastard.

"This is freakin' ridiculous," I say out loud as the brush catches when I try to pass it through my hair. I yank the brush as hard as I can and literally cringe in pain. I think I just pulled the entire section of hair out of my head. When the brush finally makes its way down the rest of my long hair, I catch a whiff.

"Mint?" I set the brush on the counter and reach for the

1

serum I just put in my hair. I put my nose to the end of the pump. "Hmm, not mint." I pick up the damp towel that just came off of my head and wet the end under the faucet in an attempt to get rid of whatever this mystery goop is in my hair. That's when I finally see the culprit.

"You have *got* to be kidding me!" I suddenly want to rip every single strand of hair out of my head in frustration. I do *not* want to deal with this mess this morning. I just want an easy morning. When do I get to have an easy morning?

"Kyndall!" I yell from the bathroom, echoes bouncing off each wall, slamming mercilessly back onto my skull. It hurts my head. Or, maybe that's just the residual pain from the recent hair assault I inflicted upon myself. I wait a couple of seconds…no response.

Hmm, this must mean that the TV which is *not* supposed to be on, *is* on.

"Kyndall!" I shout again, this time stomping my foot for added emphasis. I know she's the only one who can be responsible for this mess. Not only because her older sister wouldn't dare, or because her younger sister can't reach the sink, but because this sort of situation…well – it's just Kyndall. Like the time I found three days worth of my home cooked meals "hidden" in one of my decorative baskets in the kitchen. The brief stint at vegetarianism didn't last long, but it would have been nice if she would've at least told me about it. Lots of ground beef was wasted and I have a lot of boxed meals that require it.

Sighing loudly, I start to step out of the bathroom when I hear the steps of my lovely seven year old daughter getting closer. I watch her pink tutu skirt bounce up and down as she skips happily down the hallway.

"Yes, Mama?" Oh, so innocent.

"Baby? Can you tell me what's going on with the towel here? Can you tell me what this stuff is?" I bend down and hold the towel right in front of her face so she can see the blue goop to which I am referring.

I watch her eyebrows come together as a result of her full force concentration. "Um, toothpaste?"

"Yes, toothpaste. Can you tell me *why* there's a big glob of it in the middle of my towel?"

"Well..." she pauses briefly and widens her eyes, obviously frustrated that I haven't figured it out on my own. "It was all hard when I tried to squeeze the tube to get more toothpaste out, so I did what you told me to do last time. I wiped off all the extra toothpaste from the top and started over."

So I guess, in essence, I have done this to myself.

Okay...

"Kyndall, sweetheart. I used a paper towel...not a towel, towel. We don't use regular towels for that kind of stuff."

Kyndall looks down at the towel and back up at me. "I'm sorry, Mama. I was just trying to do it myself."

I can't help but cave when I look at her beautiful blue-grey eyes. I just don't know how this sweet child always manages to get herself, or me for that matter, into these unfortunate situations. I let out a sigh.

"It's alright, Kyndall. Let's just forget the use of *any* kind of towel. How about when it happens next time, you just rinse the top of the toothpaste under warm water to get the hard stuff off? Easy enough?"

"Yes ma'am." She reaches up to touch the toothpaste infested section of my hair. "Eww – that's sticky!" I lift my eyebrows, asking her if she really wants to reopen the argument. She drops her hand immediately. I assume that's a no.

I let out another deep breath. "Okay. Now, where are Nycole and Rylie?"

"They're watching cartoons in the living room."

Ah-ha! I knew it!

"Can you run and tell them to hurry and eat because we need to load up to leave in about five minutes or we're going to be late to school?"

"Sure."

"Thanks, baby."

"Mama?"

"Yes, ma'am?"

"I love you infinity."

"I love you infinity times infinity."

I give her a quick kiss on the cheek. I turn her little body toward the door and give her a light shove. "Now go tell your sisters!" I joke and smack her little behind. She laughs and skips down the hall. I watch her thick shoulder length brown hair bouncing up and down with a smile on my face. Turning back towards the mirror, my smile dissipates.

I look at my tired eyes and pale face. I pull the skin down under my eyes to examine the red blood vessels that seem to have taken over. I think I used to be pretty, at some point…but that seems so long ago. Lately, I'm the frumpy mom that I always told myself I'd *never* become. I mean sure, I dress decently enough for work. But I just look (and feel) so tired. Run down.

I don't generally wear a lot of make-up, so the fact that I have long dark eyelashes helps. But my big brown eyes that used to look so alive with excitement and joy have been replaced with sad, tired, mournful eyes. And my hair? Let's just say I support the ponytail look wholeheartedly.

I turn my attention back to my hair. Seriously, what am I supposed to do with this mess in five minutes? *Hmm...ponytail it is.* I sigh to myself as I think about how lovely it would be to actually *have* time to do my hair in the morning, to style it with something other than a hair band. I mean, having an actual style would be nice. But, to be able to take the time to style it, well, that would be beyond comprehension..

I would be unrecognizable at work. I would walk in to the office and it would be like one of those hair commercials; wind in my hair, hot guy gazing at me adoringly because I have beautiful *styled* hair. I would flip my hair in slow motion...

"Mama! Rylie's picking her nose again!" I hear loud shrieks as the girls start running around the living room. "Eww! Mom! She keeps acting like she's gonna wipe it on us! Help!"

Snapping out of my reverie, I quickly throw my thick brown hair back into its usual lame ass pony tail, trying to not think about the section of my hair that's starting to bubble up. The same section of hair that is slowly forming a crusty top layer as the toothpaste begins to dry.

Oh well, I think to myself, turning on the sink and throwing some water on it to make myself feel better. Who knows, maybe I'll get lucky. Maybe the water has some magical mysterious element to dissolve the toothpaste. Giving myself one last look of disapproval, I dart quickly from the bathroom. I round the corner and enter the living room, finding all three of my beauties sitting quietly on the couch.

I guess the nose picking fiasco has ceased.

Nycole, my oldest, appears to be frozen in time; her spoon has only made it halfway to her mouth and seems to be stuck there. Brown curly hair perfectly braided, headband in and big brown eyes glued on the TV.

"Nyc." Nothing.

"Nyc." I clap my hands. Still nothing. Oh my God. *She's in the TV.*

"Nyc!" I shout, giving it one last try. She jumps in response, milk and cereal immediately spilling onto her neatly pressed plaid skirt. She shoots me a glare. I shoot her one back because honestly, that's just uncalled for. I walk over and turn off the TV.

"I'm pretty sure I told you guys no TV. None of you have even remotely touched your breakfast, and now we have to go." They all look down at their full cereal bowls with huge, longing eyes.

"Sorry," I say, shaking my head in disbelief. "In the sink girls, come on...we've got to get going. We're already running late." I watch as they slowly get up from the couch and make their way to the kitchen.

"I told you not to turn it on, Kyndall. Now I don't get my breakfast. Way to go."

"Yeah, Kyndall. Nycole told you."

I stand there, arms crossed over my chest, waiting for them to make their way back to the living room. My eyes land on Nycole as soon as she enters.

"If you knew it wasn't supposed to be on, then why didn't *you* turn it off, Nycole? Lead by example. Don't just place blame. You're nine years old and fully capable of operating the TV – I know you can because I've seen you do it. You know better." I end my statement with a raise of my eyebrows.

"Yeah, but–"

"Nope. No excuses."

"But–"

"Nyc ." I'm fully anticipating another rebuttal, but evidently she gets the point and stomps off. I guess she wants to make her point too. *Noted.*

I turn my eyes to Kyndall. "Kyndall. You know better too, don't you?"

I watch as her eyes swell with tears. "Yes, but, I just wanted Rylie to be quiet. She kept copying everything I was saying. Everything Mama. She wouldn't stop. It was the only thing I could do to get her to be quiet. I'm sorry." She looks down at the floor. I walk over and raise her chin so she looks at me. "I know it's hard, but next time, just come get me. I can take care of her, that's *my* job. You just come to me when she keeps doing stuff like that."

I wipe a tear from her cheek with my thumb. "I'm not mad sweetheart, okay? Just go wait by the door. I'll be there in a second." I give her shoulder a quick squeeze. She offers me a slight smile in return and makes her way to the front door.

I turn my attention to the hellion of the group. I watch her while she attempts to do the robot. She flashes me her trademark dimples, no doubt trying to diffuse the situation. Her long spiral curly hair falls forward along with her head, dance clearly over. Right arm extended and bent at the elbow, she ends with a perfectly performed "hinge move", her forearm still swinging back and forth. I stand there until she looks back up at me from underneath her mile long lashes, trying to wipe any evidence of a smile off of my face.

"Rylie, what did I say about copying your sisters?"

She giggles and responds with, *"Rylie, what did I say about copying your sisters?"*

I close my eyes and count to ten.

"Rylie?"

"Rylie?"

"Seriously, stop it."

"Seriously, stop it."

"I stink."

"You stink." Damn it.

I attempt to use the only weapon I have at the moment. Silence.

I quickly scoop her up by her waist, wrapping her underneath my arm, and make a mad dash to the kitchen. She giggles hysterically. I could tell her I'm not trying to be funny, but I really hate the copying game, so I don't.

I manage to scoop up the three backpacks and my laptop case from the kitchen table with my other arm, *because I'm super mom,* and make my way to meet Nycole and Kyndall at the door. I set Rylie down gently. They all laugh with each other and I take a brief moment to look at my girls.

My girls; the loves of my life. Now the *only* loves of my life and I'm content with that. This is my life and I accept it 100%. Sure, I would have chosen differently if I'd been given the chance, but it's my responsibility to teach these girls to make the most of what life has handed them. If I had just given up the day our Derek had been taken from this earth…where would we be now? No, I have to be strong for all of us.

Sure, some days are harder than others. I have breakdowns every now and then, but I think that's normal. And I try to shield the girls as much as I can from moments when mommy's feeling a bit "down". But these girls...they mean more to me than my own life. I'll do everything in my power to keep them from being hurt ever again. *That* is what defines me. I already had my happiness and I live for them now. I'm okay with that.

Getting back to my already hectic morning, I take in a calming breath through my nose before opening the door. I hand the girls their lunches and back packs before herding them out of the house. While walking to the car in a single file line, Rylie (who's unfortunately walking in front of me) insists on stopping randomly every few seconds.

Bug on the ground. "Mommy, look!" She stops. I trip.

New flower identified in the yard. "Oh, smell this Mommy." She stops. I trip.

Half-eaten tootsie roll in the driveway. "We don't eat candy on the ground, right Mommy?" She stops. I trip.

Chewed up gum that Nycole spit out yesterday. *Didn't I ask her to pick that up and put it in the trash?* "Um...Nycole didn't listen to you! I listen to you, Mommy." Rylie stops. I stop. And glare at Nycole.

I patiently stare; so intently, that I can actually see the synapse fire in her brain. Nycole walks over, picks up the gum, holds it as far away from her body as she can, and throws it in the outside trash can.

"Thanks, Nyc." I try to keep a straight face as she wipes her hands on her shirt. I mean, the gum did come out of her mouth; I'm not sure what the big deal is. I watch as she grabs the hand sanitizer out of her back pack and that does me in. I can't contain my snickering any longer.

"Seriously, Nyc. Is it that big of a deal? It's just a piece of gum…that came out of *your* mouth."

"Mom, I can't believe you made me do that. It's been sitting in this nasty driveway since yesterday. That's just gross."

"Well…you could have thrown it away yesterday, like I asked you to do. Maybe next time, you won't ignore me when I ask you to do something. " I throw open the back of my Suburban and hurl my laptop case in, closing it just as quickly as it was opened. "Let's not do the drama queen thing this morning. I'd love to have just one morning where we all get al–"

"Kyndall! I called seat check!" Nycole yells while Kyndall snatches the seatbelt and quickly buckles herself in, excited grin on her face the entire time. Just *one* morning is all I ask. Just one morning where we can make it to the car with no major catastrophes or ridiculous arguments.

"Nyc…just take another seat, *please*. We don't have time for this." I step up onto the side rail and reach over Rylie to buckle her in. Right after I hear the click of the seatbelt, I find myself grabbing at the arm of Rylie's booster seat for my life while my feet slip out from underneath me. I wince in pain as both of my shins scrape against the rail, from my ankles to my knees, until my feet finally reach the ground.

Note to Self: Buy some heels with better traction. Or sandpaper.

"Shit! Shit, shit, shit!" I yell, jumping around from the immense pain radiating from my lower legs. I can feel them pulsating and the pain makes my eyes water.

"Mom!"

"Mama, are you okay?"

"Um…Mommy said shit! Shit, shit, shit!"

I immediately stop jumping and turn to look at the girls. All of them have their mouths wide open, watching my very mature reaction to what just happened. Great. I'm sure Rylie's school will be calling me later today with the wonderful news that she has taught all of her classmates to say shit. Just. Freakin'. Wonderful.

"Rylie – we don't say shit. Don't. Say. Shit. Do you understand me?" Rylie nods her head, but smiles as though she has no intention of listening to me. I point my finger at her. "Don't say it, Rylie. I'm serious!" I watch her big brown eyes glance over at her sisters, mischievous grin still intact.

I look over and see Nycole and Kyndall covering their mouths and giggling as they watch our interaction. They're definitely not helping this situation any. And, although I really want to laugh with them, I can't. I know it will only encourage her, so I force the giggle back down my throat and address the other two. I can feel my mouth start to turn upwards, but I try to keep my face straight. I'm pretty sure it's not working, judging by Rylie's smile. I turn my eyes to the other girls in a last ditch effort to remedy the situation.

"Sorry guys. I should've handled that better. Can we just forget that any of this happened?" I look at them with pleading eyes. I watch a sly smile slowly spread across Nycole's face.

"I don't know, Mom. I think you should have to buy us something. You know, to keep us quiet." She throws in an exaggerated wink to make sure I get her point.

"Nyc, have you lost your ever livin' mind? You know I don't do things like that!" I look at all of them with my serious mom face and then I can't help but let out a chuckle, pain long forgotten. I roll my eyes in defeat. "Oh, alright…One thing at the gas station and that's it! Got it?"

They all squeal at once. "Yay! Love you, Mommy!"

I sigh. "I love you too, girls. More than you know."

Sitting behind the steering wheel, I let out a long, deep breath. *Gas or no gas…that is the question.* I was just at the freakin' gas station! I can't believe I didn't notice this sooner. Actually, now that I think about it, the low fuel level warning *has* been chirping at me for a couple of days now.

Looking at the needle, I contemplate whether or not I can make the twelve mile drive from Rylie's daycare to my office without stopping for gas. 7:58 AM. It's not like I'm actually worried that Harlow will be pissed that I'm late…again. It just makes it easier to rationalize my decision to not get gas. I'm pretty sure there's a reserve gas tank built into these things, right? For procrastinators like me? Unless I'm already dipping into the reserve tank, which would prove to be rather unfortunate.

Shifting into drive, I inhale deeply and turn right to jump onto the interstate. I lose myself in my thoughts, thinking about this morning and how the chaos continued full force. After the gas station, where none of my children picked anything remotely healthy as their replacement breakfast, Nycole and Kyndall found themselves in a very heated discussion about whether or not one of Nycole's friends actually had Justin Bieber's phone number. A discussion that ended with high pitched screaming that I swear could have broken the sound barrier, and quite possibly my windows, but I had to side with Kyndall on this one.

Finally ridding my car of the feminine theatrics, I drove Rylie to her daycare. A bad habit I've developed is brushing her teeth while in the car at the parking lot of her school. A bad habit she's developed is literally aiming her sneezes at people. Both habits rolled into one? Well, that equaled another ill-fated incident involving toothpaste. Rylie laughed heartily at my expense after she aimed her toothpaste filled sneeze spray at my black shirt. I think my girls have decided to gang up on me using toothpaste as their 'modus operandi'. Seriously. With a toothpaste-splattered poplin top, I carried my four year old baby girl (who was still laughing by the way) into her classroom, quickly kissed her goodbye, and jetted out of there before she could use me as her latest show and tell demonstration.

I noticed the familiar warning regarding my gas level when I got back into my car. I guess I didn't hear it earlier this morning over my lovely children yelling and screaming at each other. Days like this, I really miss Derek. He always made sure I had enough gas to make the morning rounds. He absolutely hated when I had to get gas by myself and made every effort to make sure I never had to. After three years, you'd think I would have managed to not depend on my husband to still do certain things for me. Yet, three years later, here I am, once again on empty.

And now I find myself driving down I-35, becoming increasingly nervous that I made the *wrong* decision. I push my foot down on the gas pedal to pass some poor old couple that evidently started driving when the Model T came out, when…nothing. My car starts slowing and as I push down on the pedal, I realize that I have indeed made the wrong decision. My car has stalled. I pull over to the side of the interstate and throw my car into park.

"Seriously? Can *anything* go right today? Harlow's going to freakin' kill me!" Ten minutes late is still within Harlow's "not going to kick ass" window, but I have a sneaking suspicion that this is going to throw me into some unknown realm of Harlow fury.

I pull out my cell phone and punch in the number to our office.

"Prestige Staffing, Harlow Reed speaking." She sounds flustered already, so I'm definitely not looking forward to this conversation.

"Um, Harlow…it's Alex."

"What's up love? Are you on your way? We have that interview with the potential candidate for Synergy Accounting in, like, twenty minutes. So please, tell me you're on your way."

Not really sure how to break this to her, I opt to remain quiet while she figures it out herself.

Three… two… one…

"Tell me you're on your way, Alex! I can't do this one

on my own. We both need to be here to make the decision. This one's too big for only my opinion. It's a freaking senior executive potential hire, Alex!"

Okay, Harlow's usually a little high strung, but this is a little out of the norm…even for her. *Odd.* Maybe the pressure has finally gotten to her.

You see, Harlow and I started our own staffing firm right out of college – Prestige Staffing. We started our own business so that we could smoke in our office all day long, consume adult beverages during work hours, and do nothing but giggle and gossip all day. However, we both eventually quit smoking, quickly figured out that we were no good at *anything* while drinking and, since we couldn't get any business while intoxicated, we had absolutely nothing to giggle or gossip about. So, we decided to start taking our business seriously.

Currently, we're responsible for recruiting and interviewing potential hiring candidates for almost every company in Waco. Together, we can usually tell whether or not the person will be a good fit for the position before recommending them to the company for their own interviews. We have a proven track record, with over 95% of our referrals being placed with the companies. The commission on this potential candidate is HUGE. Yeah, Harlow's definitely pissed.

"Listen, I know you're upset–"

"*Upset?* Are you fucking kidding me? I. Am. Pissed!" Yes, just as I'd figured.

"Listen, I ran out of gas on I-35. See if you can stall him for half an hour. I'll flag down an 18-wheeler if I have to. I *will* be there. I've never let you down and I'm not going to start now. Just hold him there as long as you can, okay?"

"Okay, Alex. But hurry the hell up! I have no idea what to stall him with. We only have enough coffee for one pot and no breakfast because *you* were supposed to pick that stuff up this morning, remember? I can't stall him forever with my witty banter and mile long legs; there's only so long that the poor man can ogle me. Your ass better be here in thirty minutes. Get. Here. ASAP." I'm pretty sure I hear about three more F-bombs before catching dead air.

Oops. Maybe it's a good thing I ran out of gas because neither the coffee nor the donuts made it into my possession today. I *knew* there was an actual reason I went to that gas station this morning!

"I'll be there soon." I say to absolutely no one but myself.

I step out onto the interstate... well, the *side* of the interstate, and attempt to flag the first few motorists I see. No luck. Obviously I'm not the only person running extremely late for work this morning. Sighing out loud, I resign myself to the fact that I'm probably going to have to walk to the nearest station, which will definitely put me outside Harlow's thirty minute time requirement. Turning on my heel to start the trek, I hear the rumble of a motorcycle slowing down behind me.

I hesitantly turn around, using my hand to shield the sun from my eyes, to catch a glimpse of whatever scary biker man has decided to be my hero this morning. I fully expect to see an old man with a beer belly and bandana covered head; complete with B.O., missing teeth, and a sweat stained wife beater. *Like the hook-handed truck driver from Adventures in Babysitting!* I am, however, pleasantly surprised by the

16

delicious mirage that appears before me.

I watch the man lift his right leg over the bike and place it on the ground. Wow. This guy is huge and freakin' tall. But anything would be tall to me, considering my five foot frame.

I hear the slow clanking of the buckles on his boots as he starts to walk toward me. *Man, those are some freakin' masculine boots.* My eyes slowly graze upwards and I notice the worn look of his jeans; frayed a bit at the bottom, holes at the knee and snug at the hips. Do I dare keep going? Seriously, the temperature just raised 20°C out here. And this *is* Texas…in late August…

Not easily deterred, I do, in fact, keep going. His white v-neck t-shirt is stretched as far as it can go across his chest and biceps, falling a little more loosely over his stomach, while still managing to hug his hips. *OMG.* I'm totally not going to look any further; I can sense disappointment on the horizon.

Damn it. My eyes have a mind of their own as they keep wandering upward. I catch a glimpse of his light brown hair. It falls to his neck, with shorter layers everywhere, making the ends turn up slightly all over his head. It's a hot mess. I never knew what that term meant until this moment right now. It's perfectly messy. I wish my hair looked that good. I reach up and attempt to push down the bubbly toothpaste section of my hair. Okay, I'm actually starting to find this guy annoying.

I figure it's better to just look at his face and get it over with. Like ripping off a band aid, the quicker the better, right? Either it will be horrendous, which at this point I'd prefer because no one should be this perfect, or he'll be completely gorgeous and then I'll keel over and die right here of embarrassment. Either way, I'd like to just get this part over with.

I quickly glance to his face. I privately note his sculpted jaw, perfect nose, and his beautiful mouth, his perfectly kissable mouth. And his perfect teeth, all of which I can now see because as he's getting closer to me he's...laughing at me? *What the hell?*

I'm about to give this random man a piece of my mind when I happen to catch a glimpse of his eyes. I find them a vaguely familiar shade of green, a light olive green. I narrow my eyes, allowing myself to really look at him. I look at his eyes, then his face, then his hair, then his shirt, jeans and boots. Oh. My. God.

"Well, Blake Morgan. What the hell are you doing back in town?"

CHAPTER TWO

I watch him while he rakes his hand through his hair and shakes his head, chuckling to himself. Oddly enough, this seems to make his hair look even more perfect.

Internal eye roll.

"I really don't see what's so funny, Blake." I say his name in some weird new octave that I have never heard myself use. "I'm sure it's easy to laugh when it isn't *you* sitting on the side of the interstate at eight o'clock in the morning."

"Actually, Alex, I *am* sitting on the side of the interstate... at eight o'clock in the morning. I think that automatically gives me some allowance to laugh at the situation. However, that's not what I'm laughing at. What I'm actually laughing at is that I'm literally just driving in to this god-forsaken town when I see *you*, stranded on the side of the road and because I'm such a nice guy, I'm forced to stop and help. Fate tends to be cruel sometimes."

Um...ouch. And completely unnecessary. What the hell did I ever do to Blake Morgan? I mean, I haven't seen him since high school, so either I did something really massive back then that you'd think I'd remember based on his latent anger, or he's just a bonafide asshole. At this point, I'm leaning toward the latter.

I raise my hands in mock surrender. "Look, I didn't *ask*

you to stop so don't take it out on me that you're a nice guy, although I think your definition of nice might be a little skewed when compared to normal people's. If you don't want to help, then don't. I don't have time for this shit, Blake. I have to get to a gas station, get gas, get back here, get my car started, and get to work so that I can avoid being strangled by my business partner...all in about twenty minutes. So if you don't mind, please be on your way and find another damsel in distress so you can meet this nice guy quota that you must have to complete. It was wonderful to see you again, Blake. I hope to *not* see you around anytime soon."

I turn quickly and start double-timing it, in the opposite direction of Blake, toward the gas station. I would love to just take off running, but unfortunately Nike has yet to make a great pair of heels. Or any heels for that matter...

Note to Self: Write a letter to Nike regarding the need for athletically enhanced heels.

Directly behind me, I hear him get on his motorcycle and start the engine, revving it a couple of times for added dramatic effect. *Bonafide asshole, definitely.* I mean, what kind of man leaves a woman stranded on the side of the road? I feel a knot in my throat and my eyes begin to form tears, but I refuse to let Blake Morgan see me cry.

I'm not sure if it's the stress of the morning, or the fact that seeing Blake brings back all sorts of memories that I can't emotionally deal with right now, but I'm starting to feel that empty feeling in my chest that's never a good sign. I'm usually equipped with enough strength to keep all my emotions effectively buried throughout the day, and I mean *every* day, but I think the craziness of this morning has weakened my defenses. So I start walking faster in an effort to get out of the current situation as soon as possible.

I hear Blake's motorcycle growling as it pulls up next to me. I keep my eyes forward and walk faster.

"Get on!" I hear Blake yell over the sound of his engine.

I shake my head. "Um, no. Thanks." The Dory song from *Finding Nemo* keeps running through my mind…"Just keep walking, just keep walking, just keep walking, walking, walking…"

He continues coasting alongside me. "Get on the bike, Alex!!"

"Seriously, Blake, get on with your good deeds for the day! I. Am. Fine!" I yell back at him to make sure he hears me over his ridiculously loud motorcycle. I seriously think he's over compensating for some part of the male anatomy.

I start walking again and the sound of the engine ceases. I hear the familiar clanking rapidly approaching me from behind. Suddenly, I feel a hand grab my arm and I'm forcefully whipped around to find myself about two inches from Blake's irritatingly handsome face. We're so close that I can smell the mint on his breath as he speaks. It reminds me of how much I hate toothpaste.

"Alex, get your ass on this bike. I'll take you to your office. We can deal with your truck later. I can still get you there within the now," he pauses to look at his watch, "fifteen minute time frame to make sure you don't getting strangled by your business partner. Think about it. Is your pride more important than your business?"

I wiggle free from the vice grip holding my arm.

"Get on your bike? In this?" I move my hand, performing a perfectly executed Vanna White demonstration of the black and white striped pencil skirt I'm wearing. Does he not understand the simple design of the pencil skirt? There's no way in hell I'm going to be able to straddle that bike seat. And I'm pretty sure I can't side saddle it either, not with those pesky safety laws. Nope...there's absolutely *no way* I'm getting on that stupid ass bike. "Not gonna happen, buddy."

"Alex, if I have to pick you up, put you over my shoulder, and physically place you on my bike, I will. So yes, it's gonna happen. You can either do so with dignity, or we can do it my way. Your choice."

I stare at him with the best mommy death stare I can conjure up, and he holds it with no fear. *Shit*...this stuff always works with the girls. I'm now in a very unfamiliar territory. And unfortunately, it starts to seep into my brain that I have no more time to argue with him about this stupid situation if I want to keep both my business and my best friend.

"Fine!"

Blake breathes a sigh of relief and I notice his face slowly turning back to its normal color. He turns to walk back to his bike and I hesitantly follow him. He takes a helmet from the back compartment and hands it to me, then looks directly at the top of my head.

"Um…I think you have something in your hair." He makes a move to touch my toothpaste bubble and I knock his hand away, rather vehemently.

"It's a present from my daughter," I state with annoyance, slamming the helmet down onto my head. Not really knowing what to do with the strap, I attempt to buckle it under my chin. He in turn slaps my hand away from the strap, *the nerve of this guy*, and buckles it, tightening it until it fits perfectly. His fingers stall for a minute, grazing across my chin and as they do, I find myself looking him dead straight in the eyes. I do this for two reasons. One, to let him know that touching me is *not* okay. He must get this one pretty quick because he promptly removes his fingers from my chin. And two, as much as I hate to do it… "Thank you, Blake."

Blake looks at me for a brief second and I watch the left corner of his mouth slightly curve upward. He turns quickly and begins to fish his keys out of his pocket. When he turns back around, his face is completely void of any effect the last two seconds had on him. "Let's just get this over with."

For some reason, this sends a pang of hurt to my heart. What the hell is wrong with me? First the "almost" tears and now this…I need to get the hell out of here.

"I agree," I quickly bite back.

Approaching the bike, I mentally work through several different strategies for conquering the seating issue at hand. Landing on the most plausible, I know what I have to do. But, I need to make sure he's on his bike and facing forward for this to happen.

"Go ahead and get on," I tell Blake, gesturing with my hand towards his bike. Surprisingly, he does so with no gratuitous commenting. Once he's on the bike, I make sure his eyes are forward. I start to fold my skirt up until it hits middle of my thigh. I start to climb on, but there still isn't room for me to straddle the seat. *Shit.* I proceed with the next fold, and start to lift my leg over the bike. As I lower my body to take my seat...

"Woo-hoo!"

"Nice legs!"

"Ride *me*, baby!"

I hear horns, catcalls, and whistling as people pass us on the interstate. *Punks...*

I shudder with embarrassment, glad to have the helmet over my face. I'm sure it's turning crimson and the last thing I want Blake Morgan to see is my face beaming the exact shade of red it did when I received "the talk" from my parents. *So embarrassing.*

"Get to work assholes!" I yell back at them. I feel Blake's shoulders begin to shake from his laughter. "Shut *up*, Blake. Let's go!"

I tightly wrap my arms around his midsection; I'm actually glad that I'm so pissed off right now. Pissed off is my guarantee that my mind won't wander to places I don't want to deal with.

"Do you know where you're going?" I ask him, suddenly realizing we have yet to discuss the exact location of my office.

"Yeah, you bought Ms. Parnell's old office, right?"

"Er – yes. How did you know that?"

"My parents still live here, Alex. I know a lot of things."

With nothing left to say, he starts up his bike and we drive the whole way to my office in silence. Not that we really have a choice. You can't hear a damn thing riding a motorcycle, going what feels like one hundred miles per hour, with a helmet on.

Shortly after, we pull into the Prestige Staffing parking lot. After Blake gets off, I make him turn around so I can lift my leg over the seat. Once successfully completed, I make my move to get off this freakin' death trap on wheels. Setting my foot down on the gravel, my ankle rolls slightly.

Damn shoes again! I *really* need to get started on that letter to Nike.

I grab Blake's shirt to steady myself, immediately realizing my mistake. Once again, two inches from his face, I find myself momentarily lost.

Note to Self: Two inches away from Blake Morgan's face is some kind of equivalent to the Bermuda Triangle.

Immediately letting go, I start to take off the helmet and wince when it pulls some of the hairs out of the top of my head. Once the helmet is removed, I look down to see that some of the toothpaste has oozed off my head and found a new happy home in the top of Blake's helmet. I decide to keep this bit of information to myself.

Silently laughing at my secret, I pass the helmet back to Blake. I reach my hand up to feel that I now have long strands of hair sticking straight up from where the helmet pulled them out of my ponytail. I laugh again to myself, but this time it's more of an admission of defeat. Obviously my hair and I are in some sort of sick power struggle today.

Blake clears his throat – I think in an honest attempt not to laugh in my face – and turns his attention to cutting the engine. I finally roll down my skirt back to its original length, smoothing any wrinkles, when I look up to see Blake staring at me. I start to say something to end this wonderfully awkward moment, when the front door to the office opens and I hear Harlow yelling from the doorway.

"Eight twenty-nine, and with one minute to spare! Good thing for you the appointment wasn't really until nine o'clock," she says smiling at me, an ornery grin plastered on her face. She moves her eyes from me to focus on Blake. "Blake Morgan, is that you?" She flashes him her notorious "Harlow smile". "It's about time you got here. Took you long enough." Then, rather ominously, she slowly closes the door to leave me in an even *more* awkward moment. What the hell did that even mean? I shake my head in an attempt to clear it.

I turn my attention back to Blake. "Thanks again. Evidently, I made it with thirty-*one* minutes to spare. Sorry, I assumed my partner wouldn't use the 'change the time so you're actually on time' ploy while I was stranded on the side of the road fearing for my life."

Blake looks back at the front door of my office. "You're partners with Harlow Reed. I completely forgot about that," he snickers sarcastically.

"Um, yeah? Is that a problem?"

"No," he offers. "I'm just surprised you get anything done that's all." He puts his helmet on while still laughing. "See ya Alex."

He starts his engine and I watch him drive off.

Jerk.

I think of the toothpaste in his helmet, probably grasping the hairs on the top of his head right this very minute. *Yeah, well, who's laughing now?* I walk toward my office, ready to conquer the day. I look down at my empty hands. Oops.

I wonder if Harlow's figured out there will be no coffee or donuts until *after* our morning appointment?

CHAPTER THREE

Walking briskly into Harlow's office, I shut the door behind me. "What the hell *was* that out there?" I once again attempt the mommy death stare.

"What the hell is *that* right there?" she counters quickly, biting back a laugh. She points at my head. "Seriously, Alex, you never cease to amaze me. What are we calling this morning's hair creation? This has got to be one of the worst hair days you've had in the last, um, what? Thirty days?" Seriously, the death stare needs an upgrade...mommy death stare 2.0 maybe.

"Shut your yapper, Harlow. With the morning I've already had, you're treading on very thin ice, so watch yourself," I say, shoving my pointer finger in her face. "What the hell was that outside with Blake? Took you long enough? That was really creepy...even for you. Like...wooo-wooo, psychic lady from *Poltergeist* creepy," I say, waving my hands around mimicking a ghost. "What *was* that?"

"You don't need to be worrying about what I'm doing. What you need to be worrying about is that freaking bird's nest you've got going on up there. Complete with bird poop I see." She reaches up to touch my hair, makes a face, and wipes her fingers on her Ann Taylor pleated trouser pants. "Gross, Alex. Seriously, go fix your hair. We have this interview in 'T' minus twenty minutes. Please, go make yourself presentable. This is a big fish and we need the commission."

Rolling my eyes at her, I reach for the purse that's always draped across my body and resides permanently on my hip. Well, the purse that *usually* resides on my hip. What the–

"Oh my God. Oh my God. Oh. My. God! Harlow...I left my purse in the Suburban...I left *everything* in the Suburban! Including my laptop." I start to feel as though I'm hyperventilating. "I don't think I even locked the door. Oh my God, Harlow...what am I going to do?"

Harlow walks over and places both hands on my shoulders. "Alex, calm down. Breathe. Everything is going to be fine. Look, I have some basic toiletries in the bathroom, you know, for when I have the occasional overnighter." She wiggles her eyebrows at me. My face pinches in disgust and I shake my head, trying to clear the God-awful image. *Too much information...*

"Everything you need should be under the sink. Go, fix yourself. We'll do the interview and then we'll go take care of the truck. No worries. It'll be fine." She pivots me toward the bathroom and shoves me with just a little too much oomph.

I turn to argue but I'm given what she has evidently developed as her own Harlow death stare. "GO!"

I sigh loudly so she can note my protest and stomp into the bathroom. I turn on the light and can do nothing but stare at the reflection looking back at me.

Get a grip, Alex.

I pull the hair band from the back of my hair and shake my head until my brown hair falls across my shoulders.

Turning on the sink, I wet the top of my head and grab the hand towel from the rack. Scrubbing until I feel my hair is finally toothpaste free, I brush it out, only to place it back in a low, yet professional, pony tail. I use the flat iron to take care of any frizz that was added by Blake's helmet, making the back of the pony tail as smooth as I can get it.

I can't believe Harlow keeps a flat iron here. I open the doors to the cabinet under the sink. I take note of the toothbrush, toothpaste, make-up bag, eye-makeup remover, hairspray…all under the counter. Man, she keeps a lot of stuff in here. How many overnighters does this woman have?

Note to Self: I should totally try to get to work earlier. Maybe I could get some good blackmail material…

As I walk out of the office, I happen to catch a quick glimpse of the nine o'clock appointment in the waiting room. What was his name again? I really should have reviewed his file last night. I lean against the wall and watch Harlow as she strikes up conversation with him. I guess since we have no coffee or donuts, Harlow *has* opted to use her witty banter and mile long legs to distract this guy after all. And, for the record, I think this guy *could* ogle her forever. And if I'm not mistaken, Harlow Reed is actually enjoying herself.

I take another look at Mr. Nine O'Clock. Dark spiky hair, nice build, light blue eyes…totally Harlow's type. They would make a nice couple with his dark hair and blue eye combination and her auburn red spiral curls and light green eyes. I nod my head to myself in approval...not bad at all.

I make my way to my office, since I have about ten minutes until the official interview time. I take a seat at the organized mess I call my desk. Hearing Harlow's laughter coming from the waiting area, I can't help but think about her lack of serious relationships. Sometimes I feel I'm holding her back, like she doesn't want to move on without me. Almost as though she feels guilty allowing herself to be happy because I've been so sad.

My Harlow. The one who never left my side the entire time at the hospital. The one who comforted me while I broke down after I had to tell Derek goodbye. The one who held me while I screamed at the top of my lungs when I realized he wasn't coming back. The one who stood beside me and watched me throw anything I could find in the grieving room out of pure anger, never passing judgment.

My Harlow. The one who gave me the strength to come home and face the girls. The one who slept over every night when I needed her, making sure my children were taken care of when I felt like I couldn't go on any longer. The one who managed my entire household while I was lost in grief.

My Harlow. The one who helped me heal. The one that made me laugh for the first time after Derek's death and the same one who taught me I didn't have to feel guilty for it. She's still the one who keeps me in line, and she's still the one who insists on telling me the God's honest truth, whether I ask for it or not.

Unfortunately, I think she's also the one losing very valuable time in her life playing keeper to me. I had my time to be happy. I have my children as a result of that happiness. And honestly, after three years, I can say that I'm satisfied with where I am in my life, that I've found some sort of happiness again. Yet, I can't help but feel as though Harlow has fooled herself into thinking she's happy. That she's allowing herself to settle for less than she deserves in her life.

And I've not only let it happen, but I've been the cause of it.

Now, while watching her through my office window with Mr. Nine O'Clock, I also have a gut feeling that this guy might be the game changer for her. I pray that he is. She deserves her happiness, her happily ever after. And I'm at a point in my life where I don't need her to be there. She's always going to be my surrogate sister, but I don't need her to be my safety net anymore. What I *do* need is for her to allow herself her chance at happiness. And I can't help but hope that it will be this guy to help push her over the proverbial "happiness" fence.

I smile to myself. Watching her reaction to whatever he's saying right now, I know she isn't going to need much of a push. As Harlow gets up to lead him to the conference room, I notice her flip her hair in a very "Harlow sex kitten" manner.

Cancel that. It might be more of a nudge instead of a push.

After giving them a little more alone time, I grandly enter the conference room with a huge smile plastered on my face. I sit down quietly and place all of Mr. Nine O'Clock's information in front of me, ready to convene the interview. When I look up, I realize that I'm still donning the goofy grin. I immediately relax my face, leaving it void of any form of elated emotion. Harlow lifts an eyebrow asking me if I'm okay. I nod my head to let her know everything's fine and we start the meeting.

Trace O'Connell was Mr. Nine O'Clock. That's about the only information I retain during the interview. Well, that, and the fact that he's applying for the Senior Executive Accountant position at Synergy, but I don't really think that counts as information retained from the interview itself.

As soon as we start, my mind wanders to my crazy, off the wall morning.

Toothpaste in my hair. *Crazy.*

My Suburban sitting on the side of I-35, probably a victim of an *actual* highway robbery. *Crazy.*

The lovely encounter with Blake Morgan this morning. *Crazy.*

Harlow making goo-goo eyes at Trace O'Connell. *Crazy.* And kinda gross.

How the hell am I actually supposed to concentrate in this meeting with all of *that* going on?

Well, I don't. I find my thoughts centering around Blake the majority of the time. Why is he here? I mean, he obviously didn't sound like he wanted to be here. And why after all this time? How long has it been since I had seen him? He left for Colorado right after high school so that would be around sixteen years, give or take. Why is he so pissed at me? I really need to figure that one out. And if he *is* so pissed at me, why did he stop to help only to make a big scene about it? And what was up with him touching my face? It almost seemed like an affectionate touch.

A touch that I swear I can still feel right now. Raising my fingers and placing them over the area he skimmed earlier, I find myself back in the conference room with both Harlow and Trace staring at me, evidently waiting for me to say something. "What?"

"Alex? Do you have any other questions for Trace?" Harlow asks. "Actually Alex, do you have *any* questions for Trace?"

Oops. Busted.

"Nope, I'm all good," I say hastily, gathering my papers. I feel the sudden need to escape this room and all thoughts of Blake. Getting up from the table, I reach over to shake Trace's hand. *He has really big hands,* I think to myself as I start giggling uncontrollably. Before the laughing can get worse I say, "It was a pleasure to meet you, Trace. I'm sure we'll be seeing more of each other very soon." But it's too late. I can't keep from laughing any longer. I wipe the tears from my eyes and quickly make a hasty exit. Knowing I finally hit delirium, which has been known to happen from time to time when emotionally overwhelmed, I figure it's best to just get my ass out of that room.

Upon entering my office, I notice my purse sitting on my desk with a piece of paper lying right beside it. *What in the world?* Stepping forward, I pick up the note and slowly unfold it. As I read it, I find I have to wipe my eyes again. Although, this time the tears are not from laughter.

Alex—

I went back to check on your truck. Keys were still in the ignition. Called a friend. Got your gas. You have a full tank.

—Blake

I walk into the waiting area and see my Suburban parked right in front of our office. Harlow and Trace walk out of the conference room at the same time, in deep discussion. She laughs at something he says and then looks at me. I see concern in her eyes when she notices I've been crying. She slowly walks over to me and I hand her the note. Eyes wide, she looks at the Suburban and then back at me. I can no longer control the tears. I figure Trace understands he's in the middle of some colossal feminine breakdown because he quickly says his goodbyes and makes his own hasty exit.

Note to Self: I owe Trace O'Connell one massive beer.

CHAPTER FOUR

The rest of the day is pretty much a blur. After what was most definitely a feminine breakdown, I head back into to my office and just zone out all day. After a while, I take solace in looking at each and every knick-knack on my desk which I've accumulated from my kiddos over the years. There are many memories in those beautiful art projects and presents that now reside in my office. I pay special attention to a few of my favorites.

There's the "My Mom Rocks" picture I framed that Nycole made for me just last year. Black crayon lettering on top of alternating strips of color in a rainbow pattern, each precisely the same width because; well…that's just Nycole. I love it…everything about it is perfect. And it makes me feel like she loves me, which is actually really rare these days, with her pre-pubescent attitude and everything. She made me that picture one night and left it in my laptop bag without telling me. She's usually the silent type, not wanting to draw attention to her actions. When I found it in my bag, I was so touched that I immediately went and bought a frame; it's been on my desk ever since.

From Kyndall, I have a framed picture she drew of the day that she and Derek went to the lake, just the two of them. In the picture, there are two stick figures holding hands walking on the beach with the sunset in the background. She must have been around five years old, judging by the artistic talent, but I remember this one specifically for two reasons. One, the sunset. It's not a typical sunset. In fact, it's a very bright neon pink and green sunset. Very Kyndall-esque. Two, this was the first picture she drew after Derek passed. I was worried because she stopped drawing after it happened. Since art and Kyndall go hand and hand, the fact that she wasn't drawing worried me. When she gave this to me, I knew she would be okay. But the sight of it made me cry silently for days. Very bittersweet.

From Rylie, I have the Father's day present I gave to Derek from her the summer before he died. The "#1 Daddy" frame holds a picture that I think is one of the most poignant pictures I have ever taken. Derek is holding Rylie tightly on his hip and smiling at her. Her chubby legs draped around him and her head thrown back laughing at something undoubtedly goofy he just did. And he's looking at her as though nothing or no one else exists. I know she was only one year old when he died, but those two had a bond unlike anything I had ever seen. I honestly think it was because he knew without a doubt that she was going to be just like him. Rotten and ornery, but so lovable, they never stay in trouble. And he would have been exactly right.

Then I look over at the note from Blake. Where does that fit into all of this?

It doesn't. End of story.

So what now? I obviously have to call him and thank him. I mean, it was a thoughtful, yet extremely frustrating, gesture.

How does one go about getting a hold of Blake Morgan?

I finally walk out of my office around four o'clock and

see Harlow typing away at her desk. I walk to the leather seat in front of her desk and dramatically dump myself in the chair.

Whining loudly, and sounding much like my children, I ask her, "What the hell am I supposed to do now Harlow? I mean...how do I even get a hold of him? Am I supposed to just pull over on the interstate every morning at eight o'clock so that maybe I'll run into him?" I sigh loudly. "This is asinine."

Harlow shoots me a very unsympathetic look. "I think that you're thinking about it too much. I also think that going to I-35 every day at eight o'clock in the morning would have me calling you 'psychotic', behind your back, of course. And it would definitely get the unwanted attention of the police and some of the homeless that live under the overpass. So let's just x-nay the alking-stay. I think that you're a reasonable adult, who can make reasonable decisions." She rolls her eyes in exasperation.

"Alex, just call his freaking parents and see if they can get you in touch with him. It's not that hard. It's just a thank you. It's not like you're proposing to him. Unless you *want* to propose to him, which would make the stalking notion a little more acceptable," she says with a wicked little smile.

"Okay, first of all the interstate statement was meant merely for dramatic effect, so stop using the word stalking...both in *Pig Latin* and in *English*. Secondly, you think I should call his parents? Really? You don't think that would be weird?" I ask.

"No, I don't think it will be weird at all. It would just seem like you're calling a friend to say thanks. I mean, you guys were friends once, right? Since you were mere babes in cribs? So would it be that far off base to do something like that? No. I do think that the fact you're obsessing over this like a smitten high school girl sure does say a lot though. Just my opinion."

Before I have a chance to make a smart ass rebuttal, she jumps out of her chair and grabs her purse. "Gotta get going. I'm going to pick up the pizza tonight before I come over for Wednesday's Weekly Wild And Wacky Women's Night. So don't worry about picking up anything, I've got it covered. Just have your iPod ready with the usual Dance Party USA playlist, okay? Love you!" She hugs me quickly and runs towards the door. "Call his parents, Alex. And see ya at seven!" she shouts as the door closes. I love how she always leaves when she feels like she's made her point, leaving me absolutely no time to say anything.

Fine. I grab Harlow's office phone and dial his parent's number just as easily as if I was in junior high school. I can't believe I remember that.

After being prompted to leave a message, *thank God*, I leave one with his parents with the reason I'm calling and my number in case Blake wants to "call me back". Yeah, I said "call me back", like I'm sixteen years old again. I should've said something to the effect of "if he would like to get a hold of me" or "in case we are the last two people left on earth." *Yeesh.*

Oh well…damage done. I hang up the office phone, grab my purse and my keys, and take one more look at the note lying on my desk. I decide to walk back into my office and put it my drawer.

It's odd. It definitely doesn't fit in anywhere or with anything on my desk, but I don't want to throw it away.

Emotionally spent, I sigh as I close my office door. Leaving to go pick up my "wild and wacky" girls, I'm definitely ready for tonight.

My *non-emotional* Wednesday night.

"Seriously girls, how hard is it to actually spit the toothpaste *in* the sink?"

Looking at what appears to be a mosaic of pink (Rylie's – of course) and blue toothpaste all around my children's bathroom sink, I'm once again in shock (yet slightly impressed) at the range of toothpaste emission my children have. There's toothpaste on the front of the sink, dripping down the cabinet doors like an extremely thick coat of paint. There's toothpaste on the counter. There's toothpaste on the faucet head. There's toothpaste splattered all over the bottom half of the mirror. Best of all, there's toothpaste all over the top of toilet tank. Looks like Rylie, or Kyndall, *or both*, have been practicing their finger painting.

"I need all three of you girls in here, pronto! Harlow's going to be here any minute and you know she won't give you your dollar if this bathroom is not spotless!" Thank God for Harlow. The one room I could guarantee would be clean tonight would be their bathroom. Hey, every little bit helps.

Harlow, having a strong aversion to both filthy bathrooms and the work that goes into actually cleaning them, started bribing my daughters years ago to clean theirs once a week. The cleaning has to be on Wednesday, since that was our weekly girl's night, right before she comes over.

I chuckle to myself when the three loud shrieks come from the living room. I watch them all file into the bathroom. Kyndall in her "bohemian chic" panties only get-up. Rylie in a fairy costume, complete with wings and slippers that must have come out of her dress up trunk...undoubtedly a mess that *I'll* be cleaning up later. And Nycole in one of my old sleep shirts, which reads "Miss Be-haven". Smiles on all of their faces, they grab the cleaning supplies from under the counter.

"No cleaning spray in Rylie's hair this time, please Kyndall," I say, giving them each a hug.

"Mama! I told you I was sorry," Kyndall whines while rolling her eyes.

"I know, baby. I just want to make sure it doesn't happen again. That was *not* fun, okay?"

I look at Nycole shaking her head. We both stifle a giggle. That night was one for the memory books.

The doorbell rings and the girls scream and grab their sponges.

"Alright, I'll try to stall her as long as I can, okay? Be sure to put the toilet seat down this time. We don't want Harlow falling in like she did last week. It took me twenty minutes to convince her to pay you guys. Deal?"

"Deal!"

I listen to them in the bathroom as they giggle with each other. No doubt the idea of having Harlow fall in the toilet again is extremely tempting, but I don't want to encourage it...out loud at least. Leaving them to their cleaning duties, I make my way to the front door.

Opening it, I see Harlow, all smiles. She's holding two boxes of pizza and a bottle of Pinot Grigio.

"I already had a bottle you lush," I say grabbing the pizza from her.

"You know one's never enough for us...and *you're* the lush."

"What? I have no idea what you're talking about." I give her a quick wink, also taking the bottle from her hand. "I'll go ahead and put this in the fridge. You know, just in case." I shut the door behind her. "The girls are working on your bathroom. I told them I would stall you."

"Well, at least they're good for something. I mean, besides the obvious comedic relief. And it's good for them. It gives them a sense of purpose. Very important, you know. I only bribe them to clean the bathroom to make them better human beings," she states with a hint of sarcasm. At least I hope it's sarcasm.

"Well...regardless, they need some time. Let's get dinner and dancing ready. I'm ready to tucker these kiddos out. I need some mommy time."

"Yeah, I figured you might after today. Hence the second bottle of wine."

"Right. And what's your reason for every other Wednesday?"

"Umm..." I give her a quick smile for her efforts.

"Yeah, well, don't strain your brain. I'm so ready to get this night started. Hey – while I get everything ready, can you go check on your nieces? But peek in, *don't* let them see you. I just want to make sure there are no unfortunate incidents with any cleaning products tonight."

Harlow belts out a laugh and makes her way to the bathroom. "Yes. Let's do that. I prefer to avoid that situation from happening again if at all possible. I really don't feel like frantically jumping in the shower for fear of Rylie losing her hair...or her eyesight. I would like to remain low key tonight. Well, as low key as possible in this crazy house." I lose sight of her as she pokes her head into the bathroom.

Leaving the pizzas in the living room, I carry the wine into the kitchen and put it in the fridge.

Obviously, Harlow didn't continue "peeking in" as I requested, because about five seconds after I enter the kitchen, I hear "Harlow!" cheers from the other room. I also hear suspect murmuring and lowered voices. There's absolutely *no* telling what bargain Harlow is striking with them right now. I shudder to think.

I assume they pass the cleaning inspection, though, because shortly after I see them all carrying dollar bills around with huge grins on their faces.

"Everyone in the living room please!" I yell, grabbing the plates and heading towards the living room. Slowly but surely, everyone takes their usual seats. Harlow sits on the couch with Rylie in her lap and Nycole and Kyndall sitting on either side of her. And me...on the floor criss-cross applesauce because let's face it, I'm old news. Pizza on the coffee table, we all dig in as the girls tell Harlow about their day.

"Hah-low." Harlow has no choice but to look at Rylie as she places one hand on each side of her face and forces her to turn her head. "Hah-low listen to me. You listening?" Harlow laughs and nods her head. Rylie smiles back at her. "Guess what! I did *not* go to time out today. I was a good girl. My teacher said so."

"Really? I am so proud of you Rylie. Are you *sure* you didn't go to time out today?" Harlow asks, knowing as well as I do that when she offers up information like that, it's usually not a good sign.

Note to Self: Ask Rylie's teacher why she went to time-out today.

"Yes ma'am. I'm sure. I was a good girl, 'cause I am bigger. I'm not little anymore," Rylie says in reference to the fact that she just moved into "the big girls" class in school.

"Yes, you are a big girl," Harlow says very seriously. "You're so big I think it's time for you to move out and get your own place." She winks at me and turns back to Rylie.

Grimacing, Rylie states, "Hah-low. Stop saying that. You're makin' me crazy."

"Yeah, well, consider us even then," Harlow says right before smiling and planting a big kiss on Rylies' cheek.

"How about you, Kyndall? How was your day? Anything interesting happen to you today?" We all turn to look at Kyndall. Mouth full of pizza, she answers Harlow's question. "I played with my friend Abby."

Pet peeve number one – talking with a mouthful. Especially Kyndall because she's still got quite a bit of space left in between her front two teeth.

Harlow jumps a little and then wipes her cheek. "Kyndall, honey, say it don't spray it!" Nycole and I burst into laughter. Kyndall giggles and finishes her bite. "Sorry Harlow. I forgot to swallow first!"

"It's okay, hon. Go on with your story." Harlow glances at me with wide eyes, as though she can't believe she just got pegged in the face with a chewed up piece of pepperoni. I let out another little giggle. I can't help it.

"Well, I played with Abby today. And we both told jokes. Wanna hear 'em?" She flashes an excited, dimple filled smile.

"Go for it!" Harlow distances herself from Kyndall before she begins. I'm pretty sure this is a precautionary measure.

"What do you call a bear with no teeth?" We all wait in anticipation.

"A gummy bear!" She giggles out loud. Nycole just shakes her head.

"Want another one? What did the lion say after he ate the clown?"

"WHAT?" Rylie pipes in.

"Something tastes funny!" This time Kyndall and Rylie let out giggles. Catching on to the game, Rylie jumps off of Harlow's lap and stands in front of us. "Wanna hear my joke, Hah-low?"

"Sure!" Harlow watches Rylie twist her body from side to side.

"What do you call a bear who eats a clown?"

We all look at each other knowing this is in no way a real joke. Once she has our undivided attention again, she delivers the punch line.

"Poop!" She breaks into uncontrollable laughter at her own joke. So typical. Both her laughing at herself and her use of the word poop.

"Rylie, please don't say poop." I'm trying very unsuccessfully to not giggle myself, because now she's rolling around on the ground as if she just said the funniest thing in the world. Everyone's looking around at each other when Kyndall finally says, "I don't get it." And that does it. We all break into a collective fit of laughter. Great. I'm encouraging my daughter to say poop because it makes people laugh. Mother. Of. The. Year.

Once we all quiet down, Harlow continues her line of questioning, this time focusing on Nycole.

"Nycole – how was your day sweetheart? Did you learn anything new?"

Nycole finishes her bite of pizza before answering. *Thank you, Nycole.*

"Nope."

Harlow and I exchange glances. "Really," Harlow continues. "You didn't learn anything at school today?"

"Nope."

"Nothing at all?"

"Nope."

"Not one thing?" I can tell Harlow's trying to break her. She gets some kind of sick thrill out of it.

"Nope."

"Not one, little bitty, eensie weensie, teenie tiny thing?"

"Nope." I have to end this now. We could go on all night.

"Nycole, for the love of all that is holy, please tell Harlow *one* thing you learned today!"

Nycole sighs loudly. "Fine." She fixes her eyes on Harlow. "I learned not to sit anywhere close to Kyndall while

46

she's eating. Because Harlow still has a huge piece of pizza on her cheek." Harlow immediately puts her hand up to her cheek.

I glance over at Nycole and watch as a mischievous grin spreads across her face. She watches Harlow as she begins running her hands all over her face, making sure to remove any possible remnants of Kyndall's dinner. When she's done, she looks to Nycole for approval.

"Gotcha!" Nycole shouts and runs out of the room. Harlow jumps up off the couch and runs after her. Rylie and Kyndall follow, shrieking with delight.

And this is when the real fun of Wild and Wacky Wednesday begins. I couldn't be happier to not be thinking about anything that occurred earlier today. This was my time to *not* think. To just have fun…with all of my girls.

So after the next three hours of talking, laughing, dancing, bathing, brushing and reading…Harlow and I finally get the girls to bed. I take in a deep breath to relax. It feels like I have been going all day.

I walk over to the couch and deposit myself beside Harlow. That's when I feel her staring at me. "What?" I say widening my eyes.

"You."

"Me? What about me?"

Harlow sighs rather forcefully and I start to get the feeling I'm really not going to like this conversation.

"Are you going to say anything about what happened today? I know seeing Blake threw you for a bit of an emotional loop, a fact made evident by your breakdown at the office. I'm just wondering if you would like to have the chance to go on the offensive before I start my assessment of the situation," Harlow states matter-of-factly.

"I really don't know what you're talking about. I honestly don't think *you* even know what you're talking about. Yes, I saw Blake Morgan today. I see people around town all the time, Harlow. It's not like he's any different. The breakdown I had was from the stress of nearly dying on the interstate, nothing more. I don't know why you're reading into this so much; it's really borderline obsessive. I might actually have to call someone for an intervention."

I know by Harlow's calm tone, I'm about to get the speech of a lifetime. The calm before the storm...and the impending long lecture.

"Alex, how long have we known each other?"

"Since we were *seven*?" I ask because I'm not really sure where she's going with this line of questioning.

"Right, so that's...what...twenty...some odd years. You think after all these years that I don't know you?" She stalls waiting for an answer. I continue to pretend I have no idea what she's talking about. I don't really have to pretend that much actually. Yet, she keeps on going, like the Energizer bunny.

"Well, I do. Honestly, I know you better than yourself. Especially lately."

I feel my blood pressure begin to rise.

"Harl–"

"No, you're going to let me finish. I'm not going to give you the chance to try to rationalize out loud what you *think* is going on, because it's time for you to hear what I have to say. I know you don't want to hear it, but honey, you need to. I need you to. Your children need you to," she begins.

"You know I love you more than if you were my own

sister, if that's even possible. So saying this isn't going to be easy, but just know that I'm saying it out of love for you and your precious girls."

I open my mouth to speak but she holds up her hand, signaling she's serious about me not speaking.

Okay...

"Do you really believe that seeing Blake today had nothing to do with what happened at the office today?" I nod my head, trying to end this conversation before it starts. Unfortunately for me, it seems to have the opposite effect.

"You can't honestly believe that, Alex!" Harlow takes a deep breath, obviously trying to control her temper. She lowers her voice, but keeps her eyes on me the entire time she speaks.

"No, I don't think you do. I think you know, deep down, that seeing Blake had an effect on you. And I think that you're so used to not allowing yourself to feel anything that your brain didn't know how to cope. I don't know how long you're going to keep doing this to yourself, Alex. How long is long enough?" I continue my blank stare. Unfortunately, I think she's on to me.

"You go on, each day, as though you're happy and at peace with your life. Or at least trying to convince yourself that you are. But you also go on, each day, not really living. It's not fair. It's not fair to you and it's definitely not fair to your children, who deserve to see their mother happy. It's time to let him go and live your life without him. Derek has been dead for three years! Three. Years. Alex."

Okay...now I'm really starting to get irritated.

"Really Harlow. How profound of you." I glare at her. My voice starts to quiver as it rises.

"No shit Derek's been dead for three years! I live with that knowledge every single day of my life. *Every day*, I wake up still expecting him to be lying next to me. *Every day*, I look at these children and wonder if they have any inkling of how wonderful, caring, smart, beautiful, strong, and loving their father really was. I live my life, *every day*, with a heart that is completely empty. I have a heart that unfortunately is irreparable. Yes, Harlow, *every day* of my life is a constant reminder that Derek is dead! Is there any other mind blowing information you feel the need to share with me?!" I yell at her as the tears roll down my cheeks.

Without hesitation, Harlow moves herself directly in front of my face. "Yes, Alex. Actually there is. You've become so obsessed with living right by him after his death...you don't see anything else. Derek is dead, Alex. You are not! But you live as though you are, as though your life is done and over with too. You should know better than anyone how short and precious life is. How important it is to make the most of what you have been given. You have got to find the strength to get back out there. To *love* again. To *feel* again. You *cannot* continue this apathetic way of life. It's not healthy for you...and it's affecting you. If I see it, you know the girls see it. Is that how you want to be seen by your daughters...the children who worship the ground you walk on? Is that the example you want to set for them? Or do you want them to see the true strength their mother possesses? Because I know it's still in there, Alex. I know you and I know your fierce strength. How hard you can love. How much life you still have in you. Don't let your fear rob you of the happiness that you deserve." My thoughts automatically go to Blake.

"What...so Blake's supposed to be my second chance? Just because he happens to come back to town, that means I'm supposed to fall madly and deeply in love with him? Get real, Harlow. I have three daughters now. I don't have the luxury to just fall in love on a whim. My life is different now," I say to her, trying to control my anger.

"This has nothing to do with Blake. What it has to do with is the fact that you're so obsessed with Derek that you won't let anyone else in. He didn't do anything today but help you. Yet you're angry about it. Instead of being grateful like anyone else in their right mind would be. Although seeing you express *any* emotion at all is refreshing actually. You've completely closed yourself off from anyone else but me. You won't open yourself up to feel anything. That's what concerns me."

I try to choke down my anger, but I don't think it's really working. I'm pretty sure my anger filled tears are giving me away.

Harlow shifts her weight on the couch. "Listen honey, it could be Tony the *fucking* Tiger and I would still be having this conversation with you. You have blinders on and refuse to allow yourself to see anything else. I'm not saying you should feel *anything* for Blake. But it's okay to get help from people. Not everyone expects something in return. Blake was always there for you when you needed him, and evidently he still is." I roll my eyes. She continues.

"But while we are on the topic of Blake...I do find it very interesting that you say seeing him is like seeing anyone else around town. I know you and Derek were together for a very long time. But there was a time *before* Derek, Alex. There was a time that you and Blake were actually very close

51

friends. Best friends. We all were. But you refuse to acknowledge any of this when talking about him. Do you even remember those days? Do you remember how much he cared for you back then? Even as young as we were, he would've done anything for you. He was always there for you, whenever you needed him, both before and after you met Derek. Do you really not remember? Or is it just safer for you not to remember?"

I just stare at her when she's finished with her speech, tears now running in continuous streams down my face. I can't answer her because, honestly, I don't know the answers to the questions she's asking. I don't know anything anymore. I can say that I honestly had no thoughts stemming back to my relationship with Blake when I saw him this morning. All I really thought about Blake this morning was that I found him extremely irritating. Maybe Harlow does have a point. Because, now that I think about it, it's odd that I didn't even think about my past relationship with Blake this morning, considering he and I grew up together. She's right; we had a history together and for me not to even remember that, well…

I exhale in defeat.

"Alright, Harlow. I get it. It's just hard sometimes, ya know? Honestly, I'm tired of being strong all the time, tired of pretending. But I'm scared. It's so much easier for me to cling to the memories of happiness than to consider any possibility of losing someone again. You were there Harlow. You saw everything. I don't know if I could survive it a second time when I *barely* made it through the first time. You know that. How many times did you have to force me to get up just to take care of the girls? How many times did you have to come over to console me when I couldn't stop screaming and crying? How many times did you come over just to check on the girls to make sure they were okay – and don't say you didn't because I know you did. Honestly, how many times? So I understand your concern, I truly do. But I feel that I've earned a little leeway to be scared without being judged."

Though still angry, I feel myself conceding that she might be on to something. "But…you're right about the girls deserving better. And I'll work on that, okay. Just please, try to be patient with me."

My face is now soaked with my tears.

"It's just not easy for me to accept help from people. You also know that Harlow. I don't want to let someone in only to lose them again and asking for help is letting someone in. That scares me to death so I guess I choose to distance myself like I did this morning with Blake. Of all the freakin' people, why did it have to be *him*? "

Harlow gives me a slight smile.

"Alex. I love you. I love your girls. I just want to see you allow yourself to be happy. I'm not saying Blake is or isn't the one to do that for you. But I don't want to see you push away a true friendship that you need right now. And you need him. I know you do. And I think you know you do, too. I don't think it's necessarily a bad thing that it was Blake this morning. Maybe someone's trying to tell you something, but you're just being too stubborn to listen." She places her hand on my knee.

"Listen. You know I have no room to pass judgment. And I would never pass judgment on you. Yes, I did see everything you went through. And the fact that you're here, being a wonderful mother to those beautiful girls, shows me how strong you truly are. How strong you can be. Show the girls that strength. Your strength. Teach them. I know you can. I know you want to. And I know you will. But eventually, you're going to have to let someone else in. Even if it's just a friend. You need to start trusting people again, Alex. "

I nod my head and place my hand over hers. "I know, Harlow. It's just not that easy. I'll try, but please be patient with me. And even though I'm officially still mad at you," I give her a quick wink, "I know that you're only saying this because you care, so I forgive you."

I tighten my hand around hers.

"I love you Harlow. And I thank you, from the bottom of my heart. I wouldn't be here without you."

Harlow gives my hand a pat. "You are *most* welcome." Then, smiling widely she adds, "Now, enough of the serious shit...let's finish off that second bottle of wine."

Two hours and one fall in the toilet later by Miss Harlow Reed (for which I knowingly misplace the blame onto my children), I close the door as Harlow leaves. When I'm confident she's gone, I migrate to the attic to pull out a box full of random things I kept from my time with Derek. Old letters, dried flowers, movie tickets, etc. I don't know why, but I just feel the need to go through it right now. Maybe it's because Harlow just drilled the fact that Derek is *indeed* dead into my head tonight.

Flashlight in hand, I walk across the attic floor. I notice a box sitting in the corner that I don't recognize. It's simply labeled "Alex's Stuff." Hmm...whoever was in charge of labeling on moving day really needed to be reassigned to do something else.

I open the box and it is mainly stuff from my childhood room: dolls, cassette tapes, yearbooks…

Digging around, I notice an old shoe box at the bottom. I pull it out and open it. In the box there are many pieces of paper, different shapes and sizes, with writing all over them. Below them, something shiny catches my eye. I shift the papers over and pull the silver object out of the box. I let out a small gasp.

In my hand is the charm bracelet that Blake had given me when we were kids. He worked for years and years on it.

Oh. My. God. How could I have forgotten?

And how could I have just thrown it in a box?

I look at each charm and smile. I remember every single one. Blake would get a charm anytime we went anywhere. He would buy them when he went on summer and winter vacations with his family. He would even buy them on random occasions, making his mom take him all over to find just the right one. And since this started when we were around seven years old, there were a lot of charms, five or six year's worth of them. I flip through them quickly to find my favorite charm. Blake gave it to me when we were thirteen years old.

We went to the lake that day to go fishing, something we

always did in the summers…and since school was about to start we wanted to get as much fishing time in as we could. Enjoying the morning sun, we were both sitting in the boat, silently enjoying it as it rocked back and forth, when I felt a sudden tug on my line. I yanked the pole back and I could feel the fish fighting me; it felt like a big one. I jumped up with excitement and started bringing it in. As I reeled it out of the water, I threw my fishing pole to the side, grabbing the line with one hand and the fish in the other. Trying to unhook the fish's mouth, I could feel the fish wiggling out of my grasp.

"Blake! Help me! I'm about to lose the fish," I yelled frantically as I tried to get the hook out of its mouth. But it was too late. The fish fell and started flopping all over the bottom of the boat. We both dropped to our knees in an effort to catch it, but neither one of us could grab it, it kept slipping out of our hands. Finally, it must have unhooked itself because it flipped and flopped its way out of the boat, but we didn't care. We were laughing so hard we could hardly breathe. We both ended up on our bellies facing each other.

Finally, when we managed to stop laughing, we just stopped and stared at each other. I noticed how his hair was a lot lighter in the summer, which made his green eyes even more beautiful. I was lost in his eyes when suddenly, he leaned in and gave me a tiny peck on the cheek. Before I could say anything, he rose to his feet so quickly it made me dizzy. Well, it was either that or the rocking of the boat when he got up. Either way, Blake Morgan just kissed me on the cheek. I could feel the heat on my face as I stood back up in the middle of the boat, but I said nothing.

Blake and I both acted like nothing happened for the rest

of the day. We soon went back to normal, joking and laughing with each other. We left after a couple of hours, eventually going our separate ways.

Right before dinner, there was a knock on my front door. I went to answer it, expecting Harlow. But when I opened the door, there was no one there. There was, however, a box placed on the welcome mat. I picked it up and untied the red ribbon that held it closed. Sitting in a patch of white fluff was a fishing pole charm and a note that simply said:

Alex,
I hope one day we can be more than friends.
Yours always and forever,
— Blake

With tears in my eyes, I stare at the bracelet as the lost memory runs its course through my mind. Then realization sets in.

I think I know now why Blake Morgan hates me so much. About a week after he left me that charm, Derek Meyer walked into both of our lives and all of this was completely forgotten....

Forgotten until this very moment.

CHAPTER FIVE

Climbing into bed, I can't help but think about my relationship with Blake. We were extremely close growing up. I do remember that. Harlow's words run over and over in my mind.

"Do you remember how much he cared about you back then? Even as young as we were, he would've done anything for you."

Freakin' Harlow.

I totally blame this lack of sleep on the exhausting five hour lecture I just received. And I will be blaming her tomorrow when I am a raging bitch at work. Perfect payback for tonight's torture session.

"Do you remember how much he cared about you back then?"

Her words keep bouncing around in my head.

I begin to think back to that last summer with Blake before Derek entered the picture. While remembering that sweet peck on the cheek, I notice my cheeks, even now, start to warm. I think about the sweet gesture of the charm and a smile breaks across my face.

What the hell am I doing? I can't be thinking like this.

Aggravated with myself, I roll over and shut my eyes. I don't have this luxury. And I won't pretend that I do.

But boy…it sure would be nice, I think to myself as I

finally fall asleep.

"Ma'am, this is Officer Sanchez from the Round Rock Police Department. Are you the wife of a Mr. Derek Meyer?"

"Yes I am. Who is this?"

"Mrs. Meyer... I'm afraid there's been an accident."

"An accident? What kind of accident?" Harlow places her coffee mug down on her desk and walks into my office. She gently shuts the door behind her, her widened eyes meeting mine.

"Ma'am, we're gonna need you to come to Round Rock Medical Center. Your husband has been involved in a pretty severe vehicular accident and was airlifted to the hospital this morning. Ma'am, if you could find someone to drive you, I suggest you get here as soon as you can. We can call the Waco P.D. and see if we can get an officer to bring you if you'd like. But we'll need you to get on the road as soon as possible."

I begin gasping for air, but it doesn't work. I can't breathe. I start to fan my face to try to get some air in my lungs. I still can't breathe. This isn't happening. I look at Harlow as a river of tears begins to flow down my cheeks. I attempt to speak to Officer Sanchez.

"No," I say as I take in a much needed breath. "I have someone who can bring me. We're on our way."

Harlow, keys already in hand, grabs the phone from me and hangs it up. "What happened, Alex? Is it Derek? Is he okay? Where is he?"

"Harlow, Derek was airlifted to Round Rock Medical Center this morning. He was in a car accident." Every part of my body is shaking now. I can't feel anything but my own heart beat, pulsating in my head. My hands are balled into fists by my side, and I feel my nails start to slice through the palms of my hands.

Then it starts to actually sink in.

"We have to hurry, Harlow. Please, we need to go," I say rushing toward the door. "I need to see him."

She follows me to the door and stops. "We'll make it, honey. Try to calm down. We don't know anything yet." She takes in a long breath through her nose and exhales. I'm not sure if the breathing is more for me or for her. "Listen, I know it's hard, but you need to focus on being strong. It isn't going to help him any to see you like this. So you have about an hour to compose yourself."

She places her hands on my shoulders. "I'm right here. I'll be right beside you the entire time. So take a breath, unclench your fists because I think you're bleeding... seriously... and let's go," she says with a weak smile. She opens the door and then wraps her arms around my shoulders. "Everything will be okay."

I squeeze her tightly in response. "God Harlow, I hope so. I can't imagine my life or the girls' lives without Derek. He's everything to us, Harlow. He's all we know."

"I know, Alex. Try to stay positive. And try to remember to breathe." She pauses to give me another quick squeeze.

"Now, let's get you to Derek, sweetie. Chin up." Harlow

removes her arms from around me and puts her hand under my chin forcing me to look at her. She peers into my eyes.

"You can do this, Alex." I look at her determined face and I know she's right. I let out a sigh blowing the hair out of my face. "Okay, we can do this. Let's get going."

As we start out the door, I grab Harlow's hand. "He'll be okay, Harlow. Right?"

Smiling a little more confidently and giving my hand a quick squeeze back, she simply replies, "Positive thoughts only my friend."

The ride to Round Rock is a pretty silent one; I think we're both lost in thought. I can't help but worry about what I'll see when I get to the hospital, but I try to push all the negative thoughts out of my mind.

He's going to be fine. He'll be fine.

I wring my hands over and over in my lap.

Harlow reaches over and places her hand over mine. "Calm down. We're almost there."

"I know, Harlow. It's just hard. I'm trying," I say, letting out a little sob. There's a lump in my throat the size of a softball. I raise my arm to wipe my face with my sleeve.

I'm trying...

I look out the window. I watch the traffic go by and find myself thinking about Derek. His smile, his humor, his arms holding me tight. He's all I want, all I need right now. His arms around me. The safety I feel when he's near me. I want to hear his laughter, to feel his kisses on my face. I want nothing more than to walk into that room and hold him tight. A slight breath of relief escapes me as I imagine crawling into the hospital bed with him, his arms wrapping around me, taking all my fears away.

I feel Harlow's car start to slow, along with the traffic around us. I look out the window and see blue and red police lights on the right side of the interstate. I notice the sun highlighting shards of clear glass all over the concrete, mixed with a lot of red pieces...both of which are strewn across this section of the road. I look up to barely catch a glimpse of what looks like the remnants of a car, completely flipped upside down, sitting in the grass on the side of I-35.

I audibly gasp out loud and cover my mouth. "Oh my God, Harlow. Is that—"

"Don't. Lay your seat down. Now! Do it, Alex. You don't need to see this."

I do as I'm told, only to shut my eyes and raise my arm where the crook of my arm covers my face. I try to keep all the negative thoughts from breaking into my mind.

Think positive.

I can do this.

He'll be fine.

He's going to be just fine.

But I still can't seem to control my tears. Harlow's hand, still resting on mine, gives another small squeeze. Shortly after, I feel the car finally come to a halt. "We're here sweetheart," Harlow says gently. "Do you need a minute?"

I shake my head as I raise the seat back into its original position. *"No. I need to get in there. We need to go."*

Handing me a napkin from the glove compartment, Harlow says, *"Alright. But you're gonna need to wipe your face before we get in there."* She gives me a small compassionate smile.

I accept the napkin and blot my cheeks. I let out a deep sigh from my lungs and smooth my shirt with my hands.

"I'm ready," I say, voice shaking.

I just wish I knew exactly what the hell I am supposed to be ready for...

"Oh my God–Harlow." Every ounce of strength I think I have abandons my body. I grab my best friend as I begin to lose my legs from underneath me.

"Harlow –I ca–"

"Yes, you can, Alex. You have to. I'm right here sweetie. Just go to him. He needs you," she says, guiding my uncooperative body to the side of the bed where Derek lies, unrecognizable.

Looking at my husband, I know I'm slowly losing control. Every part of my body is shaking. More tears stream down my face. The lump in my throat is almost unbearable. But, I need to stay strong for him. As I move closer to the man lying in front of me, I try to manage the emotions that seem to be forcing their way out of my body. Taking a deep *breath, I begin to time my breathing with Derek's heart monitor in an effort to remind myself to actually breathe.*

Beep. Breathe.

Beep. Breathe.

Beep. Breathe.

I take my trembling hand and raise it to touch his cheek. His face is so swollen; I can't make out his features. There's no resemblance to the man I know. My eyes move to where his head is wrapped in a bandage that covers every lock of beautiful brown curly hair.

I physically don't have any more strength. I lay my head down on his chest. I grab his hand and let my fingers intertwine with his.

"Derek, where are you? Open your eyes for me. I want to see your beautiful brown eyes. Please open them, baby." I will myself to raise my head to once again look at his face. I place my chin on his chest because my head just seems too heavy right now. I focus on his mouth and raise my hand to run my fingers over the cuts on his lips. I can't help but think of his beautiful smile. The dimples that fill his cheeks when he laughs. Tears pour out of my eyes, soaking his hospital gown.

"I need you. Your babies need you, Derek. You have to fight to stay alive for us. Please don't stop fighting for your life. I know you can hear me. I love you, you're my life baby. You're our rock. Our strength. Our protector. I can't do this without you. Please... please.... please..." I keep repeating it, hoping he hears me.

After a while, I feel Harlow's hand on my back. "Alex, there's an officer here that wants to speak with you," she says quietly.

Sniffling, I raise my head from Derek's chest and mop the tears from my face and neck. I nod my head at her. "Okay."

With a lingering look at Derek and a light touch to his cheek, I turn to follow Harlow out of the room. Outside, I see who I presume is Officer Sanchez standing in the hall. He gives me a sympathetic smile...the same exact smile that I would come to absolutely detest over the next few years of my life.

"Good morning, Mrs. Meyer. I'm Officer Sanchez. I believe we spoke earlier on the phone. I'm glad you made it down here safely".

"Yes, sir," is all I can manage. I feel my brain slowly starting to shut down.

Taking a deep breath, Officer Sanchez places his hand on my shoulder.

"Well, ma'am, we suspect that he fell asleep at the wheel while driving on the interstate. We were called to respond sometime around 7:30 AM. We found the car right on the outskirts of Round Rock and immediately had him airlifted to Round Rock Medical. There's not much that we can tell you at this time. What we do know is that his car was hit several times before ending up on the side of the interstate. It took us a while to get him out, but when we did, he was immediately put en route to the hospital," he says nervously. "I'm sorry there wasn't more we could do for him on the scene."

I start to replay the previous night's events in my head. Derek coming to bed late. Him kissing the back of my neck. Turning to look at the clock. 3:17 AM. Making love. Waking up. Finding him gone. The unmistakable scent of sandalwood lingering on his still warm pillow.

I turn to Harlow. We were joking about our "late night" right before the phone call from Officer Sanchez.

"Oh my God. We were up too late last night," I say through the tears. "It's my fault. If I would have told him no—"

"No you don't, Alex," Harlow says through her teeth, shaking her head. "You're not going to take the blame for this. This is not your fault. It was an accident. Accidents happen. There's no one at fault here, sweetie, especially you."

Turning to Officer Sanchez, Harlow asks, "Is there anything you need from us? My friend really needs to be with her husband right now."

Sanchez shakes his head. "No ma'am. There may be some information we need to get later, but nothing that can't wait." He turns and looks at me, sad expression filling his eyes. "Ma'am, I'm truly sorry. I really hope that he pulls through."

And with that, Officer Sanchez turns and walks down the corridor.

I start to walk into the room when Harlow grabs my arm and turns me to face her.

"This is not your fault. You DO NOT walk in that room believing that, Alex. You get in there and you fight for your husband. Blaming yourself will do absolutely no good right now. No wasted energy. Go in there and remind Derek of everything that he needs to fight for." I can see her actually trying to will the strength into me. She jerks her head in the direction of Derek's room. "Go."

I nod my head and embrace her as though she's my lifeline. She squeezes me just as tightly and after a while she pats my back for encouragement. Hoping I have absorbed

67

some of Harlow's strength, I finally let her go.

"Harlow, I know you've already done so much for me today, but can you do me a couple of more things?" She nods. "Listen, I need you to please call John and Nancy and have them go get the girls from school. Let them know Derek has been in an accident. That I'm here, but I haven't spoken with the doctor yet. I think that they'll want to get here to see their son as soon as possible. Have them bring the girls. Tell them they can bring my car if they want to, remind them I put the spare keys in my kitchen drawer. Then, call my parents and let them know what's going on as well. Tell them there is no reason for them to fly down yet and that I will call them as soon as I know something." I stop speaking as my thoughts immediately go to the girls.

"What am I going to tell the girls, Harlow?" My voice shakes uncontrollably.

"You'll tell them the truth. That's all you can do sweetie." She turns my body gently toward Derek. "Now, go to your husband. I'll take care of everything else."

I give her one last look and walk into the room. As I enter, I hear the familiar and comforting sound of Derek's monitor.

Beep.

Beep.

Beeeeeeeeeeeeeeeeeeeeeeeeeeeeeeeeeee–

I watch the monitor as the last remnants of Derek's heartbeat slowly go by.

"No! No! No! Oh my god... Harlow!" I scream a guttural scream as I run to Derek's side. I push the call button for the nurse and yell as loud as humanly possible. "Nurse! Please... Help! Help me... help my husband!

Please!"

I'm still screaming when the nurses and Harlow rush into the room. I grab onto Derek and loudly cry out, "Derek, you fight! You fight for us! Don't you give up! We need you, Derek!" I'm shrieking at the top of my lungs and shaking him with every ounce of strength my weakened body can muster. I barely register that Harlow's beside me trying to pry my fingers from Derek's arms.

"Alex, you have to let go sweetheart. They can't help him unless you let go. You need to move, honey."

I wrench my fingers as tightly as I can around his arms. I can't let go. If I let go–

"Please, let go, Alex. Let them try to help," Harlow says, forcefully breaking my hold on Derek. She grabs both of my hands, turns my body away from Derek, and looks me directly in the eyes. "Alex, we need to go outside. Okay? Let them do their jobs."

I stare at her face because it's the only thing I can do. I have no fight left in me. I let her lead me out of the room. I hear the doctors and nurses fighting to save him. But I know deep down he's already gone because I don't feel him anymore. I don't feel his soul. I don't feel his presence in my heart. I don't even feel my own heart anymore. That's how I know he's gone. There's nothing I can do. Nothing I can say. Nothing I want to say. I can feel my body, my heart, my brain…everything…shutting down. There's nothing anymore. I'm completely void. Completely empty.

I should have never let go.

I awake in my room, my pillow drenched in tears. My eyes remain shut but the tears continue.

Derek.

Gone.

Alone.

Empty.

As I re-play the death of Derek, just as it was in my dream over and over again, I find myself getting angrier each time.

Angry at myself for being so weak.

Angry at Derek for dying and leaving me behind.

And honestly, I find myself angry at a certain *someone* for showing up after all these years. Trying to be my hero. I don't need a hero. I don't need anyone.

And I sure as hell *do not* need Blake Morgan.

CHAPTER SIX

Thursday morning I wake up to the sound of my alarm, evidently set to the tone of "Drill Nails into Alex's Skull". I honestly don't know if my headache is from the wine, the tears, or a combination of both. Whatever the reason, I'm being severely punished this morning. Turning my alarm off, I drag myself out of bed and make the rounds to wake up my girls. I walk into Nycole and Kyndall's shared room and turn on the light. Their heads immediately disappear under their sheets.

"Get up sleepyheads!" I shout, immediately cringing in pain.

Note to Self: Refuse second bottle next Wednesday.

I watch their beds for any sign of movement. This is going to be an extremely long morning.

"Girls....please get up. Mommy isn't feeling great this morning. Can you guys help me a little and get out of bed now, instead of waiting until the thirty-seventh time I ask? Please? I will love you guys forever." I sing the last line.

Nycole's head pops straight up. "So, are you saying there's a possibility you *won't* love us forever?"

A small smile finds its way to my lips as I look at this little girl who's growing up so fast.

"Um, no. But it was an effective way to get you two up, no?"

"Mama," Kyndall says, removing the covers from over her head. "That wasn't very nice. Are you sure you're gonna love us forever?"

"Girls, I will love you forever and ever and ever. There's *no* way I could ever stop loving you. You're both my babies. Did you know that when you are *fifty* years old, you'll still be my babies?"

They both giggle.

"So, yes, I'll love you forever. Unless you guys don't get out of bed this minute. Then I will love you *no more!*" I yell as I jump onto Nycole's bed and start tickling her. Kyndall jumps on my back in a measly effort to protect her sister. I bring her little body over my shoulder and throw her onto Nycole's bed, tickling her as well. We're all giggling when I hear Rylie's little voice as she enters the room.

"Hy-yah!" She shouts, running across the room. She jumps on my back, karate chopping and kicking like the ninja master she is. When I finally catch a glimpse of her, I break out into laughter. *Oops.* I guess we forgot to take off her swimsuit before she went to bed. Oh well, at least I did manage to remember to braid her crazy hair after her bath, which will make getting her ready much, much easier this morning.

"Nice kick, young grasshopper. Now guys, let's get out of this room and start getting ready for school."

Maybe I should have reconsidered the early morning wrestling match, because now my head is *really* throbbing. Yet, I smile to myself in lieu of my misery. It was so worth it.

The rest of the morning is pretty uneventful. The only minor hiccup is Rylie refusing to wear shoes that actually match her outfit. And since I'm running on my morning after Wild and Wacky Wednesday speed, I opt to not argue with her about it. While heading to the car, I shake my head as I look at my beautiful baby girl, brown curly hair blowing everywhere, dressed in a blue sundress that Nancy bought her with a pair of red and white checkered flats. Well, if nothing else, it's very "Dorothy in the Wizard of Oz"-esque.

While driving the normal morning route, I decide that I completely loathe the "Do you know?" game that Rylie has recently started forcing me to play with her.

"Mommy, do you know what starts with A?"

"What?"

"Apple and Art."

"That's right baby. You are *so* smart."

"Mommy, do you know what the potty is called?"

"What?"

"The toilet or the rest room."

"That's right baby. Hey, Kynd–"

"Mommy, do you know the color of brains?"

"Rylie – we don't talk about–"

"Pink. Brains are pink, Mommy."

"Rylie, that's right. But please don't talk about brains, okay? I don't think your teachers in your new big girl class would like that."

"Okay, Mommy."

"Do you know the capital of New York?" she asks. Honestly, she's got me there.

"No, honey, what is the capital of New York?"

"Albany."

How does she know this stuff? And why New York? Why not Texas?

"Rylie? What's the capital of California?" I suddenly feel the need to gauge this child's intelligence level.

"My formula." She smiles widely looking back at me in the rearview mirror.

Phew! Okay...so she isn't completely smarter than me. I grin back at her wholeheartedly.

After I drop the girls off at all of their respective drop sites, I head over to Prestige. Walking in the door, I let out a snort as I look at Harlow.

"Sporting the after Wednesday night look as well my dear friend?" Harlow is in the process of popping ibuprofen in her mouth. Her hair is in a pony tail, which is an extremely rare occurrence.

"I totally blame you for this look, actually," Harlow snaps back, obviously not in the mood for my first-rate sarcasm this morning.

"Well then, we're even because I didn't get an ounce of sleep last night thanks to you. After you left, I went into the attic and found some random box labeled 'Alex's Stuff' – did you do that by the way because your labeling is completely unacceptable. Anyway, I opened it, and found the charm bracelet Blake gave me when we were kids. You remember which one I'm talking about, right?" I watch Harlow give a slight nod yes, obviously in too much pain for a full-fledged head shake.

"Well, I had some unfortunate memories about him, and then proceeded to have some even more unfortunate memories revolving around Derek's death. So needless to say, if we're playing the blame game, I win...by a freakin' landslide."

I think I just word vomited on myself. I need some coffee.

"Okay...you win," Harlow says emphatically surrendering. "Sorry for the drunken lecture. But honestly, we don't have that many chances to really talk, ya know? I said what I felt needed to be said and what I know you needed to hear."

"I know, Harlow. It doesn't make it easy to take though. I know everything you said is true, but honestly, I'm just not ready. Maybe someday, but not now."

Sighing extremely loudly, Harlow places the ibuprofen bottle on the counter. "I'm *not* getting into this with you today, Alex. I'm too tired and too hung over."

"That's completely fine by me," I say as my cell starts ringing. "What the—"

"Who is it?"

"Oh. My. God. I completely forgot I left a message with his parents. It's Blake."

Covering her mouth in an effort to try to hide her obvious amusement, Harlow asks, "Well, are you going to answer it?"

"Hell no, I'm not going to answer it." I throw my phone back into my purse. "I don't have time for this shit, Harlow. So what, he's here after all of these years? Honestly, I don't care. It has nothing to do with me. I haven't spoken to the man in years. There's nothing to say. He did me a favor. Big freakin' whoop. I'm not obligated to answer his phone calls.

So I'm not going to."

"Okay...jeez, Lucifer. I was just asking a question. You sure are defensive about a phone call." Harlow's enjoying this. I can tell by the delighted look on her face. I decide to squash any thoughts that may be going on in that devious mind of hers.

"Well, I don't want you to get your hopes up, Harlow. I'm broken. And I don't anticipate being fixed anytime soon. And I sure as hell don't expect Blake Morgan to be my cure. Nor do I want him to be. I'm comfortable where I am in my life," I say walking into my office. "I *don't* want to hear anything else about Blake Morgan. *Ever!*" I shout at Harlow, slamming my door.

I swear I hear her laughing, but I choose to not acknowledge it. I sit down at my desk and look at my phone. Shit, he left a voice mail.

After staring at my phone for five minutes, I delete the message without even listening to it. There's nothing Blake has to say that I want to hear. Now or ever.

Well...it seems my gut feeling was spot on, as usual, about Harlow and her new potential man, Trace. He calls while I'm deleting my unheard message from Blake. Harlow excitedly rushes into my office and demands that I accompany her on Friday to meet Trace. He got the job with

Synergy and wants to meet for drinks to celebrate. Evidently this is some kind of girl code I'm unaware of....number one, because I haven't been on the dating scene in a ridiculously long time. And two, because Harlow never bothers to "date" anyone.

Very interesting.

I accept because, while I do love Harlow, I really just need a good girl's night out. So, if nothing else, it will be an enjoyable evening with my friend. With a little bit of Trace thrown in...

Friday "day" comes and goes, and now I find myself in my bathroom, putting make-up on with my mother-in-law Nancy, aka the babysitter – also aka Derek's mother, sitting on the bathtub behind me discussing the schedule for this evening.

"We're meeting Trace at George's Bar at seven. After that, I have no idea." I chuckle as I look at Nancy in the mirror. "You have met Harlow right?"

Smiling back, Nancy nods her head. "Yes, I have. I'll stay however long you need me. Actually, I'll probably just take the girls to my house for the night so there's no need to hurry back. You girls enjoy your evening. Don't worry about us. We'll be just fine."

After a few second of silence, Nancy speaks again. "I heard Blake Morgan's in town."

"What? Blake Morgan?" I ask innocently. Seriously, is there a Blake Morgan convention going on that I don't know about? "Yeah, I ran into him earlier this week. How do you know Blake?"

"Alex, he and Derek were friends, don't you remember? He used to come over to our house with Derek after the football games. Very sweet boy as I remember," she says as though lost in a memory.

"Yeah, well he may have been sweet, but Derek was the only one for me. You know that. I didn't really notice anyone else in high school. I don't really think he would have appreciated that much."

I shoot her a smug smile. I really don't want to get into this with her before my much needed girls' night.

"I know. I was just thinking that maybe –"

"Um, no. Don't start. I've already gone into this with Harlow and I don't feel like rehashing it with you. I'm still in love with Derek, Nancy. It wouldn't be fair to start something with someone else. I would think that you, especially, would appreciate that." I apply the second coat of mascara to my lashes.

Leaning forward and placing both hands on the counter, I will myself to meet her eyes in the mirror. I'm so sick and tired of this conversation.

She shakes her head disapprovingly. "It's not about me, dear. It's about you. It's about how you're choosing to live out the remainder of your own life. I still love Derek too, honey. But honestly, Alex, my son loved you more than anything. And I know that he would not have wanted this life for you. Just because you move on with someone else doesn't mean you love him any less, sweetheart. Your happiness was the most important thing to him and he would be heartbroken to see you living this shell of a life you are living now."

Well, shit. Use of the Derek guilt card by one Nancy Meyer.

"Nancy, I'm not ready. When I am, I'll be sure to let everyone know, since my love life has become everyone's favorite past time and talking point. Until then, I don't want to hear anymore about it. And I don't want to hear any more about Blake. I wasn't interested in him then and I'm not interested in him now. Actually, I would've preferred that he'd never come back here, honestly. Just thinking about him makes me angry and I think it's better that we don't discuss him right now. Okay?" Nancy drops her eyes to the floor.

"Alright, sweetie. In your own time I guess. But just keep in mind what I said. It's okay for you to let go, when you're ready," she replies.

I soften my voice and walk over to where she's sitting. She stands up and I take her hand gently into mine.

"Nancy, I don't mean to be short with you. It's just been a rough couple of days. I'm really sorry. I love you, you know that don't you?"

Bringing me into a tight embrace, she quietly says, "Yes, dear, and I love you as though you're my own daughter." She steps back and gives me a once over. "You look beautiful, Alex. You really do. You just go have fun tonight, and forget all this grown up stuff for a while. You deserve the break." She gives me a quick peck on the cheek before leaving me alone to finish getting ready.

Ten minutes later, there's a knock at the door. "Girls! Go get the door, please. It's Harlow."

"Yay, Harlow!" they all scream in unison.

Before I leave my bathroom, I take note of my appearance in the mirror. Hair down, naturally wavy and kind of messy, but cute. Silky champagne colored halter top...very simple but tight in all the right places. Black short shorts, a must for girls' night. And my favorite six inch T-strap champagne heels. Being 5'1", high heeled shoes are my weakness. I never have to worry about being too tall, so the higher the better. Plus, they make my legs look fantastic. Not that I'm trying to pick anyone up, but it's always nice to just feel sexy and with three kids, feeling sexy is something that doesn't happen too often.

Putting in my silver chandelier earrings, I take one last look, nod to myself in approval, and turn off the light.

Standing in front of the bar, Harlow runs her hands down the front of her outfit smoothing the non-existent wrinkles. "Do I look okay, Alex? I'm kind of nervous," she giggles.

I look at my best friend with her red curly hair flowing down to the middle of her back. She looks amazing. She's wearing a pale pink off the shoulder dress, which goes perfectly with her complexion, that hits her about three inches above her knees. It fits her like a glove. It's definitely tighter than my halter top. With her "hippie" wedge heels to round out the outfit, the kind with the tweed bottom, she looks absolutely beautiful. I'm pretty sure the nervous flush in her cheeks also adds to her beauty factor.

"You look gorgeous, Harlow. Trace is gonna pee himself when he sees you!" We giggle a little too loudly in the parking lot.

With a wicked smile playing on her lips, she replies. "Well, I hope not. Incontinence isn't really my forte."

God, I love this girl.

Once we finalize our appearances, we open the door and enter the bar. I yell to Harlow over the loud music coming from the deck. "How long has it been since we've been out here? It seems like forever!"

"It's been too long that's for sure! Let's grab some beers and then make the rounds to look for Trace," she yells back.

I nod my head and we make our way to the bar. Grabbing our beers we find an empty table, set our purses down and take our seats.

"Do you see him, Harlow?"

I watch her eyes move around the crowd. "No. Not yet. He should be here by now, though. Let me go check the other part of the bar. I'll be back. You stay here and guard the table."

"Okay. Be careful," I demand when she gets up to leave.

"No worries. I'll be right back."

I watch her as long as I can, just to make sure she's okay. Then I turn my attention to my cell phone, making sure Nancy hasn't called. I smile to myself as I picture the girls completing the wonderful make over they'd just started on Nancy as Harlow and I were leaving the house. Green eye shadow, very unnaturally red cheeks, and fuchsia lips. Hair teased and standing straight up...poor woman. It's gonna take her the rest of the night just to get the eye shadow off.

Throwing my phone back into my purse, I start to feel like someone is staring at me. And it's not a good feeling. I feel kind of gross, actually.

I look up to see Bobby Reeves making his way across the bar to our table. Ugh. My gut feeling was right, *gross*. I absolutely detest this man. He's one of those guys that used to be really good looking in high school, but didn't really age well…like, not well at all, but he thinks he did. You know those guys? The ones that gain fifty pounds and lose half of their hair, but they're still convinced that they're the varsity football captain. Bleh.

I dart my eyes in every direction but his, trying to scan the bar for any sign of Harlow or Trace. Just as I grab my purse and start to jump up from the table, I feel a hand on my arm, keeping me in place. "Don't worry, honey. I'll take care of it. No need to bolt," Harlow says with a smug smile, Trace in tow. *Thank God!*

Harlow protectively places her body in between mine and Bobby's. "Don't even bother coming over here Bobby Reeves. Just turn around and walk away!" She says shooing him with her hand. "She's not interested. In fact, for the record, she's *never* going to be interested. So just turn around and go back to where you came from, and I don't mean the table you happen to be parked at this evening, I mean go back to your wife!"

What? I cover my mouth to stifle my laugh.

Oh. My. God. I cannot believe she just said that. I look at Trace with wide eyes and we both start laughing. It can't be helped. What a douche bag. He deserved every bit of what Harlow gave him. I guess it *has* been a while since I'd been out with Harlow, because when the hell did *he* get married?

Watching Bobby and his defeated stride as he heads back to where he was previously "parked", I make a mental note to try to catch a glimpse of the poor woman who thought it suitable to legally wed this man. *Yikes…*

I turn back to Harlow and Trace, giving them a grand smile.

"Hi, Trace. It's nice to see you again. I'm glad to see that you have indeed survived the first few minutes with Harlow. You're definitely doing much better than that guy," I offer, throwing my thumb over my shoulder, obviously indicating Bobby. I reach my hand out to shake his and notice that this man is absolutely, 100% drop dead gorgeous. I must have been extremely side tracked in the office that day, because this man is downright drool worthy. His clear, sky blue eyes are perfectly accentuated by his extremely dark lashes and dark eyebrows. And his smile is just as gorgeous. He actually has one of the most genuine smiles I've seen in a long time. Yeah, this guy is definitely growing on me.

I look over at Harlow and raise my eyebrows in obvious approval. She giggles, and resumes whatever conversation they had been having before going on the offensive against Bobby.

A good hour and a half later, I have learned that Trace O'Connell grew up in Waco. We graduated the same year, but he attended a private school, while Harlow and I were slummin' it in public. He left Waco for a while, but returned when he heard of the recent job opportunity, deciding it was time to move closer to his family, regardless if he landed the job at Synergy or not. A decision I very much respected.

We actually had a lot of the same acquaintances in high school, but I don't remember ever meeting him. Harlow, however, remembered exactly who he was. Which was the *real* reason for her rushing me the day of his interview. She confessed this to me during one of our many trips to the bathroom.

"I knew something was going on!" I yell from the other stall after her admission. "You were acting so *weird* that day!"

Note to Self: Always trust my gut feelings.

We giggle on our way out of the bathroom, stopping at the bar to grab another round of beers. Since I'm beginning to feel a little buzzed, I grab a glass of water as well. Heading back to the table, I stop dead in my tracks.

"Is that–" I turn to Harlow with my eyes popping out of my head, probably very similar to certain cartoon characters I'm subjected to every Saturday morning. I shift my gaze back to our table where I see him, standing right in front of me, in his stupid perfect jeans and his stupid perfect shirt, with his stupid perfect hair. All I want to do right now is punch him in his stupid perfect face.

"Please, Harlow, tell me you didn't," I say walking up to him, not bothering to wait for her answer.

I slam my beer down on the table, next to the glass of water, right in front of Blake…which actually did not have the effect I originally anticipated. Instead of supporting my dramatic entrance like I wanted it to, the beer just foams up over the top of the neck of the bottle and starts flowing all over the table. I turn to Blake, trying to give off the vibe that I *totally* meant for that to happen.

"What the hell are you doing here? Huh?" I snap at him, attempting my mommy death stare. Once again, I'm reminded it needs some serious upgrading, because he's looking back at me with his own Blake Morgan death stare. I would like to go on record that mine is *much* more intimidating than his.

"ALEX!" Harlow yells. "What's *wrong* with you?"

"I would just like to know what he's doing here." I keep my eyes fiercely glued to his while I continue speaking. "I mean, I'm sure that you already know what he's doing here, right Harlow? I'm sure that this is another attempt to save Alex from her miserable existence." I turn my glare to Harlow.

"Alex, I have *no* idea what you're talking about. And I have *no* idea what he's doing here. But, last time I checked, Waco was still part of the free country in which we live. I wasn't aware that there was some sort of requirement for an 'Alex Approved' guest list for George's Bar. If I had known, I would have sent out a mass email to all of Waco!" she shouts in my face.

Did she just "finger quote" me?

Turning back to Blake, I state matter-of-factly, "Newsflash... just as much for you as for everyone else I've been in contact with lately. I don't need you here to rescue me! I don't need you here to be my hero! What the hell are you even *doing* here? I don't even want you here! Why can't you just leave me alone!" I am literally yelling at the top of my lungs and breathing like I just ran a marathon. Tears are forming at the base of my lashes, but I refuse to cry.

Blake doesn't say a word. He says absolutely nothing. He just looks at me, then Harlow, then says something that I can't hear to Trace, turns his back to me, and walks out of the bar.

"Really, Alex, you can be such a *bitch* sometimes,"

Harlow bites at me through her clenched teeth. She runs after Blake, leaving me on my own with Trace. What the hell is *her* problem? I roll my eyes in annoyance and turn my attention to the stunned man standing next to me.

"Sorry about that, Trace," I say apologetically. "I've had enough of that man this week to last me a lifetime. I apologize for losing it like that, but I warned Harlow to not push me about him. It's kind of a long story."

We stare at each other for a minute. He seems hesitant to speak. I think I scare the poor guy.

"Well, Alex," he says nervously clearing his throat. "Um, that's actually *my* fault. I invited him." Trace stops to let it sink in that I just ripped into my best friend for no reason...then continues.

"I knew Harlow was inviting you, and Blake and I have been friends forever, so I invited him. I had no idea you guys had any kind of history. He's never mentioned you. I thought you guys would hit it off," he says chuckling. "But obviously I was wrong. Honestly Alex, I had no idea. I'm so sorry."

Trace and Blake were friends? Like long time friends? And he never mentioned me? At all? Like, ever?

Well, jeez...

Don't I feel like a narcissistic asshole.

CHAPTER SEVEN

In an effort to not completely ruin the rest of the evening, I figure it best to stay and let Harlow and Trace have some time to catch up. Obviously, having already reached my drinking threshold, I drink only water for the rest of the night. While rehydrating, I do manage to get Trace to tell me Blake's top secret location.

Although staying with his parents really isn't groundbreaking news, Trace seems extremely hesitant to give up the information...most likely because of my unfortunate outburst earlier in the evening. However, approximately three shots later – shots that I bought by the way – I'm able to wrangle it out of him. I do this knowing I have some major damage control to take care of in the morning.

Harlow is refusing to really engage in any conversation with me, understandably so. After a while, I ask if it's okay if I just take her car to my house. Since I haven't had anything to drink since my run-in with Blake, which was two beers and three hours ago, it's safe to say I have no more alcohol in my system. And I kinda don't want to watch her flirt with Trace anymore. Some things are just better unseen.

She immediately responds with an enthusiastic "Yes!", since that leaves her "needing a ride". With the delighted look on her face, I'm pretty sure that all is forgiven between us.

Nancy calls to let me know that she's already taken the girls to her house and encourages me to sleep in the next morning. *Yeah, right.* That would be wonderful, except I really don't think I'll be getting much sleep tonight or tomorrow morning. I have plans to be up early.

Leaving the bar and finally making my way to the house, I find my thoughts wandering to my earlier outburst with Blake. The look on his face when he first saw me was one of complete shock, so I'm pretty sure he had no idea of Trace's matchmaking scheme. But it was the look of outrage on his face right after I first approached the table that wouldn't leave my mind. It actually sends a jolt of pain to my heart. Even in my slightly inebriated, obviously ill-tempered state, it hurt to see that he was *that* angry with me.

With the memories of the last day of summer that Blake and I shared still lingering in my mind, I start to really allow myself to think honestly about the past. I feel completely…well, I feel at a loss. Had I been so completely callused to not even acknowledge Blake's gift to me? Did I even bother to discuss the charm with him? Ask him what it meant? What he was trying to say?

No, I didn't.

My lip starts quivering as I begin to remember how much Blake was actually involved in my life. Time that I chose to dismiss. It's weird, because now that I think about it, Blake was always there. Blake and I had been best friends. We grew up together. We did everything together. But after I met Derek in junior high, I just left him behind…without even a second thought. No more phone calls, no more fishing, no more movie nights. Nothing.

No wonder he wants nothing to do with me.

I start to feel anger rise in my bloodstream, but not at Blake this time. This anger is reserved for me. I had become so wrapped up in Derek and the infatuation that started the day I met him, I completely disregarded any prior history with Blake. Thirteen years worth of history. And I continued to do it through high school. I never attempted to make contact with him during college or even to call him when we moved back to Waco. What kind of person does that make me?

No wonder he never mentioned me to Trace. And here I was convinced that he came back to Waco to save *me*. To be *my* hero. To fix *my* life…

Note to Self: I am 110% a narcissistic asshole.

Utterly disgusted, I walk into my house knowing that the first thing I'm going to do tomorrow is go to Blake Morgan and apologize for the person I was. And the person I have evidently become.

The drive to Mr. and Mrs. Morgan's house is a familiar

one. And it's a good thing it is, because I'm finding it extremely hard to concentrate on where I'm actually driving at the moment. I am, however, breaking down every possible scenario that could happen when I knock on that door. Good news is, as each and every scenario plays out in my head, they all end in one of two ways. He either speaks to me or he doesn't.

That's a 50% success rate. Not bad when considering my actions last evening...that and those many years I spent dismissing Blake entirely.

Memories begin to flood my mind as I drive up to the red brick two story house I spent so much time at while growing up.

...Blake and I climbing the huge oak tree in the front of his house to get to the tree fort we built together when we were seven years old.

...Both of us playing hide-and-seek in the garden by the side of his house with me yelling at him for cheating...there's no way he could count to one hundred that fast.

...The time we made a bike ramp and tried to jump the fence...definitely not one of our best moments. I find myself grinning widely at that memory. Mainly because Blake couldn't make the jump, ruined his bike, and had to ride his sister's very pink Barbie bike until he *learned his lesson* (as his parents put it). I tortured him with that one for years.

Parking my car in the drive, I look at the front door and breathe a heavy sigh. I glance down at my hands as I remove them from the steering wheel – they're slightly trembling. I shake them in an effort to get rid of the obvious nervous energy and wipe my sweaty palms on my jeans. I run my hair over my ponytail to smooth any fly-aways and exit the car.

Looking down while straightening my "Goonies Never Say Die" t-shirt, another memory surfaces.

Blake and I used to make homemade t-shirts all the time together. Mine were always way better than his, *of course*, but at least he tried. My favorite one of his was this army green, *G.I Joe* "Knowing is Half the Battle" t-shirt. He wore it all the time. So much so that the iron on letters started falling off and it eventually read "Koin is alf Bat." God, I would laugh every time he would wear it. I think that's why he wore it so much.

I look back at my hands. They are still shaking. It seems that even with the comfort of old memories running through my mind, I still can't shake off my nerves. Making my way to the front door, I mentally chastise my anxiety. "This is ridiculous, Alex. You're a grown woman. Act like it," I mutter while walking up the porch steps. I note there's only a motorcycle parked in the driveway, which bodes well in my favor. This is going to be difficult enough without having a parental audience.

Approaching the door, I raise my fist to knock, pausing for another second to take in a cleansing breath. Breathing out, I say a prayer and knock loudly.

I hear his heavy footsteps coming towards the door, followed by the sound of the deadbolt unlocking. I watch nervously as the handle turns, but when I look up, I'm completely unprepared for what is standing directly in front of my face.

As the door flies open, so does my mouth. Blake is standing in front of me, shirtless, wearing only his red and navy plaid pajama bottoms, bare feet on the floor. His light brown hair is all over the place, but incredibly sexy as it falls messily over his forehead and flips out from behind his ears. One look at this man's stomach renders me momentarily speechless, and I have to fight to keep myself from running my hands over every single hardened ridge of his abs. So instead, I place my hands over my open mouth and start giggling like a ten year old little girl.

Mid-giggle, I notice the door starting to close. I quickly jump into action. I immediately put my foot in the doorjamb and my hands on the door, using all of my weight to keep him from being able to close it – a trick he taught *me* by the way.

Shaking his head at me through the opening that I'm desperately trying to maintain, Blake emphatically states, "Nope. Mmm-mm, Alex. It's too early for this right now. Go home."

I start to say something when he cuts me off. "There can't possibly be anything left for you to say after the drunken tantrum you threw last night. You remember? The one you decided to throw in the middle of a bar? The one in which you embarrassed the shit out of yourself? *Very* classy by the way…"

Jeez…obviously I wasn't the only one who got zero sleep last night.

"Blake, ple–" I start to say, but as I try to push as hard as I can to keep the door open, he shoves the door making progress in his attempt to shut it and I'm thrown backward a bit, cutting off my words. "I don't want to talk right now, Alex." I push back with all of my might.

"Well…*too bad.* You need to hear what I have to say, Blake!"

Quickly turning my back to the door, I push as hard as I

can, using my legs for strength. I extend my arm and wrap my fingers around the side, to get a better grip. Unfortunately, at the same time, Blake finally manages to slam it shut.

I swear I hear four separate crunches before I can get the words out of my mouth.

"Blake! My fingers! Damn it, open the door! Now!" I'm sure my fingers have fallen straight to the floor. I don't even want to look.

The door jerks open and I hastily pull my throbbing fingers to the safety of my chest. Moisture gathers in my eyes as I move my hand in front of my face to examine the now very red, very flattened sections of my fingers where the door caught. My whole arm is shaking as the pain pulsates clear up to my shoulder. I pull it back into my chest and protectively cover it with my other hand, and turn to glare at Blake through the tears.

"Shit, Alex. Let me look at 'em," Blake says angrily. I'm not sure if he is mad at me or at himself for hurting my hand. But just in case, I continue my glare. He whips open the door and steps out onto the porch.

Oh.

My.

God.

He looks even more gorgeous in the sunlight. Almost like that day on the lake, with the sun peeking through his messy hair. If I wasn't in excruciating pain right now, I would be really enjoying the view.

Alex, control yourself.

I attempt to clear my mind from all potentially naughty thoughts. Then I remember my situation and gather my wits.

"Really, Blake? What the hell?" I ask in annoyance. "I

get that you're pissed, but can you at least act like an adult about it? Slamming the door in my face? Real mature, *jerk*." I try bending my fingers. They're stiff, but I can bend them a bit. I grimace and suck in a breath as pain shoots up my arm.

"Really? You want to talk about mature right now? After last night? You want to go there?"

I have no witty retort, so I just look at him.

"Yeah, that's what I thought," he says, holding out his hand. His voice softens. "Just let me look at them, Alex."

I timidly hold my hand out for his inspection. He's surprisingly gentle as he takes my hand and holds it in front of his face, looking closely at my fingers. I can feel his warm breath hitting the palm of my hand. I let out a small breath of air and briefly let myself look at his eyes while he examines my fingers. I forgot how beautiful they were. A cross between very light brown and olive green. As I stand, staring at him...he looks up, catches my gaze and holds it. Determined not to lose this battle, I continue to look at him until he breaks away.

"You need to get some ice on them. Come on. I'll get you something," he says, stepping aside so I can enter his house, still holding my hand.

"It's fine, Blake. I'm just going to go. I think enough damage has been done," I say, knowing I mean this in a way that doesn't pertain to my fingers. I extract my hand from his and turn to walk to my car, lump forming in my throat. I don't know what I was thinking coming here. Some things just can't be repaired. I know this better than anyone...I should be the poster girl for irreparable damage.

I take a step to leave when I feel Blake's hand hook my good hand. "Alex, don't. Let me get you some ice." I feel an electrical pulse pass through my body as his fingers slide up to wrap around my wrist, pulling me into his house. I follow him as he leads me into the kitchen. He pulls out a bar stool from under the counter and motions with his hand for me to sit down. Not until I'm seated does he let go of my wrist to walk into the kitchen. He grabs a plastic bag out of a drawer and starts to fill it with ice from the freezer. I can't help but watch the muscles in his back working as he deposits the ice into the bag. He turns, disrupting my insane thoughts, and brings the ice back to where I'm sitting. He takes my hurt hand, tenderly placing it in his own, and sets the bag on top of my fingers.

We sit in silence, probably because we're both too stubborn to be the first to break. But, knowing I came here to make amends for some things, I willingly, *for the record,* break first.

"Listen, I just wanted to come by to say I'm really sorry about last night, Blake. Things have been a little stressful over the last couple of days and I'm dealing with a lot right now. And seeing you the other day…well, it just threw me. Then you helped me and… honestly, it's been a long time since someone has helped me like that. Except Harlow of course, but that's kind of her main job right now." I laugh softly at my joke. Blake does not. So I keep going.

"Blake, you have to understand that it's hard for me to accept help sometimes. It isn't easy for me to admit that I need help, but I *needed* help that day. So, not only were you incredibly blessed with having the opportunity to help me that morning, I'm sure ruining whatever plans you had for the day, but you were also the victim of my misdirected anger last night simply because of the help you provided."

How many times did I just say help? One hundred?

"I guess you can say that I have issues with help in general," I joke to him. I decide to just stop talking. I know I'm completely rambling; I do that when I'm nervous.

I make sure I look him directly in the eyes during my explanation. Unfortunately, there is absolutely, positively, no response that I can read on his face.

Um, I guess my apologies need upgrading too? I decide to give it one more try.

"I'm sorry, Blake. Do you think we can just start over? Forget the last couple of days?"

I continue to watch his expression. He lets out a deep sigh.

"Listen, Alex. You need to know something. I didn't come here for *you*. I didn't come back to *help* you, or *save* you, or *take care* of you. I feel that I need to say that. I didn't come here to be your hero or to carry you away on a white horse. I came here solely to help my family."

Sarcasm duly noted.

"My father's retiring and I need to decide what I'm going to do with his business. I might take it over, I might sell it, I haven't decided yet. Regardless, my coming back had *nothing* to do with you. "

Jeez – Alright already.

"Okay, Blake, I get it!"

Using the only working hand I've got left, I immediately push myself up to get off the stool, because for some reason, those words take all of the air out of my lungs. When I start to stand, he holds me in place and forces me to look at him. His face softens.

"No, you *don't* get it, Alex. I need you to know that so

you can get over whatever dumb ass, anger projecting issues you have going on regarding being *helped, saved,* or *taken care of* in any way. I don't plan on doing any of that for you." He smiles and continues. "So that means we should be able to be friends, right? If I promise *not* to help you?"

Choking back a laugh he adds, "But you do realize how backwards that actually is, don't you?"

It's impossible to describe, but the relief I feel at that moment is like one thousand pounds have been removed from my shoulders. I don't know if it has to do with no longer feeling the pressure of any possible expectations from Blake, or if it's the fact that I know that with that one smile, he's forgiving me for my treatment of him all these years. But, whatever the reason, I can physically feel the release of pressure from my body.

Friends. Yeah, I can do friends I think.

Friends would be really nice actually.

Giving him a gigantic smile, I reach out and hug him, throwing my good hand behind his neck. "I would really like that, Blake."

He grins back at me while releasing me from our embrace. Then he looks directly at my hand.

"Yeah, well, don't come running to me when you figure out your fingers won't be working right for the next couple of weeks." He chuckles underneath his breath before continuing. "Oh, and by the way... It's gonna be a bitch driving yourself to the emergency room to see if they're broken. I would help you but..."

Blake shrugs his shoulder and throws a piece of ice in his mouth as he saunters out of the kitchen.

Well...

Shit.

CHAPTER EIGHT

"Stop laughing, Blake. It's not funny," I whine. "My hand hurts and your gloating is *not* helping."

I glance over at Blake. I can tell he's trying to keep from smiling and can't seem to control it any longer. He starts laughing...*again.*

"Blake, seriously. Stop it. You're starting to make me really mad. I'm in a lot of pain." I huff and roll my eyes. "God, you're ridiculous."

Blake starts gasping for air. *Ridiculous.*

"I can't help it Alex. That was the funniest thing I've seen in a long time," he says, wiping the tears from his eyes. "You're so stubborn. You should've seen your face...it was hilarious." He stops to catch his breath. "It was all scrunched up in determination, like the little engine that could." The mental picture must have sealed the deal because now he's practically doubled over, grabbing his stomach and trying to catch his breath through the laughter.

"Oh my God, did you just snort? How freakin' old are you?"

I did attempt to drive, but it was pretty much impossible. I didn't feel that shifting with my wrist was in the best interests of the driving community...I *have* to be the only person in the world who has a Suburban with a manual transmission. (Great idea, Derek) So, I had to break down and ask Blake to drive me. In *my* car. After my *huge* anti-help speech. *Typical.*

Now, as I watch Blake in his fit of laughter, I'm seriously regretting my decision. I should have just walked my ass to the hospital.

"I'm glad that you find it so hilarious that your overreaction to me, wanting to have a simple conversation with you, ended up with my broken fingers. I find nothing funny about it; my hand is throbbing right now!" I reposition the ice pack on my hand.

I guess my comment strikes a nerve, because his outburst comes to an abrupt halt.

He looks at me with apologetic eyes. "Alex, I said I was sorry. I feel really bad. I would never hurt you on purpose; I hope that you know that."

Damn those eyes.

"Yeah, well stop laughing or I'll get out and walk. Seriously." He once again focuses on the road.

I eye him for a couple of seconds. Once I'm sure he's finished his juvenile antics, I pull out my phone to make the necessary calls. First, I call Nancy to let her know that I hurt my hand and that I'm currently on my way to the ER, with one Blake Morgan. She wisely chooses to make no comment.

She's due to go out of town with John to a realty conference, so my next call is to Harlow. I ask if she can pick up the girls from Nancy's for me since they need to get on the road. I have a feeling I'll get an earful later. I think the possibility of having a broken hand trumps her sarcasm at the moment.

She in turn lets me know that she's going to have to bring the girls to the hospital because she's going out of town with Trace to help him move some more of his stuff back to Waco. At this point, I choose to leave any of my sarcastic commentary out of the conversation as well, knowing that she will *definitely* be getting an earful later.

So no Harlow or Nancy to help this weekend. Great, of all the weekends...

We finally get to the hospital, the rest of the trip laughter free. After getting all the paperwork from the registration desk, I quickly find out that writing with my left hand is almost as impossible as trying to drive my car. I scowl at Blake. He's still trying not to laugh, but this time it's at my illegible handwriting.

"Alex, give me the paperwork. I can fill it out for you. Just tell me what to write."

I don't even bother to look at him because I know his face looks just like it did the majority of the car ride here. "No, it's fine. I can do it. I have to do it. It's not like you're going to be around all hours of the day to write for me whenever I need you to. I might as well start working on it now," I say with a sigh.

After about five minutes, the only thing I have managed to write is my name and half of my address. I blow out an exaggerated deep breath. Blake reaches over and grabs the clipboard from off my lap.

"What the–?"

"Seriously, Alex. I get it. You can do it. But honestly, at this rate, your hand will be completely healed by the time you're finished. Just let me write the information for you. It'll be a lot faster and we can get you home sooner. I'm sure your girls don't want to spend the next week in this hospital because their mother is too stubborn to let a friend write some information for her on a piece of paper."

Okay, first of all – using the kids is really low. Second of all, how does he know I have "girls"? First he knows where I work, now this? I find this *very, very* interesting.

Note to Self: Open the "How does Blake know so much about me" investigation.

"Fine. But only because I want to get out of here. I hate hospitals." I say the last part without even meaning to. It just slips out, and when I turn to look at Blake to see if he caught it, he's looking right back at me with heavyhearted eyes.

Don't do it…Don't say it…

"I was sorry to hear about Derek, Alex. I can't even begin to imagine a loss like that. You had been together for–"

"Seventeen years," I finish for him. "Yeah, it definitely wasn't easy." I let out a deep breath and slap my good hand down on my leg. "But life goes on, right? Can we just get back to the paperwork?" I'm in enough pain right now without even approaching that discussion.

"Of course." Blake obviously understands and doesn't say anymore.

Fifteen minutes later the paperwork is done and turned in to the check-in desk. *Okay – so maybe he had a point.* Thirty minutes after that, we're in the exam room waiting for the doctor. Blake hasn't really said much since I shut down the attempt to have the "Derek's Untimely Death" discussion. I think he's worried about upsetting me, so I decide to make an effort and engage him in conversation.

"So, Blake, what have you been doing since graduation? You kind of just disappeared."

"Yeah. I...well, I just needed to get out of this town. There really wasn't anything for me here anymore." He shifts his weight uncomfortably in his chair. I can't help but feel there's more he wants to say, but he skips right over the comment and keeps talking.

"I headed out to Colorado and took some business classes. Then I transferred into the University of Colorado and got a degree in Construction Engineering Management. I knew I wanted to stay in dad's line of work and eventually take over his business if he needed me to. But, he didn't need me right then, so I started my own construction business in Colorado. I still own the business and luckily, I can manage it from here, but eventually I'll need to figure out what I'm going to do with it."

"Hmm. Tough one. Would you rather stay in Colorado?" I ask.

Running his hand through his hair he says, "I thought I did. Now I'm not so sure. I guess I'll have to figure something out soon though." I start to ask another question, but we're interrupted by the doctor. As he enters the room, Blake and I both look at him, then immediately look at each other with our eyes raised and mouths open in surprise. As we quietly giggle, it becomes more and more difficult to contain. There's just something extra funny about trying to cover up laughter; it makes it virtually impossible and there are only so many times you can raise your hand to your mouth and clear your throat. Yeah, it's completely obvious we are laughing at this man.

Sitting right on the end of his nose, is the largest, darkest mole I've ever seen in my entire life. It has a hair sticking out that is approximately three inches long. I feel the sudden urge to grab my purse and get my tweezers. I look over at Blake and watch his lips as he silently mouths *Guaca-mole*.

Damn you, Austin Powers.

Stop it, I mouth back at him.

When the doctor approaches the table, I feel my eyes start to cross as they continue to focus on his nose. Over his shoulder, I can see Blake still holding his hand over his mouth trying to cover his laughter. I try to straighten my face, but it doesn't work, so I just go with it and flash the man the biggest, fakest smile I've ever attempted. It seems the easiest thing to do at the moment.

Dr. Mole begins to examine my hand, and if I'm not mistaken, he's getting enjoyment out of inflicting excruciating pain on my poor fingers.

It's at that point that I decide I can't continue to look at Blake... I don't think my fingers can take anymore. So in an attempt to maintain a straight face, I move my eyes to focus on the floor. I breathe in deeply – both in effort to stop laughing and to manage the pain now radiating through my hand all the way up my arm.

The doctor finishes his exam and leaves the room without saying another word. Blake and I look at each other, finally free to laugh out loud.

"Holy Moley! Did you see the size of that thing?" Blake lets out a chuckle. I smile to myself. *Oh, Austin Powers. How you make me laugh.*

"That poor man. I feel bad for laughing. But really? He's a doctor. There isn't anything he could do to remove it? I mean, he does have to talk to people all day." I shake my head in disgust. "It was even worse up close, Blake."

Blake lets out a loud laugh. "Well, I feel bad enough you have to be here. I would feel really bad if you had been poked in the eye with that thing. Did you see the length of that whisker? It may actually be Guinness Book of World Records worthy."

I let out another giggle, this time covering my mouth in case the doctor walks in. It feels really good to laugh.

The doctor enters the room shortly after, keeping a safe distance from me this time. He throws the x-rays up on the lit board and tells me that I haven't broken any bones. I do, however, have some bone contusions and soft tissue injuries. Blake lets out a sigh of relief and pats my arm, letting me know he's sorry.

After Dr. Mole finishes his expert diagnosis, I walk out of the exam room with my fingers splinted and wrapped in gauze, and with a prescription for pain medicine. Making my way through the ER waiting room and into the main lobby, I find myself pummeled by three little girls and one Harlow. They all immediately look at my hand with huge eyes.

"Oh my gosh. Mommy, what happened? Are you okay?" Rylie asks, looking at my hand sadly.

"I'm okay baby. I just got my hand caught in the door. No broken bones so mommy will be just fine. Don't worry, cuckoo head." I give her a big hug, being extra careful with my hand.

"Mama – are you sure? That looks like it hurts a lot! Do you want me to carry your purse?" Kyndall offers.

I give her a grateful smile. "Kyndall – that would be really helpful actually. Thank you so much, my sweet baby girl." I lean over to give her a squeeze while still holding on to Rylie.

"No, Mommy! I'm the baby!" Rylie shouts and pushes Kyndall away from me. Seriously, we're doing this right now? What happened to feeling sorry for mommy?

"No, you're not," Kyndall shoots back. "You're four years old now. You're not the baby. You're a big girl. Isn't that what you're always saying? Like, all day long? How you're a big girl now? So there–" She crosses her arms over her chest and finishes with an exaggerated "hmpf".

Getting another push in, Rylie yells again, "Yes I am, Kyndall!" Then she takes a breath as if to calm herself down. "Stop talking at me Kyndall, you make my head hurt."

Kyndall lets out an angry gasp and I look to Harlow for help.

Harlow takes a chocolate bar out of her purse and holds it right in front of Rylie's face. Rylie takes one look at the chocolate and grins. Fight forgotten. She lets go of me and goes straight into Harlow's arms as she picks her up. Harlow gives her the chocolate, but not before she breaks off two other pieces and gives them to Nycole and Kyndall, giving them a wink in the process.

I take in a deep breath. "Thanks. Hey, where's mine?" I say, bumping Harlow's hip with mine.

Rolling her eyes while chewing her piece of chocolate, Nycole huffs. "You guys are teaching her bad habits, you know. You always give her stuff like that when she's bad. She's going to start being bad *just* to get candy, Mom. Jeez."

While I'm mentally strangling her, I hear the lobby doors open behind me from the ER waiting room.

"Hey Blake," Harlow says as he walks up behind us. "I'm assuming you guys have worked out your issues?" She looks down at my hand and then back at Blake. Pointing her finger in his face she adds, "You and I are going to have a long talk when I get back. I mean *really* Blake, did you have to slam her hand in the door?"

All three heads whip around and their eyes narrow as the girls take their first look at Blake Morgan. I press my lips together as I try not to encourage the behavior by triumphantly smiling. Watching all three of them practice their own versions of the mommy death stare on Blake is somewhat redeeming. I quickly glance at Blake and shrug my shoulders.

Harlow assesses the situation and I can tell she's also struggling to keep a straight face. "Oops...probably not the best time to mention the whole 'slamming the door and breaking Alex's hand' thing. Sorry about that, Blake."

Turning to me she says, "Also probably not the best time for this either, but I'm leaving right now to go meet Trace. So that means *he's* going to need to drive you home." She nods her head towards Blake and clears her throat, still trying to contain her laughter when she looks again at the girls still glaring at Blake. "I'm also sorry about *that*, Blake." I can't help but let out a small giggle. I know she's trying, but it's blatantly obvious she's finding this situation very amusing.

With all three girls standing protectively around my legs and holding on to my waist, I watch Blake as he studies them all with respectful eyes. Then he looks back at me and sighs.

"Well," he says, pulling my keys from his pocket, "This is going to be interesting."

For once I couldn't agree more.

I look at my girls and give them each a reassuring smile. I place my good hand on each of their heads as I make the introductions. "Nycole, Kyndall, Rylie, this is Blake Morgan. My very, very good friend. He was actually my *best friend* growing up." I give them a quick wink and whisper quietly to them, "Now ease up on the poor guy, he's not that bad." I grin at Blake.

Blake flashes me his gorgeous smile, but immediately turns his attention to my girls. "It's nice to meet you lovely ladies." He crouches down so he can look them each in the eyes. "I'm really sorry about the accident with your mom's hand. I promise all of you that I'm going to do everything that I can to make her feel all better, if you guys don't mind me helping her out for a while."

I internally cringe at the word help. I watch my girls, each of them mesmerized by Blake's beautiful and endearing smile, as they shake his hand. As they smile innocently back at him, I feel a wall crash down from around my heart.

Well, I guess Blake was right again.

This is *definitely* going to be interesting.

Walking into our house, I look at the living room in dismay. If I would have known how the events of today were going to unfold, I would've definitely straightened up. It looks like a tornado has been through the interior of my entire house. I vaguely remember tripping over the Lego house that Nancy and the kids must have built before she took them to her house, when I came home last night, but I didn't bother cleaning it up. Now there are Lego's strewn all over the floor along with a soccer ball, Hello Kitty pillow, Barbie dolls, Ken dolls dressed up in Barbie clothes, a couple of these tiny little dolls that I absolutely hate because trying to put their clothes on is a very daunting task, my bra and shoes from last night – *oops*...all over the living room floor.

I lean down slowly to pick up the bra as Blake enters the house with the girls following him. Quickly lodging it behind the couch before he can see it, I feel my hand starting to throb more and more. Blake, thankfully, stopped by the pharmacy on the way home for my pain medicine. The main question is when I can actually take it. I don't want to be knocked out all night. What if Rylie has another accident in her bed? What if Kyndall has a nightmare? She's had nightmares ever since Derek died. I guess I'll have to try to tough it out tonight.

I turn to watch Blake observing the unfortunate state of my house. A corner of his mouth tips up when he spots the Ken dolls.

"Don't laugh, Blake. That might be you one day. Actually, I *guarantee* that will be you if you hang around here long enough," I say, giggling. I know this is the truth.

Chuckling under his breath, he walks to the kitchen and places the prescription bag on the counter. He turns to face the girls who are still on his heels. "Well, it's a good thing I look good in pink." He shakes his fingers at the girls. "But no sequins! That's where I draw the line."

Giggles erupt. Yes, I think the girls have definitely forgiven Blake. *Traitors.*

"Girls, one accident is enough for the day, don't you

think? I need you to pick up the toys and everything else that's on the floor that doesn't belong there and take it where is does belong. Okay?"

The girls just stand there looking back at me. *I'm sorry...am I speaking Greek?*

"Girls! Please, do as I say. This place is a wreck and I want us to make a good impression for my friend Blake." At the mention of Blake's name, the girls spring into action. Shrieks and giggles fill the living room as they run back and forth to their respective bedrooms putting away their things. I haven't heard them giggle this much in a long time. Thinking back to this morning when I actually giggled as well, I'm beginning to think this is just a Blake Morgan side effect. He should come with a warning label.

Note to Self: Finding yourself anywhere within a five foot radius of Blake Morgan leads to infectious giggling.

"Mom, what's your bra doing behind the couch?" Nycole says, holding up my bra for all the freakin' world to see. I walk over and snatch it from her hand and put it behind my back. She gives me an extremely calculating little smile. "Well, you should put your stuff away, too. I mean, it's only fair, right? Lead by example – that's what you always tell me."

Oh. My. God.

Did that just come out of my child's mouth?

I tilt my head and stare at her, raising only my left eyebrow. This is my code for "You have about two seconds to think about what you just said and correct it before you *really* get in trouble." She has actually become *very* familiar with this code over the last couple of months. Needless to say, she walks behind my back and grabs the bra, still holding it where Blake can see. I'm pretty sure she's doing this as an act of retaliation. "Sorry, Mom. I'll put it in your drawer for you."

"Thanks, Nyc." I want to add a major lecture about how to appropriately speak to adults, mainly your own mother, but I figure I should wait until Blake isn't around.

I turn and see Blake silently laughing in the kitchen.

"Nice job. That was obviously a very effective form of communication."

"Yeah, well, you pick up a few useful things as a parent, such as telepathic chastisement. I've tried it on Harlow, but evidently it's strictly a parent/child thing," I state nonchalantly. I walk into the kitchen where Blake's leaning against the counter.

I turn quickly to avoid thinking about how sexy he looks in his torn jeans, army green t-shirt (slightly resembling his G.I. Joe one – minus the letters) that makes his eyes look even more amazing, and his gorgeous hair – still flipping up behind his ears, but now evidently styled to look that way. Grabbing a glass out of the cabinet, I clear my throat – *jeez, it's hot in here.* My throat feels like sandpaper.

"Want something to drink?" I ask.

"Nope, I'm good."

Glass in hand, I make my way to the refrigerator and

reach up to pull the door open. Mind obviously on all things Blake, I ram my gauze covered fingers right into the door.

"Ahh!" I scream. Tears immediately find their way to my eyes from the pain. Instinctively, I drop the glass in order to once again clutch my throbbing hand safely against my chest. Glass shatters all over the kitchen floor.

"What happened?"

"Are you okay, Mommy?"

I hear the girls cry out as they run into the kitchen to see what major calamity just occurred. Kyndall's leading the pack, but when she sees the glass all over the floor, she stops abruptly. This leads to Nycole running straight into the back of her and Rylie running into the back of Nycole. It's actually a very *Three Stooges* moment and if my fingers weren't shooting pain throughout my entire body right now, I would've found it hilarious.

Before I can say anything, Blake immediately runs to the girls and herds them out of the kitchen using his arms. I watch Kyndall and Nycole jumping up and down trying to see over them, while Rylie sticks her little head just underneath. Concern etched all over their faces.

"Alex, are you okay?" he shouts over his shoulder as he signals for the girls to stay put.

"Yeah, I'm okay!" But I know I'm not. The tears that started from the pain continue from frustration. Still holding my throbbing hand, I look down at the floor. At the sight of the glass shards that are going to be an absolute *bitch* to clean up, my lip starts quivering and I know I'm about to lose it. Just as I hear Blake round the corner, I attempt to wipe my face with my hands. I quickly suck in a breath of air as the pain once again shoots up my entire arm.

I look up to see Blake enter the kitchen area. He approaches me with extreme caution. I'm not sure whether it's because of the glass shards on the floor or because he senses my imminent breakdown. Regardless, at the sight of him my shoulders begin to shake and the tears begin to stream steadily down my cheeks. I immediately look down to the floor in embarrassment. With my eyes lowered, I watch his boots make their way through the sea of glass and stop right by my feet. I'm still looking downward when puts his hand under my chin, and tilts my head back, forcing me to look at him.

"It's okay, Alex. I'm right here. Everything will be fine," he says as his worried eyes watch the tears run down my cheeks. He gently puts his hands on each side of my face and wipes the tears away with his thumbs. Then he pulls me closely into his chest, puts his arms gently around my shoulders, and places his chin on the top of my head.

I begin to sob.

He runs circles on my back with one hand while running his other hand over my hair in an effort to calm me. In the midst of my tears, I can't help but catch a whiff of him. Leather and soap. It's oddly comforting.

"Shh, it's okay, Alex. Let it out. It's been a shit day," he says with a chuckle, still holding me protectively in his arms.

And with that, I begin laughing.

"It has been a *shit* day. Thank you for being there to experience every shitty second of it, Blake." I continue laughing. I have a feeling I am very near my emotional delirium threshold.

Blake pulls back from me and his eyes wander my face. "No problem. That's what friends are for."

We stare at each other for a few seconds. I can't believe this man's kindness. After everything, he is right here, comforting me.

"Thank you, Blake, for everything. It means a lot that you're here right now, especially after the way I treated you the last night."

"Like I said, not a problem." He ends his statement with a shrug of his shoulders.

We continue to gaze at each other for another second. The look is broken by the sound of three pairs of feet hesitantly making their way back into the kitchen

"Mom, are you okay? It's been a while. I know Blake told us to stay, but we were worried," Nycole says, eyeing the closeness between Blake and me.

I look over to see her arms protectively around her sisters, one on each side. Her worried eyes look back at me for reassurance. I release Blake from our embrace and turn to face her. I wipe the remaining tears from my eyes and sniffle. I motion for them to stay where they are. "Yes, baby. I'm fine. I'm just really frustrated because my hand hurts and I can't do the things I normally do."

Nycole's eyes light up. "Well, Mom, it's a good thing Blake's here to help. Then you don't have to do everything like you normally do. You don't have to be sad anymore."

I look back at Blake and offer him a sheepish smile, knowing that her words have a much deeper meaning than they sound. And I'm sure that Nycole, as smart as she is, knows this too.

I turn back to Nycole and nod my head, acknowledging that I understand the true meaning of her statement. I then look at the other two and let out a long sigh. "Alright girls, go get the broom and dust pan from the laundry room and bring them to Blake. He's got a big mess to clean up!" Shrieks and giggles arise again as they all three run out of the room to fetch the broom. I look at Blake and sniffle again, swiping my nose along my shoulder. I move my eyes to the floor. Definitely a big mess.

The thing is... I don't know if I'm referring to the glass all over the floor or to myself.

Either way, it seems Blake definitely has a very big mess to deal with.

CHAPTER NINE

With plenty of help from the girls...who each decide they need to be wearing a pair of my high heels to do so... Blake and I are finally able to declare the kitchen an official "glass free zone". I walk over to the cabinet to grab another glass, because I'm in desperate need of ibuprofen, when I hear "No!" coming from every person in the house. I turn around to see Blake AND the girls laughing at evidently the most hilarious joke of the twenty-first century, all while giving each other high-fives.

Note to Self: I have treacherous little children.

"Hardy-har-har," I state sarcastically, trying unsuccessfully to hide my own laughter. "You guys are *hilarious*." I roll my eyes at them and turn back to the cabinet. Grabbing a glass, I walk over to sink and fill it with water. Placing it on the counter, I grab the ibuprofen bottle and start to open it.

"Did you make sure that you can take those with your pain meds?" I turn around to see Blake standing behind me. He reaches around my body, grabs my water, takes a drink and puts it back down on the counter. *Why?*

"Um, no I didn't because I'm not taking the pain meds. I can't take them with the girls, Blake." I move the glass of water closer to me.

Blake rakes his hand through his hair, as though he's scratching his scalp. I can tell he's frustrated by the tone of his voice. "Alex, you're going to have to take the meds. You won't be able to sleep unless you do, trust me."

"Um, again, no. I'm not taking them, Blake."

The girls feel the tension in the air and slowly start disappearing from the room. Blake looks at me disapprovingly.

"I told you. I'm here to help. I'll wake you if anything happens. But the most important thing is that you rest so you can heal," he says, gesturing towards my fingers.

"Hello! You're *so* not sleeping here Blake. Like I really want to explain *that* to my girls. Plus, I don't want to keep you from anything you need to be doing. Thank you, but I don't need you to stay, I'll be fine. Don't worry."

"The thing is, Alex, I *do* worry, which evidently is the problem here," Blake says, grabbing the ibuprofen pills out of my hand. "I promised the girls I would help you and I *don't* go back on my promises. I'm not sleeping with you in your bed. I'll be on the couch. So there won't be anything to explain to them. They know I'm here to help because I'm the only person able to help right now. You *need* help and you know it. I know it. Your girls know it. I really don't think there is any reason to make a big deal about it. So why don't we just make sure you can take these with the other pills."

God he's annoying.

"Give me the ibuprofen, Blake! You're being ridiculous!" I reach for them but he quickly moves them out of my reach and holds them over his head. "Seriously, Blake! Give them back !"

I jump up to try to reach them, but it's damn near impossible. I attempt to jump again, the jerkiness of the movement killing my hand. "Damn it, Blake! I'm serious!"

"Well, you're just going to have to get over it because I'm not leaving. I can't leave; I drove you here in your car, which means I would have to take your car to my house. I don't think leaving you stranded is a safe alternative. I mean, I'm sure we can figure something out if you really want me to go..." A devious smile breaks across his face. His voice rises louder as he looks over my shoulder. "But I don't plan on going anywhere tonight, that is unless the *girls* want me to. Girls, do you think I should stay and help your mom out?"

I stop mid jump and look back to see all three girls peeking their little heads around the corner of the kitchen, watching my pitiful attempt to grab the ibuprofen from Blake. *The kid card? Again? Really?*

"Why can't he stay, Mama? We're supposed to watch a movie later, Blake promised. You said he was your friend, we don't mind if he stays. It'll be like when we have slumber parties with our friends, right? That way if you can't do something and we're already asleep, Blake can help," Kyndall says to me with a look of confusion on her face.

I'm *so* not ready to deal with this right now. This man shows up a couple of days ago and all of a sudden he has infiltrated my house.

"As I said, Alex, I don't go back on my promises. So the girls and I will be watching– " He motions to the girls for help.

"The Little Mermaid!"

"Spy Kids!"

"Willy Wonka!"

Blake shakes his head and continues, "A movie, which we'll evidently be deciding on later. And since I'll be here anyway, you might as well get some comfortable sleep."

For once, I'm completely at a loss. A man has not spent the night in this house since Derek. I'm not really sure how I feel about having *any* man in this house for an extended period of time. Short visits are fine, but we're talking overnight.

I'm in a whole new realm of confusion.

"Look girls, I know you really like Blake. I like Blake too or he wouldn't be here." I make sure to shoot him a dirty look. "But things are a little more complicated when you're all grown up. It's just not that easy."

"Mom, I don't really see what the problem is. You already broke a glass tonight all over the floor. I think that we all know you need a little help. And we think that Blake being here is good because he can help you after we go to bed. Plus, what if you need something out of the cabinet that we can't reach? Blake's a lot taller and can get it for you. Mom, please, just let him help." Nycole crosses her arms over her chest and shifts her weight to one side.

Help. That evil little word. Damn Harlow for being out of town. This would be so much easier with her here...and a lot less to explain.

"Alright, I'll make you a deal. Blake can stay for one movie. Then I'll decide if I need his help through the night, okay? I'm not making any promises. And I don't want any pouty, grumpy faces if I decide he needs to go home. Got it?"

"Yes, ma'am!" They all shout at the same time, each

with huge grins on their faces.

I snap my head back to Blake who's also grinning, but his smile is more triumphant.

I lean over and whisper, "Look buddy, you need to wipe that smug smile off your face. No promises have been made, so there's absolutely no reason for you to be smiling like that. You're lucky to get to stay for a movie. And for the record, I hope they choose something that will be extremely painful for you to watch. You deserve it."

Speaking of which…

I excitedly turn back to face the girls. "Alright, go pick a movie! Oh, didn't we just get that new Barney movie? I really think Blake would love that one! You should put it on for him!" I direct my eyes over to Blake and shoot him the best, smart-ass grin I can conjure up.

Blake simply glances at me and then turns his full attention back to the girls. He trumps my enthusiasm with an astounding, "The purple dinosaur? I love that one! Do you guys really have a whole movie? I can't wait! Go get it and let's watch it!" He then looks back at me, giving me his own smart-ass grin.

Jerk.

I decide no baths are necessary tonight. My hand hurts too bad, and there's no way Blake's doing it, so I just decide to skip them all together. And since I don't feel like cooking either, we order pizzas for dinner. After the girls are fed, I pop a few ibuprofen (after internet research confirmed that I could indeed take them with the pain pills), and we load up the new Barney movie – despite Nycole's heartfelt protests.

If Blake wants Barney, he's getting Barney. Full length, movie version Barney.

As Blake starts throwing pillows on the floor constructing a make-shift pallet, I watch the girls literally slide off the couch and onto the floor, making their way to sit by him.

"Hey!" I shout. "Isn't anyone going to sit with me? I'm pretty sure I'm the one whose fingers were almost broken today!" I push out my bottom lip and cross my arms over my chest, making my best pouty-face.

Nycole looks at me and laughs. "And you call me dramatic?" She sighs. "Okay, I'll come sit with you." She flings herself on the couch and lands right beside me. She snuggles in next to me and I put my left arm around her and squeeze her tight. Elbow positioned on the arm of the couch with my right hand sticking straight up, I yell to Blake, "Let's get this party started! Push play!"

Blake leans over to grab the remote and turns back to me with a wide grin. Then he looks at the girls and says, "I'm ready for some Barney. You girls?"

"Yeah!" I hear from Kyndall and Rylie while at the same time Nycole protests, "No!"

I chuckle and elbow her in the side. "Stop it. Be nice! I'll let you have Nycole time tomorrow in the office and you can watch whatever you want, sister-free, okay? I know you don't want to watch it, but your sisters are really excited, and evidently so is Blake." I jerk my head towards him and shake my head. We both start laughing. "So you suffer with me tonight, I'll reward you tomorrow. Deal?"

"Deal," she says and then eyes my hand with concern. "How's your hand? Is it okay? Do you need anything?"

Wow. Where's this coming from? Squeezing her shoulder, I look at her. "I'm fine, sweetheart. Thank you though."

"You should take your pain medicine, Mom. We'll be fine. I promise. I think between the both of us, Blake and I can handle Kyndall and Rylie," she says seriously.

Tears start to fill my eyes. I look away because I don't want Nycole to think she's said anything to upset me. But I just can't help myself. I feel incredibly guilty that she's been forced to grow up so quickly. I wanted her to stay my baby forever, but circumstances being what they are, she's had to shoulder more responsibility than most nine year olds. Wiping a tear that escapes my eye, I turn to her and say, "You're right, Nyc. You guys are more than capable of handling those two. If I hurt too much, I'll take them. I promise."

She smiles a grateful smile at me and then looks forward as Barney makes his appearance on the television. She rolls her eyes and exhales loudly. "You *so* owe me."

122

"I love you, you love me…" I hear Blake singing as he walks down the hall. I also hear some shuffling around so I lean over the couch to see what he's doing. He's standing in my hallway, sifting through some of the girls' movies.

"What are you doing?" I ask.

"Getting the girls something to watch. They wanted to have a slumber party in Nycole and Kyndall's room. I hope it's okay, I figured it would be fun for them. Plus, it'll give us a chance to catch up. They're about to pass out anyway so I'll move them once they fall asleep."

I continue to watch him. "Okay."

He goes back to singing the Barney song, and I find myself grinning from ear to ear. Here is this beautiful, massive man, smiling and singing the stupid Barney song in my hallway. I shift my body around to get a better look. I cross my arms on the top of the couch and place my chin on them. I find myself continuing to smile as I watch him. I also find myself genuinely happy that he's back in my life.

He was always a good friend to me. A good person, who turned out to be an even better man. He has every right to be angry with me for so many things, but yet, he doesn't hold a grudge. In fact, here he is, in my house, helping take care of my children. In the midst of all of the misery over the last few years, I guess I must have done something right.

Evidently finding the movie he's looking for, he closes the door to the "movie closet", and heads to the girls room. I hear the girls shout, "Yay!", and once again, giggling ensues. After a few seconds of getting settled, I hear Blake reading their favorite book, making different voices for the characters. I don't hear anything else from the girls. I assume they're entranced by his story telling. Maybe his awesome reading skills will lull them to sleep.

Starting to feel the effects of the day, I yawn as I drag myself off the couch to head to the kitchen. My hand's really starting to hurt again. And I'm pretty sure that Blake will be staying the night because it's inevitable…I'm going to have to take the damn pills.

I pick up the prescription bottle and stare at it. Rolling it around in my fingers, I look at the clock. 9:18 PM. Sighing, I put it back on the counter and fill my glass with water. Not quite yet. Not until the girls are asleep. Then maybe I can get some relief.

I hear the door to their bedroom close and listen for Blake. "Alex?" he asks from the living room. I place my glass back on the counter next to the pills. "In the kitchen."

Blake enters and walks right past me to grab a piece of pizza from the box on the stove.

"Blake! Don't eat that! It's been out for *at least* two hours. You're going to get food poisoning!" I can't help but look at him in utter disgust.

"No way!" he fires back as he takes a huge bite of the slice of pepperoni. Mouth completely full he adds, "Two hours is nothing. It's fine. Trust me."

Pet peeve number one. *Gross.*

Note to Self: Provide Blake with updated list of pet peeves.

"Okay, well for the record that's just gross. If you get sick I'm going to be really pissed, seeing as though you're the only help I have until reinforcements arrive tomorrow."

I watch him finish off the piece of pizza and follow it with a swallow of water...*my water*. He puts the glass in the sink and turns to face me, leaning his back against the counter. He puts his elbows on the top of the counter behind him and crosses his feet at his ankles. He watches me for a couple of seconds as I back up and lean against the stove.

"How's your hand? Have you taken the pain meds?" He dips his head toward the prescription bottle. "I'm pretty sure the girls are settled if that's what you're waiting for."

"Yeah, I'll take them soon. I just want to be sure they're good for the night. Don't worry...you've made your point. The way my hand feels right now, it's pretty evident I won't be sleeping at all *without* taking them." I'm growing extremely tired of him being right all the freakin' time.

I lean back against the counter and sigh as I replay the evening in my head. It was really fun, actually.

"You were really great with them tonight, Blake. Thank you so much. And thank you for helping me through my break down in the kitchen earlier. I don't do well when things are out of my control...as if you don't already know that."

He chuckles silently and I can't help but smile as I watch his face light up with laughter. "Yes, unfortunately I know that all too well. You're allowed to need help sometimes, Alex. Everyone does. There's no fault in that. Seeing as though I actually helped put you in this predicament, it's the least I can do. Plus, you have really great girls, so it wasn't that bad," he says with a wink. "*They* were actually the easy part."

"Shut up! I can't help the way I am. You know this, yet you continue to act surprised. I haven't changed that much since high school," I say defensively.

"I wouldn't know. You didn't really bother to talk to me in high school." I scan his face for a couple of seconds, trying to gauge whether or not he is angry or just stating a fact. Either way, his statement warrants a response.

"You're completely right, Blake, and I'm so sorry. I don't know what happened really. I guess I was just young and didn't understand that what I was doing, or not doing, was hurting you. I was so focused on Derek; I just kind of moved on and left you behind." I see his body tense and I know I've struck a nerve. Nevertheless, I continue.

"It wasn't fair to you. You were, and still are, a great person. I was lucky to have you in my life then and extremely selfish when I decided I didn't need you anymore. I can't tell you how truly sorry I am. But what I can tell you is that I'm blessed you have entered my life for a *second* time, and I hope you and I can pick up where we left off, as friends. I don't want to lose this, Blake. I was reckless enough to throw it away the first time; I hope I get the chance to prove to you that I won't do it again." When I'm finished, I continue to hold his eyes with mine so he can see my sincerity.

Still maintaining eye contact, Blake pushes himself off the counter and I hear his boots clank as he crosses my kitchen floor to where I'm standing. I want to look away, but I refuse to let myself. He needs to understand how I truly feel. So I look him in his beautiful face and stand my ground. He walks right up to me and simply puts the palm of his hand on the side of my face. He strokes my cheek with his thumb. He then moves his hand to slide a lock of my hair behind my ear and places his hand on my shoulder.

"I know, Alex. It just really hurt. You meant a lot to me. You were my best friend." He lets out a deep breath. "But you're right, that's the past. So consider it water under the bridge. I was always there for you, whether you wanted me to be or not, and I always will be."

With that, he turns and walks out of the kitchen. I continue leaning against the counter, mainly to catch my breath. It seems to have left my lungs.

Well, that was...*unexpected.* I run my fingers through my hair and focus on my breathing. Finally, after regaining my composure, I make my way to leave the kitchen. I guess there's really nothing left to say about the past. Blake Morgan is here, now, in my life and evidently plans to stay.

Smiling, I walk into the living room where Blake is sitting on the couch flipping through the channels. I casually take a seat on the other end. I pull my legs up to my chest and turn to look at him, placing my cheek on the tops of my knees.

"Nice exit strategy," I say to him with a huge smile on my face. "Very compelling."

"You like that?" he asks me, joining in my amusement. "It's my power move. Did it work? Did you find it more effective or dramatic? "

"Definitely effective Blake, nice work." Laughing heartily I add, "I'm sure that works well with the ladies."

Still smiling, Blake shakes his head. "Nope, no girlfriends. My life's too busy. I don't really have the time to devote to someone else. It wouldn't be fair to them or to me."

I'm pretty sure my eyes bug out of my head. "What? How is that possible? I don't know if you're aware of this or not, but you're freakin' hot! How do you not have a million

127

girls lined up waiting for you?"

He lets out a sexy chuckle. "Alex, I didn't say there *weren't* girls. Just nothing serious. I guess I'm just waiting for someone who I actually want to make a priority, not one that I feel like I have to."

"Oh," I say looking down at my feet. *How many girls?* I swear I feel a jealous tug in my heart. *Weird.*

"What about you?" he asks.

I glance back up and shake my head back at him. "No, no one since Derek passed. I don't really feel like I've moved on from him. Honestly, I don't know if I ever will. He was part of my life for so long; I can't imagine my life with anyone else. Plus, I do have three children and I'm thirty-three years old. It's not like I have guys lined up around the block waiting to date me and my children. Most men my age are either married or there's something severely wrong with them." I point at him and giggle. He grins beautifully back at me.

"Not to mention," I add, "dating actually takes time, of which I have none. So, no, there's no one right now."

He puts his hand up to his face and rubs his jaw with his fingers as he eyes me for a while – like he is mulling over something in his head. When he's through, he stands up and moves to take a seat so close to me, that when he sits down on the couch, I almost topple over. He leans over right in my face and simply says, "Bullshit."

"Excuse me?" I ask, raising my eyebrows in question.

"You heard me. That's complete bullshit. I get your issue with Derek. I knew your relationship personally so I know how much you loved each other and I guess you'll move on in your own time. But you can't sit here and tell me that you can't date because you have three children, because you're thirty-three, or because you have no time. Those are excuses that you're using to protect yourself. I know you, Alex. Believe or not, I still know how you work. You have to be in control all the time or you're out of your comfort zone. I'm sure dating would definitely fall into that category."

He's so close I can feel his breath on my face. "You can't keep doing this to yourself, Alex. I know it isn't pleasant to talk about, so I'm going to drop it because you've been through a lot today. But I don't ever want to hear you sell yourself short again. You're a great mom. You're still very young and extremely beautiful – something you never realized and obviously still don't. You have a lot of life left to live, Alex. I don't want to see you give up when you still have so much to look forward to." He gives me a shy smile and a shrug of his shoulders as he backs out of personal space. "I wouldn't be much of a friend if I didn't say something. I hope you aren't pissed."

I immediately look down to my feet and start picking off Nycole's bright blue glitter nail polish. "No, I get it. I understand. Harlow just delivered me pretty much the same lecture. Nancy too. I know you guys are right, but it just doesn't feel right, you know? I know my girls deserve more," I say feeling my throat starting to constrict, "and I'm doing the best I can right now. I guess I just feel like I'll be dishonoring Derek's memory if I move on."

Blake shakes his head at me. "Alex, you couldn't be further from the truth. You're not being fair to yourself."

"It's not about me or being fair to myself. It's about Derek." I feel moisture gathering in the corners of my eyes. "I guess I'm just scared that if I move on with someone else, we...," I take in a deep breath, "we...won't remember him." I lose the battle against the tears and begin to cry.

Blake moves in once again to comfort me, placing his arms protectively around my body and pulling me close to his. *And I let him.* Because, with each tear that falls down my face, I begin to feel a peace in my soul that I haven't felt in years. I have never revealed that to anyone. Not even Harlow. It's something that I've kept safely locked up in my heart.

I feel like I'm taking my first real breath in three years and I have Blake to thank for that. So, I let him stay with me as I cry. The tears washing my soul with a peace I had no idea I would ever feel again.

Thank you, *once again*, Blake Morgan.

CHAPTER TEN

An hour later, Blake and I are still sitting on the couch. With my feet in his lap, I'm giving him the "Where Are They Now" version of the Waco High class of '97.

I've been relaying to him how lucky he was not to marry his god-awful prom date, Ashley Thompson. For some reason, there has always been some unspoken hatred between us. I'm not sure what the reason was, if there even was one, for this animosity. But it was something that started when we were in junior high and *still* hasn't been resolved.

"Blake, seriously, she's slept with every man in Waco. It's gross." I make a gagging noise and look at him in disgust. "I can't believe you took her to prom. She was such a hooker."

Blake looks back at me and grins. "Hey, a man's gotta do what a man's gotta do. Don't blame me, blame my hormones."

I give him my most disapproving look. "Gross, Blake."

Elbows behind his head, he leans back into the couch and props his boots up on my coffee table. I push them off with my foot. "Don't get all huffy because I didn't approve of your date. You could've done much better. And her dress," I wrinkle my nose and shake my head at him, "was rather unfortunate. Teal? Really? And it barely covered her ass. Don't even get me started on her inebriated state. I was actually embarrassed *for* her."

Blake immediately cuts me off. "First of all, the girl I really wanted to take was…unavailable. Second, she didn't keep the dress on that long anyway. Trust me." I make a much louder, much more overdramatic gagging sound. I can actually feel the bile in the back of my throat.

Blake rolls his eyes at me and smiles a sexy lop-sided smile. "Third… what do you mean you didn't approve?"

"Okay… that's really gross, Blake. I *really* don't want to talk about her anymore." I give him a light shove on the leg with my foot. "And of course I noticed. As your first best friend, I reserved my right to judge your dates. I just never said anything." And I did. I remember that now. No one ever seemed good enough for him.

He gives me a satisfied smile. "Okay, we can drop all discussion of Ashley Thompson." He shifts his body to face me. "How old is Rylie again?"

I let out a sigh of relief. Really, that woman gets my blood pressure abnormally high. I sit up and hug my knees to get comfortable before continuing.

"She's four. She's a handful, right?"

"No, not really. I think she's pretty much a normal four year old," Blake says confidently.

"How do you know so much about kids, anyway? Is there something you aren't telling me?" I gasp and point my finger at him. "You're not the father of her illegitimate children are you?"

He lets out a laugh. "Nope, no illegitimate children. But, Rebecca does have two *legitimate* children of her own. I hang with them all the time. They actually live about thirty miles from me, so I spend a lot of time over there. It gets kind of lonely living by myself sometimes. "

"Oh my God! I completely forgot to ask you how your sister's doing! I'm such a shitty friend, Blake, I'm sorry."

"Alex, it isn't like we've had a lot of time to sit down and chat. We've been kinda busy with bar fights, finger contusions, glass breaking, Barney and his crazy adventures... don't worry, it's fine," he says with a reassuring smile. "She's good though. Happily married to her college sweetheart. She's the stay at home mom of Jonathon, who's seven years old, and Timothy, who's five years old. She's really happy."

"That's great. I'm glad for her. She was always so sweet to me. I remember that one time I fell down and ripped my skirt climbing your tree and I was freaking out that mom would find out...remember? She sewed it up like that," I said with a snap of my fingers. "Mom never knew a thing. I guess she always had that maternal instinct. Me – not so much," I finish with a laugh.

Blake smiles back at me. "Well, I don't know about that. But I do know you have great kids. They each have a different piece of your personality. Even for the short time I've been around them, that's pretty easy to see. They love you so much, Alex. You have no idea how lucky you are."

I nod my head in response. "Yeah, I definitely have great kids. I mean, don't get me wrong. It hasn't always been easy. Especially after Derek passed, it was pretty difficult. But they're strong and they made it through the hard parts. I think they're happy. I hope they are at least."

I can tell Blake is shaking his head, but I opt to keep looking at my feet.

"They're strong because of you Alex. You're one of the

strongest people I know. You had the strength to make it through the loss of Derek, carrying your children along with you. That couldn't have been easy. And look at how wonderful and loving they are, even after everything that they've had to go through. That's a powerful testament to you and your strength. You should be *proud* of that, Alex. Not everyone could have handled that. But YOU did."

I let out a sigh, finally picking off the last bit of nail polish from my toes.

"I guess. Honestly, I wasn't sure I was going to make it. Blake, telling those girls their daddy wasn't coming back – to this day I don't know how I did it, but they were strong too, and I guess that gave me strength. I think that's why we're all so close. Going through something like that together, well – it makes you really grasp how important your life is," I say to him, shrugging my shoulders.

Blake seems to hesitate for a second. I know what's going through his head before he even asks it, and I'm prepared for it.

"Do you mind if I ask what happened that day? The day Derek died?"

Seeing as though I've already met my emotional breakdown quota over the last couple of days, I actually feel okay sharing this piece of my life with him. I find myself wanting to share it with him, like, he needs to know what happened that day in order to really know me. Because of this, I nod my head yes, grab his hand, and begin to tell him my story.

He sits quietly as I tell him about the phone call to the office. I tell him how Harlow drove me to Round Rock and about both of us trying to hold it together. Next, I tell him about seeing the accident on the way – his eyes widen in surprise when I describe to him the state of Derek's car as it lay alongside the highway. I go into detail about Derek's appearance when I first saw him in the hospital and how badly he was hurt. Finally, I tell him exactly what happened when Derek passed.

He continues to hold my hand, squeezing it to help give me the strength to get through the more difficult parts. And I squeeze his hand back, because I have to keep in mind that although Derek was my husband, he was also Blake's friend. And as difficult as it is for me to relive that day, it's probably just as difficult for Blake to hear. Coming to the end of my story, I find my hand contract around Blake's rather tightly. As I lessen the hold, I tilt my head, shrug my shoulders, and smile a sad smile.

"Then I came home and had to tell the girls that he was gone. That he had an accident and he wouldn't be coming home."

Blake continues holding my hand. "What did you tell them? I mean, how did you explain something like that to your children?"

I shrug my shoulders again. "Well, I explained to them about death, about Heaven, and about guardian angels... because I believe that Derek watches over us to this day. I made sure to tell them that every single bit of him still lived through them. How incredibly blessed they were to have been able to know and understand what a wonderful daddy he was. I let them know that they were so lucky compared to Rylie. She was so young; she wouldn't have many memories of him – if any. But *they* did. I told them that they should hold on tightly to those memories and remember how much he loved them. Remember how he would play horsey on the floor with them, and wrestle, and carry them on his shoulders when taking them to bed. I let them know it was okay to laugh when they remember his silly faces, his tickles, and how he would play Big Bad Wolf or zombie while chasing them around the house."

I find myself smiling as I relay this part to Blake. Derek was a really good zombie. He kinda creeped me out actually.

Blake smiles back and nods his head, encouraging me to go on. He stays silent, allowing me as much time as I need to speak.

"I told them they should smile when they remember his hugs and his kisses, how he would throw them up in the air as high as could, and how he would often fall asleep with them in their bed reading their favorite bedtime stories. I wanted them to be proud of him and to never be ashamed that they missed him. I encouraged them to cry as much as they needed to cry and to talk when they needed to talk. I wanted them to know that even though they lost him, I would always be there for them, to help them. But I didn't really set a great example in the beginning."

I sigh heavily. This part of my life was the most painful to talk about.

"It wasn't easy by any means, Blake. There were some days I couldn't get out of bed. As much as I love my girls, I was just *so* sad. So sad I can't even put it into words. Completely broken. The pain in my chest was unbearable some days, like my insides were completely hollowed out. Some days I couldn't breathe, some days I would cry all day long, and some days...I couldn't do anything but sit there in my bed because my body was so physically exhausted from the grief. I would just lay there and think about Derek. Questioning how in the world I was supposed to make it without him. He was my life for so long, I didn't know how to live it or even function without him. Thank God for Harlow and Nancy. They took turns making sure the girls were okay while I dealt with everything. They cooked for them, bathed them, read to them, got them up in the morning, took them to school. They did everything they could to make sure my girls were completely taken care of while I took the time I needed to grieve. I mean, some days were okay, but some days were – well…they were just really bad."

I look down at my hand because it's tingling and I realize that Blake's squeezing my hand so tightly, he's completely cut off the circulation in my fingers. When I glance back to his face, I find his eyes wandering all over mine. Surprisingly, for once, it's not the look of sympathy that I have grown to hate over the last three years. His expression is one of such compassion and tenderness that I catch myself holding my breath.

But I can also tell he's upset about something. The look on his face isn't quite matching up with the death grip he has on my hand.

"Blake, I'm okay now," I say with a smile because, honestly, I'm completely dumbfounded by his reaction. I can't help but find it humorous. I look back down at my hand. He follows my gaze and when he sees my purple fingers, he immediately lets go. I wiggle my fingers to get the circulation going again.

"I only have one good hand left, Blake, please be careful with it," I say with a chuckle.

Before I have a chance to say anything else, he's up off

the couch, pacing back and forth through the living room, raking his hand through his hair. He seems extremely aggravated about something. What the hell just happened in the last couple of seconds?

I stand up and use my body to block his path. He finally stops pacing.

"What is wrong with you? What's going on? Why are you so upset?"

"It's just I... Alex..."

I put my palm flat on his chest. I feel his heart beating rapidly. "Blake, I'm fine. I promise. What's going on with you?"

He looks away and I move my face into the path of his gaze. "Blake. What is it?"

"I should have been here," he says through his teeth.

I hold his stare. "What? You should have been where?"

"I should have been *here*, with you," he says emphatically, pointing towards the floor. "I should have been here, Alex. To help you. To make sure you were okay. To protect you. But I wasn't. And you were here, all by *yourself*. Handling it all by *yourself*. Dealing all by *yourself*. All because I couldn't come back here. Because I was scared to come back; scared I couldn't face what was waiting for me here. Scared, Alex," he says a little louder, but catches it and lowers his voice. "Scared. While you were dealing with this shit, I was hiding in Colorado. Jesus, that *kills* me."

I move my other hand up to his chest. It's throbbing almost in time with the rapid beating of his heart. "Blake, that's ridiculous. There's nothing you could've done. I had Harlow and Nancy. And I made it through, eventually. It just took a while. I'm okay now."

I reach up and put my hand on his face. I pull it towards mine until our eyes meet. "Look at me, Blake. I. Am. Fine. And with the way that I treated you...you had no reason to come back here to help me with anything. I don't blame you, so stop blaming yourself."

"That's not an excuse, Alex. I told you that I would always be there for you, even when you didn't want me to be, but I wasn't. Not when you really *needed* me. I can't imagine what you went through. But to hear that you were in so much pain, so sad... to think I wasn't here to help you through that, to hold your hand, to protect you. I just..."

I turn my hand over and stroke his cheek. He puts his head down and I force him to look at me again.

"Shh, Blake. That's enough. I don't want to hear any of that right now. Derek's death was tragic. It was heartbreaking. It was too much for me some days. But you listen to me. There is *nothing* you could have done if you were here that would have protected me from that pain. You need to know that. You need to *believe* that. I refuse to listen to you tear yourself up over something you had no control over. It happened. It's over. I'm fine. End of story."

He says nothing more. He just grabs my wrist and pulls my body into his, being careful not to hurt my hand. He rests his cheek on top of mine and whispers solemnly into my ear, "Never again, Alex. Never. Again."

He leaves his cheek against mine and I feel his breath in my ear. He wraps his big arms around me and we stay like that for some time. The warmth from the closeness of our bodies and the heat of his breath in my ear cause my heart rate to triple. Yet, with my heart beating a million miles a minute, I feel a strange calm. I want to let go of everything. I want to sink my body into his and let him be strong for me. I want to let him take my pain, my sadness, my exhaustion... everything that keeps me from being truly happy. I want his arms to stay around me... his warmth and protection. But as a familiar lump forms in my throat, I know this will never happen.

I *can't* allow it.

I *won't* allow it.

Blake is more right than he could possibly know.

Never. Again.

CHAPTER ELEVEN

It's around midnight when I finally get around to taking those damn pills. Blake and I have a minor "disagreement" regarding me taking them this late at night. Obviously, I don't want to take them so I'll be able to get up with the girls in the morning, but Blake won't hear it. So here I am, at midnight, in the kitchen, glaring at the prescription bottle... *again*. I absolutely hate having to use these pills to help me sleep. But the truth of the matter is, the pain in my hand is getting worse and I really doubt I will get an ounce of sleep without some major pain relief. I let Blake think he won his stupid little argument, but I take comfort in knowing the decision was all mine.

That doesn't mean I have to like it.

After eating the last couple of pieces of a loaf of bread, I chug some water along with two of the pain pills the doctor prescribed. Putting my glass in the dishwasher, I hear Blake enter the kitchen. "How ya holding up there, champ?" he asks, grabbing the wadded up bread bag off the counter and putting it in the trashcan.

"I'm good. Just took my pills, so I'm sure I'll be feeling even better soon. I'm exhausted," I say, attempting to cover my yawn.

He smiles at me. "Yeah, me too. Let's get you to bed." He puts his arm around me and gives me a quick squeeze before releasing me. "You need to get some rest; it's been a long day."

"Yeah, it has," I say, walking out of the kitchen. I head to the girls rooms for one last peek to make sure everything is okay. I can't help but smile as I look at them, all piled on Nycole's bed, sleeping peacefully.

"Do you think we need to move them?"

I turn back to find Blake standing directly behind me. I shake my head. "No, they're fine. If they get up, then they get up. I'll deal with it."

"No, *you* won't. *I* will. You rest. I've got everything covered," he states quickly. "Otherwise, what's the point of me being here?"

I make sure to exaggerate my groan so he can note my strong objection to having him help me in the middle of the night. "Okay Blake, fine, but promise you'll wake me if you have any problems with them. Kyndall sometimes has nightmares and usually needs me to get into bed with her. Please come get me if that happens."

"Alex, I have experience with kids you know. It'll be fine, I promise. But I also promise that if I feel like they need you personally, then I'll come get you. You have my word." And as I look at his unwavering eyes, I know he will.

I nod my head. "Okay. Let me go get changed and I'll bring you some blankets and pillows for the couch. I'm sorry…" He stops me immediately.

"Alex, it's fine. It's better for me to be out there anyway. That way I can hear if they need something. Don't worry about me sleeping on the couch. Go get your pajamas on, bring me the pillow and blankets, and we'll watch some TV before you go to bed." I nod my head again as I try to cover another yawn. I am so tired right now, words just seem like unnecessary energy expenditure.

I walk to my bedroom, grab my flannel PJ bottoms and one of Derek's old "wife beater" tanks, and throw them on. I pull my hair back in a headband, *no ponytails for a while obviously*, wash my face, *one handed of course,* and brush my teeth, *that was an interesting adventure.* Then I head to the closet and grab extra sheets and pillows for Blake. I head out to the living room where he's sitting on the couch, fully dressed, flipping through the channels.

"Blake," I say, throwing down the sleeping essentials for him on the couch, "let me get you something to sleep in. I'm sure I have some of Derek's old stuff you could use."

"No, Alex, it's okay... I wouldn't want to–"

"Shut up, Blake. It's fine. They're just sitting there. There's no reason for you to sleep in your clothes." I take note of how good he still actually looks. Must be nice to have had a *shit* day, but still look freakin' awesome.

"Well," he hesitates. "Are you sure you don't mind?"

"If it was anyone else but you. But it *is* you, so no, I don't mind." I turn and walk back into the bedroom. I approach the drawer that contains Derek's old sleepwear. I grab an undershirt and some pajama bottoms. While holding his clothes, I gently place my hand on them and take in a deep breath. I'm surprised that the knowledge of handing it over to Blake doesn't bother me. I'm surprisingly okay with it. I let out the breath, carry the clothes into the living room, and place them on his lap. Taking them from me, he stands up and lingers for a minute, but eventually makes his way to the girls' bathroom.

When Blake emerges, I take in a deep breath through my

nose, hold it my lungs and brace myself against the couch. I know it is my imagination, but for a split second, I swear it's Derek walking out of the bathroom. An electrical shock whizzes through my entire body, and by the time my brain grasps the fact that it is just Blake, my heart is already nearly beating out of my chest.

Blake watches me for a second, as though trying to make sure I'm okay. I give him a weak smile. "Sorry, it just took me a little by surprise."

"Alex, if it bothers you, I can—"

"No, Blake. It's okay, really. It was just a bit of a shock. It's fine, I promise. If I wasn't comfortable I would let you know," I say, attempting to persuade both of us. I've opened up so much to him tonight; I'm not going to let something as small as seeing him in Derek's clothes ruin how far we've come this evening. I shared things with him that I haven't even shared with Harlow. This friendship is important. I trust him, and he needs to know that. Even though I'm still a little freaked out, I smile and add, "Let's see what's on TV before these pills take me to never-never land."

We both plop down on the couch. He sits at the other end, obviously trying to give me space if I need it. So to let him know I'm okay, I turn so I can put my feet in his lap and lay back on the throw pillow behind me. Putting my hurt hand above my head as I lay there, I grab the remote and start flipping through the channels.

We ultimately end up on *The Breakfast Club*, laughing at the coincidence because we lived and breathed this movie growing up. As we watch it now, in my living room sitting side by side, I feel like I'm twelve years old again. We laugh with each other as we quote our favorite lines from the movie out loud.

We're right in the middle of the scene where Jon Bender is re-enacting the life at 'Big Bri's' house. As soon as *fishing* and *doing homework on the boat* are mentioned, I turn to Blake, excitement flooding my features.

"Oh my god! Blake! That totally reminds me! I was going through some things the other day and I found something very interesting!" I bolt up excitedly to fetch my recently found treasure. Unfortunately, as soon as my feet hit the ground, the room starts spinning around a full 360° and I fall back to the couch. Okay, the pain pills are definitely working, which makes sense seeing as though I just jumped up without feeling *any* pain in my hand at all.

Blake is immediately in front of me. "Alex, we can just do it later. Seriously, you can't even stand up right now," he says with concern in his eyes.

Annoyed, I start to push myself off the couch but I'm unable to find my balance. I fall back onto the couch. Blake lets out a laugh.

"Why don't you just *tell* me what it is and you can *show* me tomorrow, when you're not under narcotic influence."

"Ha-ha, Blake," I say sarcastically. "You're the one who made me take the damn things, so you lose all right to make fun of me." I think I'm starting to feel a little drunk. I sigh loudly and notice my face feels numb. I rub it with my hand and pull my lip out. I'm not surprised when I don't feel a thing.

With a chuckle, Blake grabs me under my knees and arms and whips me against his chest. I'm completely off the ground. I look down and start giggling.

"So thisiswhatitfeelslike," I start to slur.

L. B. SIMMONS

Still chuckling, Blake asks, "What *what* feels like?"

I roll my eyes because all of a sudden, I'm super annoyed he doesn't understand what I'm saying. "Hello! To be this tall... you're a freakin' giant!" I laugh to myself because I have just become the most hilarious person in the world.

Blake looks at me, his eyes full of amusement. While he's staring, I allow myself to gaze into them. My face is dangerously close to his, so close I can feel the heat from his skin. I peer into his beautiful green eyes, feeling strangely sober all of a sudden. I inhale a quick breath. "Yeah, things definitely look a lot different from up here."

I begin to feel the room starting to spin again so I stick my head into his neck and breathe in his scent. Leather and soap. "Mmm," I let out as I smile to myself. I feel so peaceful.

It's so nice, that I almost protest when he lets go of my body to lay me down on my bed. Sadly, I'm too tired to put up the necessary fight. So I lay there as he fluffs the pillow behind my head and pulls the covers up to my neck. I put my arms over the covers and smile a drunken smile.

"Blake, I'm so glad you're here. You make my life... happy..." I say as I begin to feel the heaviness of my lids. *Jeez* – when did my eyelids become one hundred pound dumbbells?

"Thank... you..." is all I can manage to get out before sleep finds me. And for the first time in years, I don't dream about Derek's death or sadness or darkness. I dream about lakes and fishing and warmth from the sun with a beautiful boy in front of me. I can't see his face. All my eyes can gather is how the sun just barely peeks through the strands of

146

his light brown hair. The vision soothes my soul. And as I continue to sleep, I find my heart completely enveloped by a warm ray of peace and tranquility… providing a brief solace from the pain and emptiness I'm so used to greeting me every night.

Note to Self: Prescribed pain pills work for both intended and unintended purposes.

Waking the next morning, I extend my arms above my head and stretch the entire length of my body, all the way to my toes. The warmth of the sun hitting my face reminds me of my peaceful slumber. My heart feels full of joy. So much so, that I'm pretty sure this goofy grin is stuck on my face for a while. Well, I hope it is anyway.

I let out a content sigh and smile as I bring my arms back over my head. I catch sight of my hand as it passes in front of my face. I'm pretty sure these throbbing fingers were *not* part of my peaceful slumber, but I continue smiling because it seems that not even that can bring me down right now. I sniff the air and my stomach rumbles as I notice the distinct smell of bacon in my house.

What are they up to?

I swing my legs over the edge of my bed and give myself one last stretch before I stand. I reach over to grab my pink fluffy robe and throw it on over my P.J.'s. Making a quick stop by the bathroom, I wash my face (again, one handed), brush my teeth, and attempt to tame my hair. I'm really missing my pony tail look right now, because this look is not at all flattering.

Once I'm done, I walk through the living room and as I approach the kitchen, I begin to notice murmuring. I hear the rumble of Blake's low voice and the unmistakable giggles of my girls.

Coming up on the kitchen, I tiptoe as to not disturb whatever they're doing. I'm barely able to poke my head through the doorway when my breath catches in my throat at the sight before me. Rylie's sitting on the counter in her red and white polka dotted Minnie Mouse night gown, grinning up at Blake as he stands next to her. He's holding a spatula and watching whatever is sizzling in the skillet. If I wasn't completely speechless right now, I probably would be making a big deal about how close my baby is to that skillet.

My eyes graze over to where I see Nycole and Kyndall, still in their matching Super Mario Bros nightgowns, munching on some chocolate chips while adding the rest to a bowl of batter. Lucky for them I'm still rendered speechless…

I watch Nycole grab the wooden spoon from the counter and stir while Kyndall continues to pour more chocolate chips into the bowl. They mischievously look at each other and grin, and I find myself wondering how many chocolate chips they've actually got in there. My eyes move back over to Blake, still in Derek's pajama pants and shirt. Bare feet on my floor in front of the stove. His hair is in its usual sexy morning routine as it flips out everywhere on his head and neck.

Jeez, this guy seriously makes me ill. He looks completely sexy. I reach my hand up to once again try to smooth out my hair. *Jerk.*

Mid eye roll I hear, "Mommy! You ruined the surprise! You're fired! I'm gonna put you in time out!" Rylie yells to me from across the room while shaking her finger at me. She looks at me over Blake's shoulder. Blake turns to see me standing in the doorway. He gives me a wide sexy smile as he shrugs his shoulders. "Did we wake you? Sorry – the girls wanted to make you breakfast. Something super-chocolaty they said," he says as he looks at Nycole and Kyndall and winks. They both give him a sweet innocent smile and then turn to me. All I get is the evil eye. I widen my eyes at them and hold my hands up in surrender.

"What? Don't be mad at me. Bacon always wakes me up, you know that! How can anyone sleep through bacon?" I attempt to look at Blake innocently. I even throw in the eyelash bat. "Can you sleep through bacon?"

He gives me a beautiful wide toothy grin in response. "I can sleep through just about anything. Well, almost anything. I definitely *could not* sleep through three little girls tackling me this morning while I slept peacefully on the couch. They're ruthless. Really, Alex. You should be proud. No bad dreams last night though, just in case you were wondering."

I look at each of my girls proudly smiling back at me and I can't help but belt out a laugh. "Good girls. I *am* proud actually. And Kyndall, I'm glad you had a good night's sleep too, just like me. I guess we all had some good sleep, huh?"

"Yeah!" they all exclaim in unison.

"Yeah!" I say back while pumping my fist into the air and walking into the kitchen. Blake turns around to flip what I can now see is bacon in the skillet. My stomach growls when I walk past him to get a coffee mug and the ibuprofen out of the cabinet.

"Hungry?" He stays focused on the bacon, but I know he's laughing at my expense.

"Um, yeah," I say, grabbing my stomach as it continues to grumble. "I can't help it, Blake. It's the bacon. I'm telling you!"

"Well, let's get some food in her tummy, huh girls? I think she woke up the neighbors with that growl!" He looks at me out of the corner of his eye and winks.

What? Do I look like a naïve little girl? Winks don't work on me. I walk by and punch him, *with my good hand obviously*, as hard as I can in the arm. "Shut it, Blake."

"Alex, be careful," he says, feigning concern while flexing his bicep. "That right there is pure steel. We can't have you breaking your other hand now can we?"

I roll my eyes at him and immediately hear the girls' laughter. Kyndall takes the bowl over to Blake and gives him a curtsey after he takes it from her.

"Please girls. Don't encourage him. It only makes it worse. Trust me." I set my coffee on the kitchen table as I take a seat. I hear the sizzle of the pancake batter as it hits the skillet and smell the sweet aroma as it cooks. Blake turns from the skillet for a brief second and gives me a mischievous grin.

"How'd you sleep last night? You sure were tired. And quite hilarious I might add," he says turning back to face the skillet. I'm pretty sure he's trying to hide any evidence of laughter.

"Don't get me started, Blake. I couldn't help it."

He turns back around to me and continues his mockery. "I know. Doesn't mean it wasn't hilarious, and kinda cute."

Out of frustration, I put my head down in my hands and rub the heels of my hands into my eyeballs. "Blake, seriously, I'm about to not be cute at all. Trust me, I'm warning you because you are my dear friend and I care about you. Knock it off!"

Blake once again turns back to the stove and I can see his shoulders convulsing. I'm really contemplating murdering this man. But when I look at my girls as they watch our exchange, all with huge grins on their faces, all the frustration leaves my body. I roll my eyes at them and jerk my head in Blake's direction. Once they've figured out Blake is in no real danger, they all happily go back to their breakfast duties.

After a few minutes, the girls put their finishing touches on the plate of warm pancakes and bacon they prepared for me and start to carry it to the table. A couple of times, in the only ten feet of distance, they almost drop it since they all had to be touching the plate.

Rylie would get mad if they held it too high and she couldn't reach it, which would lead to her bouncing up and down in a mini-tantrum and hitting her head on the plate. Nycole would then have to bend over so Rylie could reach it which would lead to her complaining that her back was hurting. *Yes, just ten feet.* Eventually Blake steps in and holds the plate to ensure everyone can touch it and to make sure it successfully crosses the kitchen without being splattered all over the floor.

I watch Blake, his tall body hunched over gently carrying the plate. I can't help but smile at him – while he isn't looking of course – because he really is sweet with the girls.

Obviously I'm going to have an in-depth discussion with them about my relationship with Blake. He's the first man in this house, literally, since Derek. I don't want the girls to jump to conclusions. The situation is a delicate one, but one that I definitely need to get a hold of before any misconceptions occur.

Blake looks up from the plate to meet my eyes and I immediately remove any evidence of smiling and replace it with an annoyed glare. I watch as corners of his mouth just barely tip up and he clears his throat in an effort not to laugh. Honestly, I can't even remember why I'm mad at him. But I'm sure whatever it is, it's a good reason. I think I'm too distracted by the food to remember, or care.

I turn my attention to the yumminess in front of me and struggle to not immediately start shoveling the food in my mouth. I wait patiently while Blake helps Kyndall and Rylie get their plates ready, which goes surprisingly well, brings them to the table and goes back to get his own plate with Nycole. While they head to the table, I look down at the pancakes.

"Um, guys. Why are these pancakes brown? Are they burnt?" I say picking up the top one and turning it over for examination. I lift it to my nose and sniff. Chocolate.

I look up at Nycole and Kyndall as they attempt to use the "bat the eyelashes and smile" technique to proclaim their innocence.

Raising my eyebrows at them (they *so* don't have me

fooled) I ask, "How many chocolate chips are left in the bag?" They look at each other, obviously deciding who's actually going to be representing the guilty parties. It's Kyndall that steps up to the plate – I mentally applaud their effort. It's nice to see them working together actually.

"None, Mama. But we *had* to use them all. We wanted to make them really chocolaty for you. We wanted you to have the best breakfast ever, since you hurt your hand yesterday. We did it for *you*," she says, her eyes as wide as saucers.

Well played, child of mine. Well, played.

I narrow my eyes at her and look over at Nycole who's nodding her head in support of her little sister. I then glance over at Blake who's obviously having shoulder problems this morning because they're shaking again. Then I look at Rylie who couldn't care less about this conversation and has already started eating her "chocolate extreme" pancakes. She looks up and flashes her dimples at me.

"Okay," I say, looking back at Kyndall. "Just next time, ease up a bit on the chocolate. I don't buy a whole bag of chocolate chip for a single use. Got it?"

"Got it Mama. Love you!"

"Love you too, sweetie. Now let's eat! I'm starving!" I say picking up my fork.

I take a bite of the pancake and actually, it's pretty good. I smile at the girls. "Delicious! You guys did a great job. So are you guys gonna start cooking every morning or is this just a weekend thing?"

"Well... Blake helped," Nycole says a little too sweetly. "It depends how much he's here."

I laugh. "Well, Blake isn't going to be spending the

night with us again. Sorry guys. That was just a onetime thing since Harlow and Nancy were both out of town and I needed someone to help me."

I notice Blake spit some of his coffee back into his cup and start to choke when the word "help" is used. I ignore him and keep speaking.

"There won't be any reason for him to spend the night again." I watch all of their faces fall. Yeah, we're going to need to have this conversation ASAP.

With their poor grief-stricken faces looking back at me, I add quickly, "But that doesn't mean he can't come over for breakfast some mornings. But that's up to Blake. And," I say with emphasis, "it's not going to be *every* weekend. I know how you guys work. Blake has his own life and won't be able to come over every time you guys ask, okay?" I say, shooting a quick glance at Blake to make sure he isn't hyperventilating from a panic attack in the corner of the kitchen. Although the spitting of the coffee was completely unnecessary, so I doubt I would help him if he was.

"Girls," he says, wiping his mouth with a napkin. "How about we start at breakfast two times a month? Two Sundays every month, we'll have breakfast that we'll cook together, to remember the weekend that your mom and I became best friends again? How do you guys feel about that?"

"Whooo-hoooo!"

"Yay!"

"So cool!"

I can do nothing but mouth a silent *thank you* to him from across the table. He nods in acceptance and takes another sip of his coffee while striking up a random conversation with the girls.

It seems that Blake Morgan has an uncanny ability to take my breath away constantly. Wow. I'm honestly in awe at how giving this man is. I'm so lucky to have him back in my life. As my best friend. And hopefully for a very long time.

After taking a sip of my own coffee, I smile at him once again and then at each of my girls.

Yes, this is definitely the beginning of a beautiful friendship... *again.*

CHAPTER TWELVE

After breakfast the rest of the day went pretty quickly. Nycole got her 'Nycole time' as promised, in which she locked herself in the office and watched her own movie. Blake, Kyndall, and I played the only thing I could play one handed on the Wii. Wii Tennis. However, I was evidently becoming, as Blake put it, a little too competitive since I threw the remote across the room after he landed an ace on me.

So now, while Blake and Kyndall battle it out, I'm curled up with Rylie on the couch reading *The Very Hungry Caterpillar* – slightly aggravated at Blake's version of 'time-out for Alex'. But regardless of what mood I'm in, reading this book with her always makes me laugh. It never fails that she calls the plums – blueberries, the Swiss cheese – pineapple, the salami – pa-slami, and the pie – pizza.

Wrapping up reading time, I almost feel better about being kicked out of the tennis game... *almost*. I'm still a little peeved actually, but listening to Kyndall's infectious laugh as she gets a point in against Blake, I can't help but giggle myself.

"You know, Blake, I can beat her. Just let me know if you need my help," I say, watching them from time out.

"No thanks, Alex," Blake says through his teeth, jumping up and down as he hits the ball. *Wow, he's really into this game.* And now *I'm* really into the game because he just got beat by my seven year old. *Ha-ha-ha!*

I hear Nycole finally exiting from the office, probably because Kyndall's laughing incredibly hard at Blake throwing an oversized fit in the middle of the living room.

"Come on, Nycole," Blake finally says. "I need rest. Your sister's killin' me over here. Come beat her so her head doesn't get too big." He walks by Kyndall, palming her head and ruffing her hair.

"She can't beat me either, Blake. I. Am. The. Champion!" Kyndall shouts in a booming voice. "But she can try I guess." She walks over to the "Wii" drawer to get Nycole her own controller.

My mouth drops open as I stare down at the two biggest traitors in the world. "What?" I exclaim. "I said I wanted to – oh, forget it! You guys are no longer my friends." I say with my best pouty face.

Laughing at me, Kyndall says, "I'm not your friend, I'm your daughter, silly Mama."

"Yeah, well, you know what I mean," I say, still pouting.

Blake looks over and I roll my eyes at him. *You suck*, I mouth to him so none of my children can hear me. He gives me a grin and turns back around to watch Kyndall and Nycole play. I sit there for a few seconds, secretly envious that I can't show these people how to *really* play Wii Tennis. *Oh well, their loss…*

I hear my phone vibrating on the table. Harlow's name appears on the screen and I smile. I miss my best friend but, oddly enough, not as much as I usually would. Probably because Blake was here to watch *The Breakfast Club* with me and regularly make fun of the girls…Harlow's two favorite past times. I reflect on how much I've actually enjoyed spending the last day with Blake. I guess when I decided to open the floodgates of my past with him, I connected with him in a way that I didn't think I would be able to do with anyone besides Harlow. I know that we still have a lot of our friendship to rebuild, there has been some damage done there, but I think we're off to a pretty solid start. I feel really good about it.

It *would* be really nice to have someone to lean on besides Harlow. She has spent the last three years, three of her prime years, taking care of me and my children. I honestly hope and pray that she'll be able to move on with her own life without feeling guilty now. Hopefully this moving on includes Trace, because I see the way he looks at her, and I know deep down in my soul he is what she needs and deserves.

So as I let go of Rylie and lean over to grab my phone, I find myself making a mental note to find out all I can about Harlow's feelings for him. It will be nice focusing on her for a change. Smiling, I hit the answer button on my phone.

"What's up love? How are you? Where are you?" I shoot the questions out before she even has a chance to say hello. Wow, I guess I miss her a little more than I thought.

I watch Rylie pick a plastic grape off of the centerpiece on my table and pop it in her mouth. "Hold on, Harlow." I put my hand over the receiver so I don't deafen my best friend.

"Rylie Meyer! Get that grape out of your mouth before you choke on it." She spits the grape into her hand. She then turns, looks straight at me, puts her hand on her hip, and says, "Well… I didn't die last time I did it, did I?" Blake immediately starts cracking up. She pops the grape back in her mouth.

"Stop laughing, Blake. It's not funny. Please get that grape from her." I watch nervously as he chases her around the living room, grape still in her mouth, which isn't as easy as it may seem, because my baby girl is fast! But finally he catches her and she spits the grape into his hand. I'm shocked that he isn't completely grossed out. I would be, and she's *my* child. But once he has it, he does a quick celebration dance, making the girls giggle, and then throws the spit covered grape in the trashcan.

I breathe a quick sigh of relief and turn my attention back to my conversation with Harlow. "Go ahead, sorry. Rylie's just trying to kill herself again. You know…the usual." Harlow laughs out loud, almost deafening *me*.

"Well, we're on our way back now. We should be there in a couple of hours. We're gonna stop to grab a bite to eat first. How are you feeling? Is Blake still there? How did it go with him there? Did he stay the night? Have the girls forgiven him yet? So sorry about that by the way. You know I generally speak before I think. I apparently lack whatever mental filter God gave everyone else in the world," she says with a bit of laughter in her voice.

I smile at her thousand questions. I guess she must have missed me a little too.

"Yeah, he definitely has worked some Blake Morgan charm on them. I've been completely forgotten in this house." Unfortunately, Blake chooses that time to re-enter the room and catches my pseudo-compliment. He smiles widely knowing that he just heard something that he wasn't supposed to. I roll my eyes and turn my body away from him.

"Harlow – they won't even let me play tennis with them. There has been a coup d'état in this house, I tell ya. I'm no longer the queen of my own castle. My reign is no longer."

She giggles into the phone. "Excellent, that's what I want to hear. Listen, I have to go. I just wanted to check on you before we stop for lunch. Like I said, we'll be there soon. Do you need us to pick up anything for you on our way?"

"Wait, I have questions for you about this little excursion you decided to take without even asking me for my permission. What's going on with you and Trace? Are you guys dating? Because I'm pretty sure you don't date at all! " I ask her with obvious amusement in my voice.

"Alex, we will discuss this in depth at a later time. Like, as soon as I get to your house. So be patient, because I'm sure you want every single detail, which I am not at liberty to discuss fully at this time. Get me?" she says while giggling into the phone. Obviously Trace has caught on to the topic of our conversation.

I find myself unable to control my grin. "Sure, but you better lawyer up because *you* are getting the fifth degree when you get here. Get *me*?"

"Yeah, I got ya. Love you sweetie. See you very soon. And don't worry, you'll also be getting your own line of questioning, so be prepared to spill. Bye, Alex."

"Bye hon, be safe and see ya soon. Love you," I say, hanging up my phone. Blake crashes down on the couch beside me leaving Kyndall and Nycole to their game. Rylie immediately crawls into his lap and continues to watch her sisters.

"Harlow?" he asks, still grinning.

"Yeah, they're on their way back. You'll be relieved of

your duties in a couple of hours."

"Well, thank God for that. I mean, hanging out with kids and playing video games all day...it's been really awful. I'll be glad to finally be done with all of this hard work," he says elbowing me in the side.

"You know what I mean, Blake. I'm sure there's stuff you need to do. You can't take care of me forever. You have your own life." I elbow him right back.

"Ouch!" he cries out as he grabs his side. "You have some sharp elbows, Alex." Rylie looks as him with concern, but Blake winks at her. She smiles back at him and crawls off of his lap to sit closer to Nycole and Kyndall.

"I know. They're lethal weapons so watch out. I plan on using them next time you guys decide I can't play. Jerks," I add with a roll of my eyes.

Blake laughs and looks forward, focusing on the game.

"It doesn't make you a weak person if you let people help you every once in a while," he says quietly.

I look over at him but he continues facing the TV.

"What's that supposed to mean?"

"You're so stubborn, Alex." He finally turns and faces me. He looks me directly in the eyes and doesn't hesitate. "It doesn't bother me to be here no matter what you think. I enjoyed the time I've spent with you and your girls this weekend. This is the most fun I've had in a really long time, longer than what you probably realize. So stop trying to push me away, Alex. I know what you're doing."

I break his gaze as I look down to the floor. "I have no idea what you're talking about, Blake."

He doesn't force me to look back at him as he continues. "Yes, you do, Alex. You know exactly what you're doing.

You're trying to push me away. You're trying to make yourself believe that I don't want to be here. Trying to convince yourself that my life can't include you. This is the second time you've attempted to make a point regarding me having my own life. I do have a life, Alex, but that doesn't mean it can't include you. I'm not going to let you push away this friendship because you feel scared, or guilty, or whatever is bringing this on. I'm not going anywhere. So stop pushing."

I look up from the floor to once again meet his eyes. They're full of determination. And a little anger. I immediately reach over and give his hand a gentle squeeze.

"I'm sorry, Blake. I can't explain why I do it. I guess part of me feels like I've already taken advantage of Harlow's kindness and I don't want to do the same to you. I don't want you to miss out on your life because of me. You have so much of it left to live. I don't want you to get sucked into my life, only to look back one day and realize you missed out on yours. That's all," I say, letting out a deep breath.

"Well, why don't you let me make that decision, Alex? That's all I ask." He offers me a soft smile and squeezes my hand in return.

"Alright, Blake." I take my hand back and use it to push myself off the couch. "But don't blame me when we're eighty years old and you have to stop by my house every day to help me clean litter boxes. I plan on being one of those old ladies with like a hundred cats. Just remember this moment when that becomes your inevitable future." I give him a huge smile and walk to where Blake left his Wii remote and push the "A" button to turn it on.

"But for now, all *I* ask, is for you to work your magic and get me into this game. We'll play doubles," I say giving him a wink of my own.

Evidently there's a John Hughes marathon on VH1 which is freakin' awesome… for me anyway. Blake and I have now taken over the TV and are watching one of my favorite movies of all time. *Some Kind of Wonderful*. Sigh.

I love Watts. There's something about her that I really identify with for some reason, I always have. I don't know if it is her tomboy persona, her tough exterior, her mad drumming skills, or the fact that she told the evil Amanda Jones… "You break his heart, I'll break your face." Probably all of the above.

My favorite scene in the movie is the end…of course. When Keith gives Watts the diamond earrings. Walking down the street she asks him how they look and he says, "You look good wearing my future." I used to *live* for that line, yet every time I see that movie randomly on TV, I never get to hear it. It never fails that my children somehow manage to distract me.

Well not today! I have Blake here to distract *them*.

So as the movie starts to come to the end and I see Watts walking down the street crying with Keith running up behind her, I scoot to the edge of my seat in anticipation. When he kisses her, I smack Blake on the shoulder repeatedly out of pure excitement. He looks back at me like I'm crazy.

"I can't help it Blake! I never, ever, ever, get to see this part. You know I love it!" He rolls his eyes and sighs. "Yes, Alex, I know you love it. I know the scene by heart thanks to you. It's stuck, right here," he points to his head, "in my brain, taking up very important space that could have actually stored something useful."

I roll my eyes. "It *is* useful, Blake. You never know when you need a good line to use on the woman of your dreams." I wink at him. "Now you have one ready for use. Now shush! He's gonna say it!"

I eagerly turn back to the TV, writhing with excitement, when right on cue, the girls run into the room screaming something about the computer and sharing.

"No! No! No!" I jump up to look for the remote... thinking maybe I can pause it. "Blake, do you know where the remote is?" I literally grab Blake with one hand and pull him up off the couch. I start pulling up the couch cushions... nothing.

Blake's laughing hysterically.

"Mommy! Kyndall and Nycole won't let me play my games. They aren't shaaaaaring!"

"Mom, she's been playing on it since we got in there! She is *lying*!" Nycole's voice gets a whole octave higher at the end.

"Am not!"

"Are too!"

I tune them out, dropping to my knees to scan for the remote under the couch. I see a few candy wrappers and a couple of eating utensils. Where in the world –

I look up at the TV and see the credits beginning to roll. I sprawl out face down on the floor, fighting the overwhelming urge to kick and scream and wail and roll around... Kinda like Rylie when she doesn't get her way. Just as I feel like giving in to the tantrum temptation, I hear Blake addressing the girls.

"Hey! Let's play hide and seek! I think that would be safer than sticking around here right now." I continue laying on the floor in defeat. "One... two... three..." The girls squeal and run out of the room. Blake sits down next to me. I can feel him staring at the back of my head.

"Don't even start with me, Blake. You know that's my favorite part. I never get to hear my favorite line. Ever. Is it really asking too much? It's like they have radar or something." I lie there for a couple more seconds. "I'm selling them Blake. So don't get too attached."

He chuckles. I push myself into a seated position right next to him. "I'm serious, Blake." I stare forward at the wall...specifically the crayon drawn hand holding stick figures that have been there for a couple of months now.

"So this isn't the time to go into the fact that those people are called actors? And how that is what you call a movie? And that it's not real?" He puts his arm around me. We sit in silence a couple of seconds before Blake yells, "...ninety-nine... one hundred! Ready or not, here I come!"

What? I totally knew he never really counted to one hundred when we were kids!

Cheater.

He jumps up and rustles the hair on the top of my head. "Don't worry Alex. Since it's a movie, you can buy it at this thing called a store–" Lucky for him, the doorbell rings, cutting him off.

"Harlow! Yay!" the girls scream as they run, all tripping over each other trying to be the first to reach the door. Shortest game of hide and seek *ever*. How come I never get that lucky?

"Girls! Be careful!" I shout at them getting up off the floor. I roll my eyes and let out a sigh while looking back at Blake. He just grins while following the girls to the door.

"Who's there?" all three girls shout.

"The big bad wolf to bloooow your house down!" Harlow shouts back through the other side of the door.

"Not by the hair of our chinny chin-chins!"

The girls giggle as they open the door and throw themselves at Harlow so hard she almost loses balance. She wraps her arms around all three of them affectionately, giving them all kisses on the tops of their heads before letting them go.

I glance back at Blake, standing behind me. "Now you know how it feels to be yesterday's news," I say with a teasing grin on my face.

"They'll be back. They ALL come back," he jokes while reaching down to grab Rylie who's already made her way back to him in the two nanoseconds since I took my eyes off of her.

He flashes her a huge smile before meeting my eyes again. "See?"

I give him a smirk and turn back to the door. I greet Harlow with a big hug of my own. "I missed you. Thank God you're back. These children have completely abandoned me while you were gone. At least I know *you* still love me."

"That I do, sweetie. Now let me see that hand," she

firmly states while releasing me from our embrace. I hold it up to show her and watch as the corners of her mouth turn down in obvious disapproval. She immediately looks over my shoulder at Blake.

"You and I are gonna have a chat. Seriously." She shoots him a dirty glare.

"Yikes," I say with a giggle, "I'm outta here. I've already been injured once this weekend. No way am I getting caught in the middle of this."

Blake sets Rylie down, obviously noting the seriousness of her tone. I watch Harlow grab his arm and lead him away from the door. She then pulls him down the hallway into my bedroom and closes the door. *Jeez, overdramatic much?*

"Um! Blake's in trouble, Blake's in trouble," the girls sing in the doorway. I hear them all "shh" each other as they tiptoe after them. Shaking my head, I turn to close the door.

When the door is almost shut I hear, "Hey, Alex." I look up just in time to see Trace approaching the door with Harlow's overnight bags draped over his shoulder. *Oops...*

Opening the door, I let a little giggle escape. "You still out there? I thought you snuck in behind Harlow," I say in an effort to cover up the fact that I had completely forgotten about the man standing outside my house.

"Nope." He chuckles. I'm pretty sure my cover up didn't work as planned.

I attempt to give him the same "innocent/apologetic" eyes my girls use on me. Either it works or it's just really that bad because his chuckle turns into a laugh. I plaster a huge smile on my face and I let him in the door. I lead him into the living room, passing the hallway that leads to my bedroom. I make eye contact with the girls, who each have their ears up to the door, and hold my finger up to my lips reminding them to be quiet so they can hear. If I can't do it myself, might as well send in my troops to get the job done.

"Where's Harlow?" he asks setting the bags down on the floor by my couch.

"I think she's chastising Blake right now. Don't worry, if she's not out in a minute, I'll go check for collateral damage," I say to him, heading to the kitchen. "Want something to drink? Eat?"

"Nope, I'm good. We ate on the way here."

I slow down a bit in an attempt to have him follow me. I don't know him that well, but I would prefer to keep him out of earshot. I have no idea what's going on, but the look on Harlow's face told me she meant business.

He eventually catches up and falls into step with me. We enter the kitchen and I grab my glass from off of the sink. Filling it with water, I grab some ibuprofen and swallow them down with a big gulp.

I take the glass with me and motion for him to have a seat at the table. "How was the trip?" I ask full of curiosity.

"It was good. I took Harlow dove hunting with me this morning before we left. My cousin has a place right outside of Dallas. So I took her over there to show it to her. We got up pretty early. Around five o'clock this morning. She was wonderful about the whole thing though. It's hard to find a real morning person."

"Ha!" I immediately cover my mouth as I let out a giggle. I have spent a lot of mornings with that woman and one thing I know without a doubt is Harlow is *not* a morning person. Like, not ever.

Eyebrows raised in surprise, I look at Trace. "Sorry. I've

not had the pleasure of meeting Harlow 'the morning person'. Are you sure we're talking about the same Harlow?" I bring my knees up to my chin and place my feet on the chair.

He laughs a deep laugh and nods his head. "Yeah, I'm sure. Unless you know some other curly headed, hot tempered woman, who has no mental filter named Harlow?"

I let another giggle. "Nope, that's definitely her."

I hear the girls shriek loudly. I just barely catch sight of all three of them running through the living room screaming and laughing loudly. A second later I hear the slam of one of their bedroom doors.

I smile at Trace who looks back at me, face full of surprise. "Those are my wonderful children who you've not had the luxury of meeting just yet. Once I make sure that Harlow isn't going to kill them, I'll bring them out for a meet and greet if you'd like."

Trace shakes his head. "Actually Alex, I've got to get going. I need to get some of this stuff in my new apartment. It's looking kind of bare in there. I was going to take Blake off of your hands for a while and give Harlow a break, seeing as though loading my furniture is pretty much all we've been doing this weekend. I'm sure he'll need a ride home anyway; I don't see his bike out there anywhere. He drove you in your truck right?"

I suddenly find myself both shocked and saddened that Blake is leaving. I guess I didn't realize he would be going so soon. I was hoping he would be here for dinner. I was going to have the girls make him a cake, as a thank you for helping me these last two days. I take a deep breath to force down the soccer ball in my throat. Seriously, I must be hormonal right now. There's nothing to be this upset about.

"Yeah, he did. I can't drive right now so he'll definitely need a ride. Thank you for offering," I say politely.

I look up from Trace to see Harlow and Blake walking into the kitchen arm in arm. When did they get so chummy? He must have used his charms on her too, just like he did with the girls. I guess no one is immune to them, not even Harlow.

Very interesting.

Still completely confused, I give them both my best fake smile as they walk up to the table. "Trace is going to take Blake home, I think, right Trace?"

"Yeah, I think so. If that's okay with him," he says looking at me. He then turns toward Blake and adds, "Sorry buddy, I need your help moving some of my heavier furniture. My cousin and Harlow helped me load it, but I'm gonna need help unloading it. That okay with you? Then I'll drop you at your place."

I watch as Blake looks at Harlow and as Harlow looks from Blake to Trace. Then Harlow gives Trace a look I know well, the 'we are so gonna have a talk later' look. What the hell is going on? I feel like I've landed in some weird episode of *The Twilight Zone*. Trace looks at Harlow with his eyes wide. "What?"

"Nothing, *honey*," she says a little too sweetly. "Alright, well, you boys get out of here then. I need my girl-time with Alex."

Trace and I both get up from the table and all four of us walk into the living room.

Blake stops by the couch and turns to me. "I need to change and then we'll be off. I'm pretty sure most people are out of their pajamas by this time."

I look down and laugh to myself because it didn't even dawn on my until this very moment that we are *both* still in our pajamas.

"Um…evidently not in this house." I motion toward the bedroom. "I moved your clothes into my room. They're in my armoire on the bottom shelf. You can change in there or in the bathroom."

"Thanks." He turns to walk to the bedroom. "I'll only be a minute and then I'll be out of your hair."

This is not how I planned the rest of the day going. I really wanted to watch *Pretty in Pink* with Blake – next up in the John Hughes marathon, play some more tennis – because I wanted a rematch… *I know his last serve was out*, and make him his "thank you" cake.

This sucks.

I turn to Harlow to ask her if *she* wants to watch *Pretty in Pink* with me, but she and Trace are evidently knee deep in a very involved conversation. Sighing loudly, I make my way across the living room to go find the girls. They're going to be just as happy as I am about the turn of events.

"Girls!" I shout walking down their hallway. I open Nycole's and Kyndall's room and see all three of them all setting up for a tea party. Even Nycole. I take a second to observe them, because I have a feeling this is the last time they'll be in this good of a mood for the rest of the day. And quite possibly tonight. Harlow and I definitely have our work cut out for us.

"Girls." Three sets of eyes land on my face. "Blake has to go now, so I need you to come say goodbye to him. Be sweet and tell him thank you for being such a big help, okay?"

Immediately, Rylie's eyes begin to tear up, but I can tell she's trying to be strong. Frowns on all of their faces, they slowly put down their tea cups and walk out of the room. Following them into the living room, I see Blake exiting the bedroom in the same clothes he wore yesterday. Yep – he still looks as good as he did then.

Immediately, Rylie runs across the room to Blake and he opens his arms to catch her. He gives her a big bear hug and then gently sets her back on her feet. He crouches down to the floor so he can look Nycole and Kyndall in their pitiful faces. "No sad faces, girls. Remember, we have a date for breakfast soon."

He extends his arms to each of the other girls, one on each side, and squeezes them tightly – with Rylie right in the middle. "Promise me that you'll help your mommy as much as you can. No fighting – deal?" They all nod their heads at him. "I'll be getting reports from her. I expect to get only good ones. And if I do, I might bring something super special to our next breakfast date, okay?" The girls continue to nod at him as he rises from the floor. They each hug his legs and turn to look at me.

"Why don't we watch some TV girls? Harlow? Can you put something on for them?" I'm starting to feel bad for Trace having to listen to Harlow ramble on. And seeing as though I know very well how it feels, I figure I'll toss him a bone and attempt to distract her. She looks up at me, gives me some version of a smile, then looks at the girls giving them a real smile. I'm so gonna figure out what's going on if it kills me. I turn to look at Blake.

He clears his throat and jerks his head toward the door.

"Um, Alex – can I have a minute?"

"Sure," I say in my pretend happy voice. I follow him to the door where he stops and turns around. He puts both arms around me, giving me a gentle hug. When he pulls back, he puts his hands on my shoulders and looks into my eyes. I get the feeling that he wants to tell me something.

"What?" Maybe his response will shed some light on what exactly has been happening since Harlow and Trace arrived.

"Nothing, Alex," he says moving his face right in front of mine. "Listen, I just want you to know that you can call me if you need anything. I know Harlow's here to help you if you need it, but I really want you to know that you can call me anytime. For anything...or for nothing at all. This weekend, well, it's been one of the best weekends I've had in a really long time. I'm just sorry I had to mangle your hand in order for it to happen."

He flashes me a brilliant smile and I think my heart literally just skipped a beat. God this man is beautiful. Especially when about two inches from my face. I shake my head to regain clarity.

Note to Self: Two inches away from Blake Morgan's face is most definitely some kind of equivalent to the Bermuda Triangle.

I clear my throat because all of a sudden it feels like I've swallowed a bucket full of sand.

"Blake, spending the last couple of days with you, I've had the most fun I have had in years. Even though my hand was mangled and I seemed to cry...*a lot*," I say with a little giggle. "This weekend, well – it made my heart feel whole again...if that makes sense."

I wrap my arms around his waist, place my ear against his chest, and say quietly, "Thank you, Blake. You've helped me more than you could possibly ever realize."

Through his chest, I hear a long exhale before he answers. "Alex, I would do anything for you. I hope you know that," he says with his chin placed on the top of my head.

Squeezing him tighter, I chuckle lightly.

"Well if that's true... then promise me you won't let the girls use the whole freakin' bag of chocolate chips next time."

And then another wall collapses.

CHAPTER THIRTEEN

After quickly introducing Trace to the girls before he and Blake walk out the door, I find myself in my bedroom, lying flat on my back across the bed. Holding my hurt hand against my chest, I stare at the armoire where I put Blake's clothes just hours ago.

So much has happened over the last twenty-four hours. I guess that's the sign of a true friend; you can literally go years without speaking, but when you meet again you just pick up right where you left off, never skipping a beat. I smile to myself as I think of Blake joking with the girls in the kitchen, quoting movie lines with me, humming the Barney song, making breakfast…yeah, there's something very comforting about this friendship. My heart feels peaceful, a feeling I haven't felt in years.

I hear Harlow shouting something to the girls about "her" bathroom while she approaches my bedroom. Opening the door, she looks at me and smiles.

"There you are! I've been looking everywhere for you. Sorry, I had to run and catch Trace before he left. When I came back in, you were nowhere to be found." She grabs a pillow and lies down next to me on the bed. "I know this sounds overly dramatic, which I am completely *not*, but it's going to be weird not seeing him for a while." She lets out a frustrated breath and covers her face with her hands. "What is *wrong* with me?"

Turning my head to face her, I laugh.

"Well, the list is so long that I have to break it up into categories and then subcategories…where would you like me to start?"

"Alex! I'm serious. I've never felt this way about a man. I usually just sleep with them and then conveniently lose their phone numbers." She lets out a heavy sigh. "It's weird. I feel like I can't get enough of Trace. He's different. I don't know…it's hard to explain."

"Harlow, there's nothing to explain. I've been there. I know how it feels when you start to *fall in love*." I watch her eyes double in size. I can't tell if the look on her face is from surprise that I actually said it or the idea of her actually being in love with *anyone*. I begin to laugh so hard at the look on her face that warm tears begin to stream out of my eyes and into my hair. Only Harlow can make falling in love this funny.

Trying to control my laughter I clear my throat and try to speak. "Harlow, seriously, it's okay to have feelings for someone. It doesn't make you a bad person. Actually, it makes you almost *human*." Her mouth shoots open and she gasps dramatically. Then, she reaches over and smacks my arm. I, in turn, smack her back with my good hand which leads to a two minute long smackfest.

"Okay! Okay! Truce!" I shout. She gives me a long look, waiting for me to smack her one more time, something I've been known to do in this situation. She relaxes when she realizes she's no longer in danger.

I smile widely at her, declaring my victory. "Well, glad we've gotten *that* out of our system." I clear my throat again to finish what I started to say before our very mature smack battle. "Anyway...Harlow, I think it's a good thing you to want to be around him. I know it scares you, but it's scary for most people, not just you. Just look at all the happy couples out there; don't you want even a little bit of that for yourself? Because, my dear, if anyone deserves that happiness it's you."

"Alex, I'm not even going to say how much you need to heed your own advice." Harlow shakes her head. "But I will say that yes, it does scare me. I mean, I was there when Derek died too. I lived everyday with you, watching his death almost break you. It was then that I decided I would *never* allow myself to become that vulnerable with anyone. But I find myself thinking that Trace might be worth it."

I can see the sadness in her eyes when she looks into mine. I know it's hard for her to talk about what happened with Derek. We were all really close; those two were like brother and sister. I'm not even sure she had a chance to grieve because she jumped straight into "help Alex function in day to day life" mode. I give her a slight smile and turn my head in the opposite direction, looking once again at the armoire.

I understand how she feels. "Yeah, I get that Harlow. Completely." The comfort of Blake's friendship, the way it makes me feel, definitely makes me vulnerable. I never thought I would *ever* let anyone else into my life after Derek passed. But after spending the weekend with Blake, I can't picture my life without his friendship. And I don't want to. So, yeah, I completely understand where Harlow's coming from.

I turn back to her and shrug my shoulders. "I guess you

just have to figure out if he's worth taking the chance. I have to agree with the old adage…'It is better to have loved and lost than to have never loved at all.' Luckily I had that love once, and I think you deserve to have it too, hopefully with a happier ending. But you'll *never* have your happy ending unless you're brave enough to open the book and start your story."

Harlow sighs heavily.

"Alex, you can have more than *one* happy ending. It bothers me when you say things like that. You still have the rest of your life ahead of you. Are you really convinced that you have to spend it alone?" she reluctantly asks.

"It's not that I'm convincing myself, I just can't see it happening. I have too much going on to make time for that stuff and my girls get priority. Maybe when they're older I can take time for me, but until then, I'm not going to abandon them while I pursue a failed love life. It's just not going to happen. I've already accepted that and I really wish you would. You have someone in your life who makes you happy, let's just concentrate on that for a while, okay?"

"Oh alright, Alex," she huffs at me, "But I'm not dismissing this conversation completely, I'm just postponing it. Understand?"

I shoot a wide grin at her and exhale a sigh of relief. "Now," I say with heightened amusement, "Tell me about this dove hunt!"

I don't think Harlow understands anything at all about dove hunting, but she evidently enjoyed herself. Though she does admit, in strict confidence of course, that she absolutely hated getting up at five o'clock in the morning. *Duh.* She must have put on an academy award winning performance with Trace, because the poor man has no idea how much Harlow hates mornings.

Or maybe she only likes mornings with Trace?

I really hope this is the case. I would hate for him to have to witness the early morning, long-winded, and ridiculously loud temper tantrums she has when woken up before she's ready.

She also admits to having a wonderful time during the hunt; he was very "up-close and personal" when he was trying to teach her how to shoot. Needless to say, they didn't shoot a thing.

But, she *did* make wise use of the pockets in her vest that were supposed to hold the shells, throwing a lip gloss in one and a compact in the other. Trace evidently found this hilarious. This is extremely good to know, because that right there is 100% all Harlow Reed. She also refused to wear the ear protection he got for her, because it would've messed up her hair, so he gave her some ear plugs as a compromise. Flexible. Another trait that makes him perfect for Harlow.

While I'm extremely happy for her, I'm also careful not

to push. I can't stand when she does it to me, and, if I do push her, she'll just do the opposite; I know this from much experience. I lay next to her as she tells me about the trip with Trace and keep my mouth shut, but inside my head, I'm doing the happy dance.

We decide after she finishes her story to actually make an effort to check on the children. We walk out of my room and down the hall while still talking about her weekend. Once we reach the living room, I can no longer concentrate on what she's saying because I'm completely overwhelmed by the smell of bleach and pine scented cleanser.

"Harlow, seriously?" I ask her rounding the corner heading to the bathroom. "Do they have to clean the bathroom *every* time you're here? Please tell me you reminded them about the bleach spray?" I ask, picking up the pace.

"Yes, I did...I don't know why you're freaking out! They asked me! They wanted to do it. They said something about saving money to buy stuff for breakfast...whatever that means."

Knowing exactly what it means, I smile to myself as I open the door and see my children hard at work.

Rylie is wiping the outside of the toilet with a sponge...the one we use in the kitchen for the dishes.

Note to Self: Buy a new kitchen sponge.

Gross.

Watching her strain to clean the underside of the toilet, I

shake my head. Poor girl, one day she's going to figure out that cleaning the toilet is not as "glamorous" as her sisters make it out to be. Sisters will be sisters I guess, and Rylie's *very* smart, so once she figures it out for herself, I'm sure they'll get what's coming to them – with interest.

I look over and see Nycole bending over, rinsing the tub with water. She takes all of Rylie's bathtub toys and puts them in the mesh frog hanging from the shower head. Water from the toys drips all over the back of her shirt when she bends down to grab the last one. She looks up in frustration, and it takes every ounce of strength I have to not laugh.

I then glance over to Kyndall, who's biting her bottom lip as she tries to clean the toothpaste spots off of the mirror. She's almost tall enough to reach over the sink without stretching, but not quite. She stops a couple of times to shake her arm as it's evidently getting very tired from having to scrub the mirror so hard. Good – maybe that'll teach them to not spray their toothpaste spit all over the place.

I watch all of them and their hard work. I guess when they really want something they'll actually work together without almost killing each other. *Good to know.*

"Wow guys, you want to do my bathroom next?" I watch their faces turn to me in horror. "Whoa! I'm totally kidding – *Jeez!*" These kids really need to get a sense of humor.

Once I feel that I'm no longer in danger, I place my hands on Kyndall's shoulders. "Seriously, girls...It looks awesome in here!" Then, I bend down so they can all hear me as I lower my voice. "Listen, be sure to get as much as you can out of Harlow. I plan on having a big breakfast."

Nycole lets out a sigh and they all flash me their pearly whites. I think they're relieved I'm not getting on to them for focusing on the breakfast with Blake already. How can I? I kinda miss him too. The poor man has only been gone for not even an hour and we're all acting like a bunch of Blake-fiends.

"Now – I'm gonna go keep Harlow busy so you can finish, although it looks like you're almost done. Just remember girls, no bleach spray on or around anyone's body. This includes the head and hair. You got it?"

"Yes ma'am!" they shout back.

Once again lowering my voice to a whisper, I add, "Alright. And," I motion for them to come close, "I'm completely serious, get as much as you can get. Think big, big breakfast." They nod at me with full understanding. "Okay," I say while giving them all an embrace and a quick wink before leaving them to their cleaning.

Walking out into the living room, I glance up to the TV and see Duckie from *Pretty in Pink* singing "Try a Little Tenderness". I stop by the couch and giggle as I watch Harlow slide out of the kitchen across the floor of the kitchen into the living room, *Risky Business* style, broom in hand for microphone, singing the infamous Otis Redding song.

"I love Duckie! He should've ended up with Andie. Blane was such a jerk," she says, now dancing across the living room. She removes her socks and slides on a pair of my old flip flops. "Hey – I found a huge chunk of glass on the floor in the kitchen under the pantry door. Be careful if you walk in there. I'm going to sweep, but just in case, we might want to wear shoes. What happened?" she asks, turning from the TV to face me.

"Well, I kind of had an emotional breakdown when I dropped a glass in the kitchen, *clearly* not one of my better

182

moments. Blake and the girls cleaned up, but they evidently missed some pieces. This is why I like to do things myself." I hold up gauze covered fingers in her face. "I don't know how much longer I can do this."

Harlow rolls her eyes and pokes me with the broom handle. "You'll do it as long as you have to. Now, go get some shoes on and come into the kitchen. I want to hear how your weekend went."

"*Jeez*... pushy! Alright, let me go grab my boots. I'll be in there in a sec."

I walk to my bedroom and grab my trusty ol' imitation UGG boots, slide them over my bare feet, and shuffle into the kitchen. Seeing Harlow's backside in the air sweeping debris into the dustpan, I just can't help myself. I snicker as I push it gently with my foot. She stumbles a little before she catches her balance.

"What was that for, *heifer*?" she smirks in my direction.

"For you, *heifer*!" I say through laughter. "Because I love you."

"Whatever, *heifer*! If I fall forward and ruin my gorgeous face, you will have muy problemos!"

I could go 'round and 'round with her, because trust me, we've done it before. But I make the decision to stop it before it turns into hours of "heifer" quotes. There's nothing like the satisfaction of lovingly calling your best friend a female cow...over and over again.

"You asked about my weekend?" I say with challenging eyes. I clearly win because after dumping the pan's contents into the trash, she turns to me with a delighted look on her face.

"Yes, please, *do* tell," she says, unsuccessfully trying to hide her excitement.

I downplay as much as possible. I don't want her getting excited and pushing anything with Blake.

"Well, it was really nice actually. Harlow, I don't even know what to say. He was... perfect. I mean, the girls obviously really like him. He watched Barney with them, read to them, and put them to bed when I couldn't. He helped me with basically everything I would let him do." I stop and look at Harlow's disapproving face. "What?"

"You know that you aren't the master of the universe, right? Do you understand that you don't have the ability to control people's minds? I'm just asking because I'm pretty sure Blake is an adult and you didn't have any say in what he did to help you. I mean, he helped you with what he *wanted* to help you with, and judging from the state of your hand, that was just about everything. I don't know why you have to rationalize it to yourself that you *let* him do it."

Um, okay. Not really where I was heading with this conversation, but it seems she thinks she has a point, so I amend my previous statement.

"He helped with everything because he's *so* wonderful and I should marry him and have *twelve* more kids. Is that what you where looking for?" I add, managing a smile. I really hope she didn't pick up on the thick layer of sarcasm I laid out for her.

She must still be coming down from her Trace-high because she only laughs. I have gotten worse reactions from saying much less.

"Alex, I get you. I know you don't want to depend on anyone and I understand that. But people help you because they want to, not because you let them. So if it makes you feel better to think that Blake was here and helped you because you allowed it, then that's your prerogative. But it's my job, as your best friend, to point out that we're going to help you no matter what you allow us to do. Otherwise, what kind of friends would we be?"

I let out an obvious groan. "You know, I really hate when you pull that philosophical shit. It makes me feel stupid, because you're always right."

Smiling as though she just won a gold medal in the Olympics, she motions for me to continue.

"Okay, so I had a couple of breakdowns while you were gone," I continue as fast as I can, hoping that if I speak quickly, she won't actually hear what I have to say.

"I, um, broke a glass trying to do things by myself... breakdown number one. But the second one wasn't my fault. He asked me about the day Derek died, so I think I deserve a 'get out of jail free card' with that one."

"Acceptable. Go on." she replies.

"Well, after the breakdown sessions were over, we actually had a great time. I haven't laughed like that in forever. I don't know. There's a comfort I have with him that I can't explain. It feels really... good. I don't feel like I have to pretend with him, you know?" Harlow nods her head in response.

"Yeah, I understand. There's nothing you need to explain. Just let it be and enjoy the friendship. Let him in, Alex. You don't have to be *strong* all the time. You don't have to fight *everything*."

I absolutely adore this woman.

I walk over to her and give her a tight embrace. "I love you, you know," I say, pulling back and placing my hand on her shoulder. "I don't know what I would do without you."

"Yeah, yeah. I'm wonderful. I know. I love you too, sweetie. I must, because I don't get all mushy over just anyone."

"Except maybe Trace?" I ask her with a mischievous grin on my face.

She lets out a laugh. *"Definitely* Trace."

"I'm really happy for you, Harlow. I hope it works out for the two of you. There's definitely something there. You would have to be blind to not see it."

She gives me a love struck smile and I know my friend is in trouble, a good kind of trouble. A, jump in both feet first and lose yourself, kind of trouble. I give her a nudge with my elbow and smile back.

"I'm gonna go check on the girls. They've been pretty quiet for a while, which always makes me nervous." I turn to leave the kitchen. Rounding the corner to head to the bathroom, I almost run over Rylie.

"We're done, Mommy!" she says beaming with excitement. "I'm gonna ask Harlow for our money. Nycole and Kyndall said I was littler so I would get more than they would." I watch her skip away to collect their money. I can't help but laugh to myself. *Jeez*…my kids never fail to surprise me with their ingenuity.

I check out the bathroom and it is indeed sparkling clean. I continue on to the older girls' room since I can hear Kyndall's voice getting louder as I make my way down the hallway. I stop by the door to listen before I open.

"I had so much fun with Blake! He was so nice and he let me ride on his shoulders! I can't wait until we get to see him again!" Kyndall say enthusiastically. Okay, I guess this would be an opportune time to discuss Blake with the girls. I know it may be premature, but I want to make sure they understand my relationship with him.

I slowly open the door. Both girls' heads whip around to look at me and they stop mid-jump on the bed. I raise my eyebrows giving them my "you know better" look. They both fall immediately on their bottoms.

"What are you guys up to in here, besides the obvious jumping on the bed that you know you're not supposed to be doing?" I sit down on the bed with them.

"Talking about Blake, Mama," Kyndall says with a smile.

"What about Blake, baby?"

"Well, I was telling Nycole how much I like him. He was really fun and he made us laugh! I can't wait 'til he comes back over!"

I nod my head at her and turn to look at Nycole who's watching me closely. I have a feeling she knows where this conversation is headed.

"What about you, Nycole? How do you feel about Blake?" I reach out and pat her leg, encouraging her to speak.

"Well… he was fun. He was really nice to us. He read us each a story last night. And he didn't even mind reading Rylie's book. I like him," she says hesitantly.

I move closer to the girls, making sure each one is on either side of my body. Putting my arms around both of their shoulders, I begin the 'Blake' discussion.

"Well, I like him too. You know, we've been friends since we were very, very little. I have known him a very long time, and I'm glad that you like him as much as I do. But I need to talk to you about my relationship with him. We're friends and that's all. I am not in love with him like I was with your dad. I don't want you to think I'm trying to replace him with Blake. It's really important that you understand that. Your daddy will *always* be your daddy, okay. No one can take his place in your heart. Do you understand?"

They both nod at the same time so I continue. "So, you're okay with us being friends then?" Smiles from both. "And you understand that we are *only* friends." Still smiling. Good. "I also gather that you're alright with him coming over sometimes?" I ask this with my own smile because they're now nodding their heads so hard I'm worried they might fall off. "And I say *sometimes* because he's not going to be able to come over *every* time you guys want him to. He just spent the weekend with us and I think he deserves a break so we're not asking him to come over for a while, okay? "

"Yes *ma'am!*" I grin at both of them as they simultaneously shout their response.

"Alright – well, listen girls, if there's anything you want to discuss with me about Blake, now or ever, I want you to come and talk to me. You know we don't keep things from each other in this family. So I want you to always be open and honest with me, okay?"

"Okay," they both respond as I bring them in close to my body, squeezing them tightly.

"Mom, can I say something?" Nycole asks, suddenly looking very serious.

"Of course, honey." I release them from my embrace, but leave my arms draped over shoulders.

"I just want to tell you that another reason I really like Blake is because, well…,"she hesitates.

I let go of Kyndall and turn my body to face Nycole.

Urging her on, I place my hand on top of hers. "Go on baby, its fine. Tell me."

"Well, it's just that you were different when he was here. You smiled and laughed a lot more. And you didn't seem so sad, that's all. It's been a long time since I've seen you happy like that. Blake makes you happy and that's why *I* like him." She makes her statement while focusing only on our joined hands. She then looks up at my face and shrugs her shoulders. "That's all I wanted to say."

I squeeze her hand. Wow. I guess I'm not hiding things as well as I thought from them. Harlow's right. My sadness is affecting them. I never knew.

"Thank you for telling me that, Nycole," is all I can manage to say. I can feel the moisture beginning to form in the corners of my eyes.

I wrap my arms around her and give her a hug. "I love you, Nycole. Thank you for being honest," I say, quickly swiping a tear from my cheek.

"You're welcome, Mom. I didn't mean to make you sad," she whispers in my ear.

I release her and look her in the eyes. "It's not you, baby. I promise. I always want you to be honest with me, okay?"

She nods at me and I give her shoulders a quick squeeze. Turning to Kyndall, I ask, "Is there anything else you would like to say?"

"Um…you're the best mommy ever? Oh, and Rylie's *really* annoying. That's about it."

I can't help but break out in laughter. "Kyndall…I don't know what I would do without you!" I say, giving her a hug too. She giggles and squeezes me back tightly.

"Mama?" she asks while still in my arms.

"Yes?"

"Is it too early to ask Blake to come over tomorrow for breakfast?"

"Kyndall Meyer!" I shout in astonishment. I let go of her and give her my well practiced look of disapproval. She giggles and runs out of the room.

Surprising me more than her request is the fact that I actually consider it for a second. I mean, I know I won't, but the fact that it even crosses my mind rattles me a little.

Great…It's official.

We're *all* Blake-fiends.

CHAPTER FOURTEEN

Harlow and I quickly fall back into our routine over the next week. She stays over every night, helping me with baths, fixing the girls hair, making dinners and lunches, and of course, driving them to school in the mornings. But by the end of the week, my hand feels a lot better and my fingers start to work normally so I don't really need help anymore. As much as I enjoy her company, I decide I can be declared officially "Harlow free" by Friday. Plus, that leaves her the weekend to spend as she wishes...aka Trace O'Donnell.

So waking up Saturday morning, with no company for the first time in a week, I was already feeling a little restless. But since Nancy came by to pick up the girls, leaving me completely alone, I'm beginning to feel absolutely stir crazy. While sitting at my kitchen table and drumming my fingers, trying to enjoy "mommy time" as Nancy put it, I'm actually relieved when my phone rings. I pick it up expecting the girls, but when I look at the screen I'm pleasantly surprised.

"What's up, Blake?" I say with an obvious smile in my voice.

"Not much. I was just calling to see how my favorite girls are holding up. I understand Harlow's services are no longer needed. I assume your hand is better?" Blake asks in a sexy tone. Man, I've missed his voice.

God, I'm *such* a fiend.

I purposely didn't call him this week even though I fought the temptation every night. I wanted *him* to call. I didn't want to bother him; I figured he would call when he had time. So, hearing his voice on the other line, I can't help but feel a *little* bit of satisfaction knowing I wasn't the first to cave in the calling department.

"Yeah, it's healing. It still aches a little sometimes, but it's much better. Thanks for asking." My heart is racing for some reason. I've known this man for an eternity; I don't know why I'm suddenly so nervous to talk to him. "Hey," I hesitate before I continue. "Let's do something. I'm going out of my mind. The girls are with Nancy for the day and I can't stay in this house any longer. Please, Blake!"

I can hear his sexy chuckle over the phone and my heart flip flops in my chest. Man, I must *really* be going crazy from the fifteen minutes of no social interaction.

"Actually, Alex," he starts off. "That's why I was calling. I was hoping to do something with *all* the Meyer girls today. But I guess *you'll* do." He finishes with that damn sexy chuckle again and my stomach feels like a thousand butterflies have suddenly taken flight inside it.

Note to Self: I'm no longer allowed to go without prolonged human interaction for fear of random physiological responses.

"Ha. Ha. Ha. Get over here and entertain me, damn it."

"Will do. I'll be there in ten. Wear something comfortable," he adds mysteriously and hangs up.

Jeez – if this were a real live date I'd be pissed. No wonder he doesn't date anyone. Ten minutes to get ready. *Seriously?*

I jump up out of my seat, catching it before it falls backwards onto the kitchen floor, and make a mad dash to the bedroom. I throw on my yoga pants, the ones that make my ass look good, *not that it matters*, my favorite homemade purple tank top which reads "National Sarcasm Society: Like We Need Your Support", and my black blinged out flip flops, because every woman needs a little bling now and then. I brush out my hair and put it in a pony tail, a*hh...how I've missed you ponytail*, and throw on my NY Yankees baseball hat. I add a bit of mascara and some lip gloss to my face and poof...I'm done. Giving myself a last appraisal in mirror, I'm satisfied with the outcome of my appearance.

Ha! Take that Blake Morgan with your *ten minute* ready requirement.

Walking into the living room, I hear the rumble of his motorcycle coming up my driveway. I open the door and watch him get off his bike. He removes his sunglasses and shakes out his windblown hair, which of course looks sexy as hell. The ends of his hair turn up around his ears and fall to the collar of his very well fitting v-neck black t-shirt. His blue jeans, frayed at the bottom, just barely drag the ground over his black boots.

Mmmmm-mmmmm.

He turns around to take the keys out of his ignition and my breath hitches as I drop my glance and note (privately of course) that his bottom looks very nice in those jeans. Very nice indeed. Turning around to face me, he gives me a sexy lop-sided grin while he tucks the sunglasses into the front of his shirt so they hang from the "V" and runs his hand through his hair.

I try to swallow, but my throat is really dry...probably because I have been watching him with my mouth wide open. I immediately start to cough.

"You okay, Alex?" he asks with a knowing smile.

"Yeah," I say, trying to breathe through my coughing attack. "I think I swallowed a gnat. *Gross.* I'm gonna go get some water. Come on in." I whip around and head into the house as fast as I can so he won't be able to see that my face has turned a new shade of red. *So embarrassing.*

I hear him laugh as he enters the house, which makes me walk even faster, trying to increase the distance between us. I'm actually breathing hard by the time I get to the kitchen. I should *really* start working out more.

I quickly grab a glass of ice water and take a swig, hoping it will help with my face. *Not really sure how that will work...*

I set the glass down and turn to see Blake walking into the kitchen. "You sure you're okay?" he inquires.

"Yeah. I'm fine."

I pop myself up on the counter by the sink and take a seat with my legs dangling over the dishwasher. "What's the plan, Stan?" I ask him. I really have no idea what we're doing.

Blake walks right over to me and reaches to grab the water that I just placed on the counter. *Really? Can the man not get his own freakin' glass of water?*

My body responds to his closeness when he brushes my

leg with his. I feel a shock race throughout my entire body and I unintentionally jump. He looks over at me with a hint of a smile. God his eyes really are amazing.

"Well…I was hoping we could take the boat out. Like old times. But if we do, we're gonna have to use your truck to pull it. I hope you don't mind. Mom and Dad are still out of town and I can't pull it with my bike, obviously. Or, we can just find something else to do. Up to you." He places the glass back down beside me. Another electrical pulse radiates through me when his arm grazes mine. I scoot over a centimeter. He chuckles again under his breath and I hop off the counter.

Jeez…What's going on with me today?

"Fishing sounds great!" I respond. I'm not really sure why I sound so excited.

I really need to get out of here. Maybe I'll be normal again with a little fresh air. "We can take the truck, that's fine! Let's get going then!" Okay, I seriously need to tone down the over enthusiasm a bit.

I grab the keys off the counter and speed walk towards the door. I have to get out of this house because, honestly, I'm extremely freaked out. I haven't felt anything like this since Derek. I don't know what's going on but it *has* to stop; I'm friends with Blake and I intend for it to stay that way. Friendship is comfortable – crushing on Blake, not-so-much.

Jumping in the truck and starting the ignition, I wait for Blake to exit the house. I watch as he closes the door behind him and holds his hand above his eyes, looking across the driveway.

"You have sunglasses, dummy!" I shout from the safety of my Suburban.

"I know!" he shouts back. "I was just making sure you weren't taking one last speed walking around the block before we head out." *Sarcasm. Noted.*

One major internal eye roll and a deep sigh later, I motion for him to get his ass to the truck. "Are we fishing or are we just going to stand around today?" *Looking like a freakin' Diesel Jeans ad. Dumb.*

He takes his sunglasses off of his shirt and slides them over his eyes. "We're fishing," he says, walking to the Suburban. He slides into the passenger seat and flashes me his trademark smile. I jokingly roll my eyes at him and lightly punch his arm. "Don't pull that sexy smile on me, Blake Morgan. Sarcasm is only acceptable when I use it." I point to my shirt. "I don't see your 'National Sarcasm Society' shirt. Therefore, I'm the only one with free reign to use it. You can just keep yours to yourself."

"Yeah, I noticed that. Still in the t-shirt making business I see. I'm in the need of a new one, in case you get bored. Poor G.I. Joe didn't make it, I'm sorry you had to find out this way." He gives me a fake frown and a quick wink.

"Aww, that's too bad. I loved that shirt. I'm sure I can put something together for you." I give him a quick wink back. "Hmm…G.I. Joe replacement. That's gonna take some work. Gimme some time."

Blake turns to look me dead straight in the eye. "Take all the time you need, Alex. I'm not going anywhere." The seriousness of his statement makes my heart flutter like crazy. I immediately feel the blood rush to my cheeks. I let out a quick breath.

"Um, okay. You ready?" We really need to get out of here, *like now.*

I can tell Blake's trying to hide his evil little smile. He enjoys making me blush and he seems to have caught on to my random physiological responses. *Jerk.* Maybe that's what his shirt should say. "J-E-R-K". Or "I live to make Alex Meyer Uncomfortable".

"Yep. Let's get going." He moves his eyes from mine to the front of the truck, letting his smile finally reveal itself.

I shake my head and start the engine. After a short ride, a lot of arguing, and even more hand slapping over radio stations, *I really, really hate country music*, we round the corner of his street and his house comes into view.

Pulling into the driveway, Blake directs me to the side of the house. "The boat's around back. Go ahead and pull up here. I'll take care of hitching it to the truck. I have some drinks and snacks in the fridge and a cooler on the kitchen counter. You can load it up while I take care of the boat. Meet me back here in about ten minutes."

I raise my eyebrows in question. "You must have been pretty convinced I'd say yes, considering all your preparations. What if I would've said no?"

"Well, I guess I'd have a lot of sports drinks and ham and cheese sandwiches. No big deal." He opens his door and jumps out of the truck.

No big deal? I'm not really sure what to think about that statement. I lean against the door and watch him walk around the front of my vehicle while I'm still trying to decipher his cryptic code. What does he mean by "no big deal"? Am I not a big deal? Is fishing not a big deal? Is having pre-made ham and cheese sandwiches not a big deal?

The next thing I know, while I'm lost in deep thought, the door flies open. I tumble sideways out my truck and have no choice but to grab the inside handle to prevent falling on my ass as my feet land on the ground. "Damn it, Blake!" I press all my weight onto the handle and straighten my body, making sure my feet are firmly planted before letting go.

"What?" he asks innocently.

"You know what! I was leaning against the door, *trash hole*! You totally did that on purpose!" I silently laugh to myself at my insult. Blake and I used that word all the time growing up. I really don't know why it hasn't caught on yet.

He coughs, I suspect in effort to cover up a laugh. "Alex, I have no idea what you're talking about. I was just opening the door for you. It's not my fault you weren't paying attention."

"Shut up, Blake." I really need a quick escape plan…this is just embarrassing.

"My keys are in the ignition. I'll go grab the snacks from the kitchen. *Don't* mess up my truck." I turn hastily to make my grand exit and start walking to his porch.

"Watch that door!" he shouts from behind me. "It can do some real damage I hear!"

"Shut. *Up*. Blake! I think I'm safe as long as you aren't behind it!" I yell back. Even though I try to sound mad, I can't help but laugh as I walk onto the porch. Yeah, I definitely missed Blake.

Approaching the front door, I catch my reflection in the window. I straighten my cap that must have been knocked to the side during the truck door debacle and then open the door. I feel the rush of cool air and taking in a deep breath, I'm surprised by the familiarity of the smells in this house. I must not have noticed it last time I was here, with my fingers falling off and all, but now I do. Mrs. Morgan's house always smelled of apples and cinnamon. I remember how, when I was younger, I would come over and immediately run into the kitchen to see if she was making her award winning apple pie. Most of the time she was, and she would always give us both a fresh slice with an ice cold glass of milk. I smile at the memory.

Knowing that Mr. and Mrs. Morgan are out of town, I'm not really sure how the house *still* smells like her pies. Maybe she has some scent oils around the house or something. I walk through their living room, slowing down to look at all the pictures she has placed throughout the room.

There's a family picture of them in the mountains, probably at Blake or Rebecca's house in Colorado. I see his two nephews in the picture and giggle to myself because they both bear a strong resemblance to their uncle. He is crouched down beside them in the picture, arms around them with huge grins on all of their faces.

Next, I come to a picture of Blake and Rebecca in high school. It's taken right on the front porch; Blake is dressed in a pair of khaki dress pants and a blue button down shirt with a red tie. His light brown hair is styled the way he used to wear it, with tons of gel to spike it up in the front. Seeing him at that age in the picture, I feel a stab of pain in my heart.

Floods of memories enter my mind. I remember Derek's hand in mine as he walked me to class, the quick kisses he would give me before school. How we'd talk for hours in the back of his truck, my back leaned against his stomach, his legs on either side of me. We planned our future wedding, discussed our future children, designed our future house. I would have made each moment with him last as long as I possibly could if I'd known that future would be cut so short.

Wiping a tear from the corner of my eye, I move to the next picture. It's a candid shot of Blake and me when we were about twelve years old, sitting on his front porch, eating popsicles. We're sitting on the porch rail, feet dangling, looking at each other as we're caught by the camera mid laugh. I pick up the picture to take a closer look. Inspecting our faces, I'm taken aback at how happy and peaceful I look. God, I used to love to laugh with Blake. Even though I was very young in this picture, it reminds me of the way I feel when I am with Blake now...the comfort...the familiarity...the warmth. I don't remember ever being around Blake and not feeling that way.

Now that I think about it, my feelings around Derek and Blake were actually very similar. They both had a way of making my heart feel happy and full of life.

I place the picture frame back on the table and think about Derek and Blake. Is it wrong that I feel so comfortable around Blake? Is it wrong that I've also begun to feel somewhat *uncomfortable* around Blake? Would Derek hate me because of it? Would he be disappointed in me if I develop feelings for another man? Or would he want me to move on, like Nancy suggested?

I really wish he was here to explain to me what the hell I'm supposed to do now. I almost feel like I need his permission to move on and that I'm stuck in some kind of limbo until I get it. And seeing as though he's no longer available for consultation, I don't anticipate getting any answers anytime soon.

Still lost in thought, I make my way to the kitchen. I open the refrigerator and grab the two bottles of grape sports drink and the two bottles of orange. How did he remember I love grape? There's no way he could have remembered that. We haven't had this stuff since we were in junior high. Maybe it was just a lucky guess…or maybe the orange ones were for me?

I grab the sandwiches and close the refrigerator door. Hands full, I turn to place all of our goodies on the counter next to the cooler, but when I see what's already beside it, I almost drop everything to the floor. There's no way.

Next to the cooler, is an apple pie with the sugar and cinnamon on the top just like his mother used to make. "Mrs. Morgan?" I say to myself, half expecting her to pop her head around the corner. I notice a piece of paper lying by the pie. In Blake's handwriting it reads:

It's probably not as good as Mom's, but pack a couple of pieces if you want. There's also a thermos with milk in the fridge.

—Blake

Smiling, I cut two pieces of pie for us and place them in the plastic container that he laid out. I grab the thermos of milk, put the sandwiches and drinks in the cooler as well, and zip it closed. Throwing it over my shoulder, I make my way to the front door.

Walking out onto the porch, I close the door behind me and smile. Blake is leaning against my Suburban, waiting for me. He looks amused when I approach him.

"I found the pie," I say, removing the cooler from my

shoulder and handing it to him. Taking it from my grasp, he grins back at me. "How'd you remember I loved that pie? And how'd you remember I love grape drinks? Seriously Blake, it's been *so* many years."

He moves his body closer to mine and looks me directly in the eyes. "Well...the pie was for me. I'm just sharing it with you. And it's kind of hard not to remember the grape drinks. You would always end up with a purple mustache after you'd drink them. I'd laugh at you behind your back for hours," he adds with a chuckle.

I involuntarily move my hand to cover my mouth. "What? No way, Blake. No one gets a mustache from drinking a grape sports drink. You're *totally* making that up."

"Whatever you say, Alex. I'm the one who had to look at it," he says, giving me a wink. He turns to open the passenger door and motions for me to get in. "Come on, *mustache*."

I shove his shoulder as hard as I can in annoyance and climb in the truck. Before he closes the door, he puts his arm up above my head, and leans his whole body forward so that he's actually inside with me. My whole entire body begins to vibrate and my heart pounds against my chest. The breath in my throat catches when he leans a little further, his face right in front of mine.

"Okay fine – you got me. I *did* make that up." He pauses for a brief second.

"I actually made the pie for *you*." He shoots me a sexy grin, withdraws his body and closes my door.

Note to Self: I'm definitely drinking the

orange today...just in case.

After Blake backs the boat into the water, I drive my Suburban up the ramp and park it. I grab the cooler and trudge to the boat dock where he's waiting for me. I pause for a brief second to take in the lake and its surroundings. I let my body sway with the movement of the water. I can feel it under my feet as it rocks the dock from side to side. I breathe the lake air into my lungs and listen to the sound of the water hitting the rocks on the side. I sigh out loud.

God, I've missed this.

I scoot my feet to the edge where Blake is waiting for me and attempt to step into the boat. But as soon as I lift my foot, a huge wave knocks the dock and with the weight of the cooler, I lose my balance. I decide it's safer to just drop straight to my bottom than to land in the lake, so I do just that. I fall backwards and brace myself by throwing my arms behind me. Once I've successfully landed, I look up to see Blake staring at me with his mouth open and his eyes widened with surprise. I lie back on the dock and belt out a laugh. I can't help it. I lift my head to glance back at Blake. Although he's managed to cover his mouth, his eyes are still huge, which makes me laugh even harder. I look up into the sky and try to gain my composure.

"If it wasn't nine-thirty in the morning, I'd be worried that you're drunk!" Blake shouts from the boat. "What is that? The second time you've had balance issues this morning?"

I giggle while I bring myself back to my feet. I dust off my bottom and the back of my tank top. "Maybe it would've been better for me to have a few drinks this morning. It couldn't get any worse, that's for sure." I grab the strap to the cooler that luckily landed right side up so there's no damage to its contents. Hoisting it on my shoulder, I feel another huge wave knock the dock and I tip a little to the side.

"Get me off of here! I'm getting a complex!" I fight to regain my balance once again, and scoot closer towards Blake. He's moved the boat as close to the dock as he can. Another big wave crashes into the dock. "Ahh! Help me, Blake!" I yell.

Blake leans forward as far as he can and reaches for me. I hand him the cooler. Throwing it to the side, he shouts through his laughter, "Not the *cooler*, Alex, *you*!" He grabs my hands and pulls me so hard, he loses his balance and falls backward into the boat, bringing me with him. I land flush with his body, my arms against his chest, his arms curved around my body. Blake squeezes me tightly and I can feel his entire body shaking from laughter. Giggling along with him, I finally raise my head off of his chest. "Well, *that* was interesting," I remark as my laughter dies down. Looking at his face, I realize the intimate position our bodies are in right now. I watch the smile on his lips disappear and I'm pretty sure he just noticed it as well. I slowly move my eyes to his. I hold his stare because there's something in his eyes calling to me. I want to lose myself in them. To give in, completely lose control, and stay like this forever.

Okay... I need to get my body off of his ASAP.

I put my hands on both sides of him to push my body off of his. When I get to my feet, I offer him my hand to help him up. He takes it and I force all of my weight backwards to offset his pull. Standing up, he looks me right in the eye. "Yeah, that *was* very interesting."

We definitely need a subject change.

I clear my throat and I smooth out the wrinkles in my clothes. Looking over to the cooler, I shake my head in disapproval. "Well, I hope my piece of pie is still edible."

Blake gives me a slight apologetic smile. "Sorry about that. I just wanted to get you in the boat. You weren't doing so hot up there."

"Yeah, well, I guess I'm a little out of practice." I walk over and turn the cooler to its rightful position. "Okay, now that I'm successfully in the boat, let's go catch some fish."

I deposit myself into the seat next to the driver's and prop my feet up onto the side of the boat. "Come on captain. Put this baby in gear!"

Blake takes his seat behind the wheel. "You might want to hold on to your cap. I plan on letting her spread her wings."

I pull the cap lower on my head making it snug as possible. Blake puts the boat in reverse and soon after we're coasting out of the "no wake zone". When we pass the final buoy, he opens her up and we race across the lake. The speed is exhilarating. I lean my head back and allow myself to enjoy it. I feel the breeze all around me. My hair is whipping crazily as the wind blows it whichever way it wants. I breathe in every smell around me; the water, the air, the fish, the trees…it feels good, like home.

We drive around for a bit before slowing. Making our way into a cove, I immediately let out a gasp and cover my mouth in surprise. He responds with a shy smile and a shrug of his shoulders. "I thought you'd like it."

I can't believe he remembered this place. This is *our* cove. We used to haul all of our stuff down the hill and fish off of the bank. It was a trek, hiking through the trails with our tackle boxes and fishing poles, but it was always worth it.

I inhale deeply as my eyes survey the beauty surrounding me. There are willow trees, whose leaves dance just barely on the surface of the water, and a number of wisteria trees with beautiful purple blooms layering the bank all around us. The scent makes my heart swell.

Turning off the engine, we drift until we find our spot. I'd forgotten how serene it was here. The water was always so smooth; there were hardly ever any ripples on the surface. The only sound was the water just barely running into the bank. When I was younger, I would come to this very place anytime I needed to get away. It was the perfect haven. Evidently it still is.

I lean my head back as the boat gently rocks back and forth and inhale one long peaceful breath. "This is perfect, Blake. Thank you. Absolutely perfect."

And for the first time in years, my head and my heart feel as calm as the waters below.

CHAPTER FIFTEEN

Sitting in the boat, Blake and I finish off our pieces of pie, *which did in fact taste just like his mother's*, with our poles in the water, waiting for the next catch. While I lick my fork clean, I glance over at Blake; he's watching me with an amused smile.

"What? It was good. I should have packed a couple of more pieces. I'd have never pegged you for a baker." I put the fork back in the cooler, grab my pole, and resume watching my bobber float on the surface of the water.

"There's a lot you don't know about me, Alex," he says mysteriously.

"Like what?" I look over as he approaches and takes a seat next me. I watch him cast his line in the water.

"What do you want to know? Ask me anything."

Hmm. Anything?

He turns to face me and I can't help but notice the reflection of light from the water dancing off of his green eyes, making them look even greener. His light brown hair is flipping up at the ends, but where it is shorter by his eyes, it falls forward a bit. There's a matching shade of scruff on his face that somehow I missed this morning. He looks amazing.

"Why no girlfriend?" I brazenly ask. Really, I want to know. The guy is gorgeous.

Facing forward, he lets out a long deep breath and scoots

down to prop his feet up on the side of the boat. "Impossible standards, I guess."

I feel a tug on my line and immediately turn away to look at the bobber. I eye it for a couple of seconds before I turn back. "What kind of impossible standards?"

Still facing the water, Blake seems to contemplate what he wants to say. "I don't know, Alex. It's hard to describe. I was in love with someone once but that was a very long time ago. Ever since then, no one seems to measure up. Impossible standards."

A long time ago? When? I don't remember him ever dating anyone seriously in high school. Eww...it wasn't Ashley Thompson was it?

"What? When? I don't remember that." I feel another tug on my line. I jerk the pole a little.

"You probably weren't paying attention. But you were there, I remember." He tilts his head and angles his body towards mine. "You don't remember?" He searches my face for some answer I obviously don't have.

Another damn tug on the line.

This freakin' fish could not have worse timing. I yank the pole backwards as hard as I can, not to hook the fish, but out of frustration. The line flies up out of the water, sails over my head, swings back in my direction, and seems to be gaining momentum as the hook heads directly for my face.

"Whoa! Alex, watch out!" is the last thing I hear before Blake slams his body into mine, wraps his arms around me, and pulls me protectively to the floor of the boat. As we're crouched together, I notice that I can feel the scruff from his cheek tickling mine. I feel his warm breath in my ear and on my neck. I can feel his chest thumping against mine. I feel everything that is Blake.

I can't help myself. With my arms still wrapped around him, I grab onto the back of his shirt with both hands and pull him closer so I can press my nose into his neck. Leather and soap. With one whiff, I am completely overwhelmed. So many feelings at one time.

I feel safe.

I felt protected.

I feel relief.

I feel scared.

I feel vulnerable.

I feel desire.

I feel...

Everything.

I don't think I have felt anything in years. My wall has completely crumbled. The numbness of protection is gone.

My entire body is shaking while Blake holds me. And while I know that it's from the flood of feelings I've just encountered, I'm sure that Blake thinks it's in response to the near assault from the runaway hook. I stay in the comfort of his arms until I'm no longer trembling. When I've regained my control, I release his shirt and unwrap my arms. I lean back a little to look at his face and offer him an apologetic smile. "I thought I had one. Sorry."

The tension in Blake's face eases. I watch his eyes soften as they continue to hold mine. Slowly, he brings his hand to my face, curls his fingers around the back of my neck and lightly brushes my cheek with his thumb. We remain there in silence, just watching each other. After a couple of seconds, he leans forward, places his prickly cheek against mine and whispers softly in my ear, "Are you sure you don't remember?" He presses his warm lips tenderly on my cheek.

Memories rush to my mind.

The lake. Blake's boat. Laughing on the floor. A kiss on the cheek.

Then it all clicks.

Blake Morgan had been in love with me? I knew he loved me as a friend, but, *in love*? That's a completely different ball game.

As I finally come to this realization, Blake's warm lips leave my cheek and his arms move to circle my waist. He leans his head back and scans my face. I raise my eyebrows at him in disbelief. "*I'm* impossible standards?"

Blake's lips form a breathtaking crooked smile when he looks directly into my eyes. He chuckles under his breath. "Yep. *You're* impossible standards."

I shake my head in disbelief. "No way. How could I have not known? We were around each other every day until..." The smile fades from Blake's face. He drops his gaze and looks over my shoulder at the water. "Until Derek," he says.

Guilt consumes me. I had been so wrapped up in my own world that I completely left Blake behind and never looked back. My best friend – Blake Morgan.

Blake – who helped me every time I skinned my knee doing stupid bike stunts when we were kids.

Blake – who always let me have the last slice of his mom's pies, even though he acted mad about it.

Blake – who took me fishing and always baited my hooks for me because it was gross.

Blake – who stepped aside as soon as I met Derek.

Blake – who watched helplessly while my life moved on

without him.

Blake – who evidently was in love with me the whole time.

I look up at his face and feel the tears forming in my eyes. "I didn't know." I look down at my toes and reach up to wipe a tear before it has a chance to run down my face. I now fully understand his anger during our first interactions when he came back home. I feel Blake's fingers under my chin as he presses me to look back at him. Once my eyes meet his, I just shake my head. "I didn't know. I'm so sorry."

He pulls me close to his chest and holds me tight. "There was no way you could have known, Alex. I should've told you how I felt, but I didn't. After you met Derek, I hoped I'd still have my chance. I waited, but the timing was never right. Then you guys got together. And that was it. All I could do was watch it happen and hate myself for never saying anything. I should have fought harder for you. I won't let that happen again."

He pulls back and looks me directly in the eyes. "I love you, Alex. I loved you when we were just kids...and I've continued to love you *every* day since."

I pull him close and bury my head in his chest, letting my tears fall onto his shirt. He had every right to be disappointed in me. I get it. He loved me, and I left him behind, without a second thought.

But, I also understand that even though he was upset with me, he helped without hesitation when I needed it. He forgave me when I simply asked. He put his weekend aside to help me take care of my children. He held me when I cried. He did all of these things because of the person that he is. I know I won't allow myself to take this relationship for granted again. I lost it once by being selfish. I refuse to allow that to happen for a second time. I've already lost too much in this lifetime.

With his arms still around me, I pull away from his chest and wipe my face with my hands. Taking a deep breath, I look up to see his concerned eyes looking down at me. "I'm okay, Blake. I promise. It just caught me by surprise, that's all."

"The last thing I want to do is hurt you, Alex. I guess, after all these years, I feel that I owe it to myself to at least tell you the truth so I can stop being angry at myself and running every what if scenario through my head." He watches my face carefully while he speaks. "I'm sorry if I shocked you. But I also want you to know that having you back in my life as my *friend*...well...I've missed you. And I hope that what I said doesn't ruin that for me. I just needed you to know the truth."

I reach back and grab his hands that are resting on my lower back and bring them to the front of our bodies. Holding them tightly, I scoot closer to him. "You won't lose me. I know you would never hurt me." I hesitate, trying to plan my next words carefully.

"I'm not sure what's going on between us. It scares me. I feel things for you that I never thought I would feel again. You make me feel alive. I can't thank you enough for that, Blake." I lower our hands and shift my body backwards.

"But I need time. This isn't the same as when we were kids. I have three little girls who are very affected by the decisions I make. I have to be responsible. I can't get wrapped up in something just because it feels good. I don't have that luxury anymore. I hope you can understand that."

Blake lets go of my hands and reaches up to gently stroke my face.

"Alex, I've waited this long. Turns out I'm a very patient man," he says with a smile. "I can wait. I understand about your girls, and I wouldn't let you rush into anything you're not absolutely sure about...for their sakes. I understand that completely. I can wait knowing that in the end, if you choose me, then I'm a lucky man. If you don't choose me, we'll still be friends, but then I can move on. There will be no more what ifs."

His thumb moves down my jaw line until he holds my chin between his thumb and forefinger. He inches forward closing the distance I just created. He leans over slowly and puts his face in my line of sight. My eyes involuntarily watch his mouth as he licks his lips. In one swift movement, he leans forward and plants a soft kiss on the corner of my mouth. I feel his hair as it falls forward and tickles my face. His scent washes over me. A smile breaks across my face and, with his lips barely touching mine, I feel him do the same.

"So, just friends, right?" he teases.

With the same smile plastered on my face, all I can manage is a small nod and a simple, "Friends."

Totally. Just friends.

I think.

A couple of weeks have passed since our romantic recreation on the boat. Blake regularly shows up at my office to take me to lunch. I can tell Harlow is secretly pleased, but she never says anything to me. I keep our "lake discussion" from her; I feel guilty doing it. There's nothing I keep from Harlow, but anything between Blake and myself I want to remain private, for now. The last thing I want is her interjecting her every opinion. I need to make this decision on my own.

During our lunch dates, Blake and I discuss the girls, Harlow's love life, his dad's retirement and his impending decision. The conversation is effortless and we easily fall back into being friends. It's nice, yet different. When I'm around him, there's definitely no shortage of longing gazes, heart flutters, and jolting touches. We both know there are feelings involved. I think he's waiting for me to make the first move. I never do, but that doesn't mean I don't think about it every now and then.

In fact, he's been invading my thoughts way too much lately. I know I need to take control of this issue... like, *now*. But deep down, I don't think I want to. Which is probably the reason I'm giggling like a school girl, on this very early Sunday morning, as I hit the send button on my phone.

"Hello?" I hear his sexy raspy voice; I'm obviously waking him from his sleep.

Note to Self: Blake Morgan sounds seriously sexy in the morning.

"So, my lovely daughters have taken my coffee hostage and refuse to give it back to me unless I call you and officially invite you to breakfast this morning." Blake laughs loudly into the phone. "Blake, we have a hostage situation. This is very important so stop laughing! I need you to get over here because I *have* to have my coffee."

I shift around in my bed to make myself more comfortable with this conversation. This is the first time I've called him to ask him for anything. Only for my children...I tell myself.

"Really? I've actually been waiting on this phone call...but if you want me to come over, just ask me. You don't have to use your children...or coffee. Really, Alex?" he says, snickering on the other end of the line.

This is exactly what I've been dealing with these last few weeks. Innuendos from Blake and me deflecting them like Wonder Woman. For someone so sweet, he's seriously full of himself. Unfortunately, I seem to be finding it sexier and sexier. This does not bode well in my favor.

"Look, the girls would like to cash in their breakfast date. I'm just relaying the message. If there's some weird fascination you have with me asking you to come over, that's your issue...not mine." I smile to myself. *Ha! Take that.*

"Alright." I hear him moving under his sheets. My mind goes places I don't even want to describe. "I'll be there at nine o' clock. Is that too early?"

"No, you know as well as I do that they get up at the crack of dawn. We'll be up and ready...unfortunately. Come on over. You're more than welcome to keep them busy so I can enjoy my morning."

I hear his familiar chuckle. "I could help you enjoy your morning even more, you know?"

"Shut up, Blake! Seriously, my children have requested your presence...not me. So you're officially *their* guest, not mine." Luckily I'm used to this from him by now so I'm not taken by surprise. "I'm going to tell them nine o'clock. You better be here."

"I'll be there. There's no place I'd rather be on a Sunday morning." I sigh out loud. I don't know why he has to go and say something like that... always making it hard for me to breathe. *Jerk.* But not. *Damn him.*

Rolling my hair around my finger like I'm in high school, I sit up in bed to catch my breath. "Okay...so I can go get my coffee now?"

"Alex, I'll bring you any kind of coffee you want... within a twenty mile radius, just name it." *Damn him... again.*

"I've infiltrated their quarters and located the target. I just need to be sure negotiations are secured so 'Operation: Get My Freakin' Coffee Back' can commence. So, just be here at nine. You aren't the one that has to deal with 'Where's Blake?' every five seconds. If you really want to make my morning, just be here on time."

"You got it. I'm there. Tell the girls I can't wait. What do you need me to bring?"

I literally laugh out loud, picturing the shopping trip we made in preparation for this phone call. Once Harlow paid the girls, I made them wait a while. I didn't want them to think every weekend was going to involve a visit from Blake. So, once I finally caved after their millionth request, they insisted we go right then to the store. Buying two bags of chocolate chips this time.

"Nothing, Blake. We have it covered, trust me. Just bring yourself... that's enough." I cringe at the last part of my statement. Really? I hope that doesn't sound too obvious. I want him here, but I don't want him to *know* I want him here.

"Alright, I'm there. Nine o'clock." I feel my heart race triple speed.

"Okay, see you then." I hang up before he has a chance to say anything else. I look over to my end table. Opening the drawer, I smile as I pick up the last thing I put in there before going to bed last night, and every night recently.

I flip through all the charms that Blake had given me. Reliving each memory, I hold the bracelet and let it intertwine between my fingers. When it falls to the base of my fingers, I wrap them around the bracelet and clench it tightly in the palm of my hand. Turning into my pillow, I take a breath of contentment and close my eyes.

Everything in me wants this man. I can't deny that. I'm drawn to him and unfortunately I can't seem to control it. And I don't know what to do about it. I can't go through another loss like I did with Derek. I can't put my girls through that. It feels much safer to just not allow it to happen. But the warmth I feel inside when I'm around him, the life I feel...it's undeniable.

While still clenching the bracelet, I feel the peace it brings to my heart. Something about it is familiar, it eases my soul. So for now, even if I don't know anything about my life and the course it will run with Blake, I keep him close every night when I hold these charms.

And something within me knows I'll continue to hold on

until there's a reason not to.

CHAPTER SIXTEEN

I belt out a laugh as I walk out of my bedroom to start cooking for the much anticipated breakfast. I see all three girls running around the living room, dressed like they're about to attend prom. We've had lots of dress up outfits over the years that now reside in trunks on the floor of Rylie's closet. Most of them are dresses covered in sequins, which I see my daughters have chosen as their attire for this morning.

Nycole's dressed in a bright red sequined "clapper" dress that she wore last year for Halloween. Complete with matching feather.

Kyndall's dressed in an old hot pink dance dress with black polka dots and black sequined trim. Complete with black tap shoes...which are *not* quiet as she runs around on the tile in the hallway.

Rylie's dressed in her favorite Sleeping Beauty dress and matching plastic Sleeping Beauty shoes. Complete with a set of cat whiskers that her sisters must have drawn on her face while I was in the shower. I *really* hope they used the washable markers.

I can't help but feel underdressed. I glance down at my beautifully made "That's What She Said" t-shirt and jean shorts.

"So, do I need to go change? I didn't know we were dressing up today." I turn around slowly displaying my outfit. Nycole's face lights up. "I know exactly what you can wear. Stay here," she says bolting out of the room. When she re-enters, she's holding one of my favorite dresses. I knew this is the one she would pick. It's the one I wore for my last anniversary with Derek. It's a sequined tube dress that's nude in color with darker sequins sewn onto the mesh overlay. It's beautiful. In her other hand she's holding my favorite six inch T-strap champagne high heels. I shake my head at her and the wide grin on her face. "No way. The dress I'll wear, but no shoes. I'll break my ankle running around in those things."

Nycole nods her head in acceptance. "Deal. But you need to go put some makeup on and fix your hair. It would look pretty dumb to be dressed up with no make-up." She throws the dress to me and points to my bedroom. Gee, thanks.

"Fine." I start to head into the other room to change. "But no whiskers on my face – I think that would also look dumb with my dress." Stopping to look at Rylie I add, "But on you, my dear, they look gorgeous!" Rylie giggles and continues spinning around the room in her dress…something she's been doing since I've been in here.

I walk into my bathroom and turn on my curling iron. I dry my hair quickly and apply some make up. Just a little because I don't want to look like I'm overdoing it. Not that the dress itself isn't overkill enough. I slide the dress over my head and walk over to the full length mirror on my bathroom door. I turn from side to side and watch the dress swish back and forth hitting the middle of my thighs. I forgot how short this dress is. *Yikes.*

I quickly add some loose curls to my hair and slide a

light lip gloss over my lips. Smacking them together, I take a final look in the mirror, surprisingly pleased with the outcome of my efforts. Not bad for nine o'clock in the morning.

"Alright girls," I say, once again entering the living room. "Let's get started!"

All three girls stop what they're doing and stare at me. I spin around and look back at them seeking approval. Nycole flashes me the thumbs up sign and a huge smile.

"You look like a model, Mama!" Kyndall runs up and hugs my waist.

"Mommy – you look so pretty!" Rylie exclaims as she runs to me and embraces my leg. I look down at them and smile. "Well, Blake isn't going to know what to do with all of the beautiful Meyer girls this morning, is he?"

Giggles ensue followed by high pitched shrieks when the doorbell rings. Great – we have absolutely nothing ready. I hope he isn't too hungry.

"Blake's here! Blake's here!" they all shout once again, trampling each other as they run out of the living room. Nycole reaches the door first and turns around to face them holding both hands in front of her signaling for them to calm down. "Shh! You're both acting crazy. I'm not opening the door until you settle down." I couldn't have said it better myself.

Once they're quiet, Nycole gives then a quick nod and turns to open the door. As soon as they see Blake, Kyndall and Rylie push Nycole aside and run to him. He's already crouched down, waiting for them, with four roses in his hand...three pink and one yellow with red tips along the petals.

I raise my hand to my mouth to cover my smile. He never ceases to amaze me. I know the meaning of that yellow rose. It is symbolic of falling in love from friendship. I swallow the basketball lodged in my throat and giggle as the girls almost knock Blake over when they reach his open arms. He gives them a tight hug and then looks up at me. Releasing them, he stands up and smiles a sexy grin while approaching me. "This is for you." He puts his arms around me gently and whispers in my ear, "You look beautiful, Alex."

I squeeze him a little tighter. "Thank you, Blake," before letting him go. Stepping back from him, I accept the rose.

Turning to the girls, Blake exclaims, "Well, don't you all look gorgeous. I'm such a lucky man this morning to be surrounded by such beauty." He takes the pink roses and gives one to each girl. "I couldn't show up to our breakfast date without flowers. What kind of gentleman would I be if I didn't bring roses?" He gives them a wink and they each grin back at him, all sniffing their roses.

He looks at Rylie and chuckles. "Rylie, I love your whiskers. I didn't think it was possible, but they make you look even more stunning." She giggles and skips into the house with her rose.

We all turn to follow her into the house. Blake reaches forward and gently hooks my hand from behind, causing me to turn around. His eyes move slowly up my body. When his eyes finally meet mine, he lets out a quick breath and gives me a sexy lop-sided smile. "Seriously, Alex...breathtaking."

I look him over for the first time this morning, noticing how handsome he looks. Trading his signature faded jeans for darker ones, he's wearing a light blue button up dress shirt with the sleeves rolled up to the middle of his muscular forearms. I also notice his motorcycle boots have been replaced with black Kenneth Coles. He looks absolutely gorgeous. I bite my bottom lip to avoid drooling all over myself. "You look handsome as ever, Blake. Not that there's ever a time when you don't."

I glance over to my driveway. "No bike today?" He runs his hand through his hair as he turns to look as well. "Nope. I wouldn't take the bike on a dress-up breakfast date. What kind of man do you take me for?" He turns back around and offers me another sexy grin. "The girls have been planning this one for a while; you *really* should keep an eye on your cell phone, Alex."

Oh my devious, devious children.

I shake my head and lightly laugh. "Good to know, on both accounts. I will *definitely* be putting a pass code on my phone ASAP." I laugh again. "And we both saw what happened last time I tried to ride your bike in a skirt." He lets out a laugh and I grin back at him. "Let's get inside and see what *else* they have planned."

As I turn to enter the house, I notice that our hands are still joined. I continue to hold his hand until we enter the kitchen where the girls have already started the preparations for breakfast. When I let go, I make sure to give him a quick reassuring smile. He nods his head in understanding.

When Blake approaches the stove, Rylie holds her little arms straight up in the air for him to pick her up. He gently lifts her and places her in her usual seat by the stove. "Not too close, Blake." He looks back at me and laughs. He scoots her over a millimeter. Laughing under his breath, he turns to face me again. "Better?"

I roll my eyes, walk over and slide her much further away. "Better."

He shakes his head and grabs the mixing bowl and the eggs from the counter. He cracks one and lets Rylie help break it open into the bowl. I leave them to it and turn to help Nycole and Kyndall. "Not the whole bag!" I shout as the last chocolate chip falls into the mix. They giggle together. "Sorry! We used *both* bags!"

I try to suppress my laughter, but when I look at their not so innocent little faces, I break. "You guys are so bad!"

They continue mixing the pancake ingredients. There are so many chocolate chips it takes both of them to stir the batter. I'm a little worried about how these pancakes are going to turn out. I think the two bags of chocolate chips are a recipe for disaster, literally.

Walking over to the other side of Blake in front of the stove, I grab the skillet and the bacon. "I'm going to make the whole package. I'm starving and I think the girls have officially ruined the pancakes." Blake turns his body slightly to watch Kyndall while she tries to mix the pancake batter by herself since Nycole has moved on to setting the table. We both laugh at her determined expression. "No, that seems about right. I remember her making that face last time."

I turn back to face the skillet. "Well, just in case."

The rest of the cooking goes smoothly. We only had one egg not make it into the bowl…not too bad, especially since it was Blake who had to clean it up. With all the food finally ready, we all migrate to the table. I compliment them on the beautiful centerpiece they created. All of Blake's roses are bobbing up and down, floating in a lemonade pitcher full of water. Well – it's the thought that counts.

Note to Self: Get my nose to safety after breakfast.

The girls rush and grab their seats. I plate up their food and Blake delivers it to the table for them. They crack up when he brings them their plate, sets it down in front of them, and bows as he says, "My lady, breakfast is served." He does this each time he brings one of them their breakfast and they laugh every time.

I peek around the corner to watch his deliveries and I can't fight the smile on my face. I love to see the girls so happy. It makes my heart feel like it's going to explode. I make my way back to the counter and lean against it with my arms crossed and a goofy grin on my face. "You're ridiculous," I say when Blake once again enters the kitchen.

He walks right up to me and leans past me to grab the salt. His whole body brushes against mine. I grin to myself because I know he's doing this on purpose. But I allow it because it feels too good not to. I lean into him and he puts his arm over my shoulder. I can feel my pulse racing. My whole body responds to his.

He puts his hand under my hair and places it on the back of my neck, pulling me even closer. I turn my head to place my cheek on his shoulder and my nose in his neck. I inhale deeply and wrap my arms around his waist. He turns so that we're now standing with our entire bodies touching. Every part of me is pulsating. He moves his hand to gather my hair and gently pulls it to the side. He bends his head down and places his forehead on my exposed neck. I grab his shirt and pull him as close as I can. I can't seem to be close enough.

"Mommy!" I involuntarily jump when I hear Rylie. "Nycole is spitting her pancake out into the trash!"

I knew it!

Blake lifts his head and places a warm, gentle kiss on my neck, lingering a little before releasing me. Chills break out all over my body.

"I think you're being summoned." He clears his throat and raises his head to meet my eyes. Releasing my hair, he runs his fingers over the place on my neck where he just kissed and smiles. Jerking his head to the table he says, "Go ahead. I'll bring you a plate." Blake turns away and I feel cold as the warmth from his body leaves mine.

I can't speak because my mouth is completely parched now, so I just nod my head in response. I push myself off the counter to leave the kitchen. Before exiting, I stop and turn around. With Blake's back to me, I watch him prepare our plates. "Blake?"

He turns around and his eyes follow me as I walk up to him. Using the same body graze technique he used on me, I reach around and grab the spatula. I pull back slowly, deliberately pressing my body against his, and give him a wink.

"Extra bacon please. Sounds like the pancakes are inedible." Without another word, I hand him the spatula and I walk out of the kitchen. I can't help but be pleased with myself.

Two can play at this game, buddy.

"I'm taking off tomorrow to get ready for Rylie's surprise party." Blake and I are standing beside each other doing the dishes from breakfast. Well, he's rinsing them and I'm loading them into the dishwasher. We discussed Rylie's birthday at breakfast. Although her birthday isn't until Thursday, we have a tradition that started after Derek passed.

I throw them a surprise party. The excitement is in the anticipation. All they know is that it's sometime during the week of their birthday. I invite some of their friends and Nancy and John always come. My parents usually can't make it because they live so far away, but I always tell them when it is so they can call for birthday wishes. Tomorrow is Rylie's."I have a lot to do. I just wanted to tell you so you don't waste your time going to the office to pick me up for lunch." He hands me a plate.

"Well, I'd be happy to come by here and pick you up. You still have to eat, right?" I place the plate in the dishwasher and look back up at him. "I'll eat, no need to worry about that." I give him an ornery smile. "I just can't go *out* to eat. I have too much to do. Presents, cake, balloons, banner...I don't think you understand the Meyer surprise party. It's kind of a big deal." I bring up the door to the dishwasher and push it closed with my hip.

Blake leans with his back against the sink drying his hands. "Want some help? I don't really have any plans tomorrow. I'll have my cell in case anyone from work needs to get a hold of me. I don't mind. I'm actually really good at blowing up balloons," he says with a smile.

Do I think it is safe to spend the day with Blake alone in my house? *Definitely not.* "Sure."

Wait! What? Argh – Freakin' subconscious!

Blake's smile gets wider. "Great! I'm looking forward to it." He throws the towel over his shoulder. "We done in here?"

"Yeah, I think so. Let's see if the girls are ready."

We told the girls we would take them to the park after breakfast, so as soon as we were done eating, they immediately scampered from the table and went to change out of their formal attire into something more park friendly while we cleaned up the kitchen.

We walk into the living room. Nycole and Kyndall are giggling as they push Rylie in Blake's direction. She's holding a piece of purple construction paper in her tiny hands.

When she reaches him, she lifts the paper as high as she can to give it to him. He takes it from her and sits down on the fireplace ledge, placing her on his lap while he opens it. As he reads it, I watch the most beautiful smile slowly makes its way across his face. Rylie eyes him with anticipation, with a big grin also stretching across *her* face when she sees Blake's reaction. She looks at her sisters and giggles. He lowers the letter and pulls her into an embrace. "Rylie, I'd love to. If it's okay with your mommy." He releases her and leans over, handing me the purple piece of paper.

This has Nycole written all over it. Not only because I know that Rylie can't spell or because Kyndall's handwriting isn't this legible, but because of the incriminating look on her face right now... and all the glitter on the paper.

Blake

You are invited to Rylie's surprise party. We don't know when it is because Mom won't tell us. So ask her.
Please come.
Love,
Nycole, Kyndall, and Rylie

I look at Nycole and raise my eyebrows in suspicion. She shrugs her shoulders proclaiming her innocence. I give her a knowing smile before turning to Blake. "It's okay with me. But I'll have to give him the top secret details later. When little ears aren't around." Rylie throws her arms around his neck and then jumps off his lap, screaming, "This is gonna be the best birthday party ever!" like a mad woman running down the hall to her room. The girls turn to follow her and I put my hand on Nycole's shoulder as she passes by me. "Well done, Nycole." She looks up at my face and confidently says, "You're welcome."

I bend down and put my face right in front of hers so she can see I'm completely serious. "Thank you, Nycole."

She kisses me on the cheek and wraps her arms around

my neck. Then, so that I'm the only one who hears, she whispers in my ear, "I love you, mom." When she lets go of my neck, I look directly into her beautiful brown eyes. "I love you too, baby." She nods her head and runs out of the room after her sisters.

I turn to Blake who's been watching our interaction. "She reminds me of you, you know. Smart, sarcastic, ruthless..."

I widen my eyes in shock. "*What?* I am totally *not* sarcastic."

I let out a laugh as I walk over to the fireplace and hold my hand out to help him up. "Well, I'm obviously not wearing *this* to the park. I'm gonna go change. How about you? Do you need anything?"

He reaches up to grab my hand and pulls himself up. "No, I'm okay wearing this." He reaches over and pushes a section of hair off of my shoulder and runs his hand down my back. "You look stunning today, Alex." He places his hand in mine.

"Thank you for a wonderful morning. I enjoyed every bit of it." He raises my hand to his lips. "But I think my favorite part was holding you in the kitchen. Thank you for that." He gently puts his lips on my hand and holds them there for a second before letting go. The heat from his mouth ignites my entire body. I exhale deeply, fighting the urge to grab him and kiss his face off. I wish I could just let go and give in to my body's demands. I want him. *And not in a friendly way.* But in the back of my mind is the knowledge that I can't afford to be wrong with my decisions, so I push away my desire and drop my hand from his.

"I'm gonna go change. Think you can handle them for a

second?" He watches me closely as I put distance between us. "Yeah, I've got them. Go ahead."

I turn on my heel, walk into my bedroom and shut the door. I take in several deep breaths, trying to clear my head. Opening the armoire, I grab the t-shirt and jean shorts I had on earlier in the morning. I pull my hair back into a ponytail then throw on my socks and tennis shoes. Inhaling deeply before I walk out of the room, I open the door and shout, "Alright girls! Let's get going!"

I don't know what's going on inside my head today. I don't know if it's fear, rational thought, or something to do with Derek, but something keeps holding me back from Blake. I'm riding a roller coaster of emotions; sometimes I want off and other times I want to stay on and enjoy the ride. My eyes move across the living room to meet Blake's. "You okay, Alex?" He walks to me and puts his hand on my shoulder. "I'm sorry if it feels like I'm pushing. I don't mean to. I'll back off."

I shake my head. "It's fine, Blake. I promise. Sometimes it's just a little overwhelming. Not you or anything you're doing, but the feelings. It scares me. That's all. I'm sorry if I seem all over the place. But I hope you understand it isn't you." I move my hand to my shoulder and briefly place it on top of his before letting go. "Please be patient with me," I plead.

He strokes my shoulder with his thumb and looks into my eyes. "I'm not going anywhere, Alex." He runs his hand lightly down my arm and gives my hand a quick squeeze before releasing it when we hear the pitter patter of little feet running down the hall.

"We're ready, Mama!" Kyndall says, as she runs up to

me completely out of breath. I glance at the peace sign backpack she's holding. "Why do you have your back pack?"

"Well, Tommy and Sandy wanted to come too!" She opens up the bag to show us her favorite stuffed bear and turtle. "See!"

I watch Nycole emerge with her iPod Touch and headphones in her ears. "Okay – Rylie, is there anything you want to bring with you?" She walks over to Blake and grabs his hand. "Just Blake!" she says, leading him toward the front door. He winks at her and gives her a beautiful smile which she happily reciprocates. I watch her skip towards the door, holding Blake's hand the entire time.

"Alright, let's go," I say to absolutely no one since they're all outside. I turn to lock the door, hoping the fresh air will ease my mind. I walk to the Suburban and climb in. Blake's already turned around in the passenger's seat talking to the girls. I turn the key in the ignition and start the drive to the park.

After two new songs from Justin Bieber's new album, accompanied by horrendous dance moves from Blake, which leads to many contagious giggles, we arrive at the park. The girls jump out and scatter all over the place. Rylie pulls Blake with her to the swings. Poor guy. He'll be there all day.

I hear her yell "Collar roaster, Blake! Do the collar roaster!" I smile as she refers to the swings. I wonder how old she'll be until she actually says it right. I chuckle to myself.

Blake is definitely good for a roller coaster ride, my dear. You definitely picked the right person for that.

I walk to the bench that sits on the edge of the park and watch Nycole and Kyndall as they sit under the slide setting up various toys that Kyndall must have had in her back pack. Judging by the amount of toys they have, it's no wonder she was out of breath.

I observe Blake pushing Rylie on the swing. He's laughing with her singing some song about a donut and a nickel. He must know it, or is an incredibly fast learner, because by the second time through he's singing it with her. They both look incredibly content.

I sigh as I allow myself to imagine this is actually my life. A gorgeous man who loves my children as if they are his own. A man who loves me. A strong man who can handle anything. A caring man who will take care of his girls. A family. A happy family.

I try to contain the tears as they start to surface.

I had that with Derek and it was taken away from me. Am I lucky enough to experience it again? I swipe away a tear as it starts to escape my eye.

Derek, I'm scared. I don't know what to do. I need your help.

Tears start to stream down my face.

Would I be wrong to allow this to happen with Blake? I'm tired of fighting it, Derek. I want so much to feel. To let myself be happy. But I can't help but worry that if I do, I'm dishonoring everything we had together. You were my first everything. I don't know if I could do it with anyone else. I wish you were here to tell me what to do. To give me your blessing. I think that's what I'm waiting for. Which is unfortunate because you aren't here. Am I crazy for waiting for you to give me the okay?

I look to the sky, half expecting him to appear like an angel floating down to give me all the answers.

Yeah, I'm definitely crazy.

I watch all three girls, now running around the park, chasing Blake. He jerks his body from left to right, barely missing their hands when they try to grab him. He finally lets Kyndall win and scoops her up in his big arms, spinning her round and round. He sets her down and takes off around the swings and the chase begins again. I watch their determination as they try to catch him. And I watch him as he contemplates who he's going to let win this round. They're all so full of laughter I can't help but smile through the tears.

Derek, I want the girls to know a normal life; to know true happiness, like what we had when you were here. I really think that Blake could give us that. Actually, I know he could. But I also know I'm holding back. There's a threshold I can't seem to cross. Is he worth the gamble? I know nothing is guaranteed in this lifetime. Trust me, no one knows that better than me. But I want so much to believe he's worth it. Worth taking the chance.

A small breeze blows over me. I breathe in deeply, trying to force fresh air into my lungs. But then, I take in a deeper breath, except this time it's not to clear my head. It smells...familiar. *Sandalwood.* I gasp out loud.

Blake looks over at me with concern on his face and starts walking in my direction. I wave him off. "I'm fine! You'd better hurry. They're tag teaming you now." He looks back and dodges Nycole as she leaps forward to catch him. He takes one look back at me and I motion for him to run. "Hurry! They're gonna get you!" He turns and changes direction running towards the slide.

Another breeze blows over me and the smell of sandalwood lingers in the air.

Derek?

Okay – I'm definitely losing my mind. I shake my head and start to get up when the most beautiful butterfly I've ever seen lands right on my knee. It looks like some exotic sort of butterfly; I've never seen anything like it. The arches of its wings are marked with bright yellow and black. But it's the bottom part of the butterfly's wings that catches my attention. The lowest section of its wings is a beautiful almost electric blue color.

I place my hand beside the butterfly on my leg, being careful not to touch its wings. Instead of flying away, it climbs onto my finger. I lift it up to my face to get a better look. Amazingly it doesn't move. It just sits there looking back at me. Another breeze blows and I'm momentarily distracted from its beauty. There's no mistaking it. Sandalwood is all around me. I can smell it on my clothes.

I look all around me. I don't see anything out of the norm. I look back at the butterfly.

Derek?

All of a sudden, it leaves my finger and begins to flutter around my head. I hear the girls run up out of breath.

"Mama – look at the butterfly. Isn't it beautiful?" Kyndall watches it land on her shoulder. She stands as still as possible and twists her head to the side to get a better look. "Oh… It's so pretty!"

Nycole and Rylie make their way over and the butterfly jumps off of Kyndall's shoulder and begins to fly all around her sisters. It lands on the top of Rylie's head and she stands like a statue while we all laugh at her, then it flutters to Nycole and lands on her finger when she holds it out in an attempt to lure it close to her. She brings it very close to her face and the butterfly flies off her finger and lands on her cheek. She giggles. "It tickles!"

Then, as Blake finally makes his way over, the butterfly flies over to him and lands on his shoulder. He takes his hand and places it right next to the butterfly. It climbs on without hesitation. "Alex, look at this. I don't think I've ever seen one like this before. Not even in Colorado. It's beautiful." Blake brings it around for a closer look. As he's inspecting it, it flies off of his hand and flutters in the air for a second before it lands back on my knee.

Okay. I'm completely losing it if I think that this butterfly is Derek trying to tell me something. I have officially lost my marbles. There is no way that –

The butterfly flies up and lands right on my nose. I look at it cross-eyed, watching it flap its wings slowly in front of my eyes. Taunting me.

Derek? Is that you?

It begins to flap its wings faster, finally leaving my nose. It makes its way back to Blake and flutters above his head for a few seconds before another breeze comes and it flies away. We all sit in silence watching it as it disappears behind the trees.

"That was weird," Blake says quietly. Turning back towards the girls he claps his hands loudly. "Hide and Seek? I'll start. One... two... three..." The girls take off running. Blake turns and sits beside me on the bench. "You okay? You look a little upset." He twists my ponytail around his finger. I nod my head. "Yeah, I'm okay. Nycole just went under the slide... in case you need a hint."

He studies my face intently and wipes a rogue tear from my cheek. "Okay, well, I'm here if you need me." He gives me one last look before I point to the slide. "Go get her. She's getting too big for her britches." The corners of his mouth tip up and he runs his knuckle across the bottom of my chin, catching the last tear before it falls. "Don't worry. I'll knock her down a couple of pegs," he says placing his palm on my cheek. "You sure you're okay?"

"I will be once you get her. I still owe her for the surprise invite... even though you were already invited... maybe I should have told you?" I lean my face into his hand and take in a much needed breath. He strokes my cheek one last time before getting up from the bench. "Good to know." He shoots me a quick wink. As he turns to walk away, he crouches low and covertly sneaks up behind the slide.

Another breeze passes through my hair but there's no trace of sandalwood. I feel a little saddened. Maybe I'm crazy, but part of me feels that nothing that just happened in the last few minutes was random. In fact, I feel like it was pretty deliberate. My heart fills with joy as I watch the girls playing with Blake.

I'm going to assume that I have your okay? The second the breeze hits, I smell it.

A happiness fills my soul. I smile looking up at the clouds.

Alright, I was just testing you.

Don't worry... I get it.

And stay tuned, because I'm going for it.

I smile even more when the clouds break and the warm sun shines on my face. I know I'm headed in the right direction now.

I just needed a little guidance.

CHAPTER SEVENTEEN

The next morning, after dropping off the girls, I make my way to the house to start the preparations for Rylie's surprise party. Pulling into my driveway, I turn off the ignition and let out a deep breath. There's a nervous excitement running through my veins; I know Blake's coming over today.

Walking into the house, I throw my purse onto the couch and make my way to the kitchen. I pull the mixing bowls out of the dishwasher and grab the cake mix. I figure I'll start with the cake because I want to have enough time to work on it. I know I have more time than usual though, since Harlow offered to pick them up and keep them busy for a while after school. The benefits of owning your own business never gets old.

Regardless, I want to get a head start. I wrapped most of the presents last night after the girls went to bed, so all I really have to focus on today is the cake, the balloons and the banner.

I throw the mix in the bowl. A little too quickly I guess because as soon as the contents of the bag hit, a white cloud flies up and coats my face. I cough as the flour enters my lungs. And of course, right at that very moment, my door bell rings.

My heart beats wildly in my chest and my stomach feels

like there's a gymnast inside it performing a gold medal winning floor routine. I wipe my hands on my black yoga pants leaving white trails from my fingers all over them as I walk through the living room. Entering the front hallway, I take a look at my tattered iron on "Save Ferris" t-shirt that I made no telling how many years ago. Well...I guess this will have to do.

Opening the door, I find it difficult to breathe when I lay my eyes on Blake. One would think I'd be use to how gorgeous he is, but for some reason, I seem to have the same reaction every time I see him. He stands before me, once again in my favorite faded jeans, wearing a black button down shirt – untucked and sleeves rolled up in true Blake style – and his clanky motorcycle boots. His hair is flipping everywhere as it tends to do. He takes one look at me and the corner of his mouth lifts. He looks down at his black shirt.

"So I'm thinking black wasn't such a good idea." He gives me his sexy chuckle and it takes everything in me not to jump on him right now, wrap my legs and arms around him, and kiss him senseless.

I giggle at the thought. "I think you're right. But don't worry. You're on balloon duty so you should be safe." I move aside allowing him to step in the entry way before closing the door. "Are those for Rylie? You didn't have to get her anything. I know it was short notice."

He holds my eyes for a brief second. Then he breaks our gaze to look down at the smaller box on top. "Not both of them. The smaller one is for you."

"Really?" I giggle like a little girl. I grab the present and skip into the living room, plopping down on the couch. "What is it?" Blake follows me but remains standing. "Open it and see."

"Okay," I say, my smile getting larger. I look down at the Disney Princess wrapping paper and smile so wide my face hurts. I glance back up at him. "You sure this is for me?"

Blake grins sexily. My eyes wander all over his body before looking back down at the gift. I rip the paper open to find a black box. Flipping it open, I can't help but gasp from surprise.

Inside the box is a new charm to add to my collection, but it isn't just any charm. This one is an exact replica of the butterfly from yesterday. Exact. Same black, yellow, and blue palette. I pick it up and let it dangle between my fingers as I examine it closely.

"Blake. You remembered the bracelet? It's beautiful." I haven't had a chance to tell him I still have it.

"Yes. Of course I remember it. I only looked for a charm every chance I had growing up. I thought this one would go nicely with your collection." His eyes break from mine and land on the charm.

"I found it yesterday while shopping for Rylie. I had to get it for you. That butterfly seemed to have some kind of connection yesterday with you and the girls. And with it being so unusual, the chance of me finding an exact match…well, I just had to get it. I think it was meant for you, for some reason." He looks at me shyly. "It seemed like some kind of sign or something. I know…that sounds weird."

When Derek was alive, he was notorious for making sure I understood what he was telling me, making me repeat what he said to make sure I was listening or quizzing me after a long discussion. I find myself rolling my eyes in my head.

Yes, Derek... I understand. No further pushing required. I get it.

Thank you.

I put the charm back in the box and gently set it on the coffee table. Smiling at Blake, I walk over to him and wrap my arms around his waist. I put my forehead on his chest and smell him yet again. Something about doing that comforts me. Blake puts his hand on the back of my head and runs his hand through my hair. Placing my chin on his chest, I tilt my head back to look him directly in the eyes. "Thank you, Blake. I have a feeling you're right. This charm was meant for me. It's absolutely perfect." He removes his hand from the back of my head and grazes his fingers across my forehead, moving the hair out of my eyes. "I'm glad you like it."

Giving him another wide smile, I remove my chin from his shirt. And then I see my mistake. In an effort to suppress my laughter, I immediately cover my mouth with my hand. I watch as Blake looks down at his shirt and then back up at me with wide eyes and a half-grin on his lips.

Oh my God.

I completely forgot about the flour all over my face. The flour that is now all over his shirt. "Oh, Blake. I'm so sorry." Unfortunately, I can't hold it in any longer. It starts with a giggle that barely escapes, but when I turn him around and see the two handprints on his back, I can't help but break out into full on laughter. I start hiccupping as he turns back around and I watch his face light up with laughter. He attempts to dust the front of his shirt, but it does absolutely nothing. Taking in a couple of breaths to regain my composure, I wipe my eyes and attempt to straighten myself back into standing position. Once I'm able to function, I grab his hand and lead him into the kitchen. "Come on. Let's get you cleaned up."

I feel a zap all over my body when he intertwines his fingers with mine. I turn back and give him a reassuring smile. I'm completely okay with this.

I grab a towel and turn the faucet on to wet it. I turn around to see Blake leaning back on the kitchen counter, legs crossed in front of him. When I approach him, he uncrosses his legs and stands up straighter allowing me to get close to him. Stepping in between his legs, I take the towel and dab it on his chest, removing the traces of white powder. I can see his muscles tense under his shirt. I let my eyes wander over his chest and slowly look up to meet his beautiful green eyes. I can feel every bit of nervous energy as it courses through my body. He holds my stare.

Keeping my eyes on him, I place the towel down on the counter beside him. I reach my hand up and run it over his chest. The muscles in his jaw tighten.

I slowly bring my other hand up and place both palms on his chest. I can feel his heart racing, encouraging me to keep going. I slowly move my hands down the ripples on his stomach. I break our stare to watch my hands roam over his body. When I reach the bottom of his shirt, I move my hands under it, slowly tracing them up his naked body. Palms still flattened, I turn my hands so that my thumbs fall into the ridge in the center of his stomach. I continue to move them up until I feel the muscles of his chest underneath each of my hands. I move my eyes back to meet his. This time, not breaking his gaze, I let my hands graze downward once again. His muscles quiver slightly as I glide over them. I remove my hands and step closer to him, grabbing fistfuls of his shirt in pure desire.

Blake watches me the entire time. Letting my hands roam where they want. But once I grab his shirt, he moves his hands to my waist and pulls me so that our bodies are now touching. He tightens his hold. I feel his thumbs pressing into my stomach. But I can see in his face that he's holding back.

"Alex, are you sure?"

I nod my head, eyes still on him. He wraps one arm around under my bottom and places the other on the center of my back. In one quick swoop, he lifts me and I wrap my arms around his neck and my legs around his waist. He turns and places me on the counter. We're eye level with each other. Legs pulling him as close as I can, I run my hands through his hair. God, I love his hair.

He places both arms on the sides of where I'm seated, his hands squeezing me from behind, pulling my body into his. He moves to press his face into my neck. I feel his nose as it grazes behind my ear. I can feel each chill bump rise all over my body. Breathing heavily in my ear, Blake whispers, "Once I start Alex, I don't know if I'll be able to stop. I need to know that you're sure. There can be no doubts moving forward. This is *your* decision."

I place both hands on the side of his face bringing his eyes to meet mine. "I'm tired of fighting it, Blake. I can't do it anymore."

My eyes find their way to his mouth and I lick my lips in anticipation. Blake slowly moves forward, giving me every chance to back out. My heart's drumming uncontrollably in my chest. He lets his face linger in front of mine and I feel his warm rapid breaths on my mouth. Licking my lips for a final time, I move forward and feel his soft lips lightly skim mine, still testing the waters. I wrap my arms tightly around his neck and pull him so there's no doubt in his mind of what I want. Then, I crush my mouth against his. I kiss him with every bit of emotion that I have been holding in since I first saw him on the side of the road. I completely let go and lose myself in this kiss. And he kisses me back, just as eagerly.

Grabbing the back of my neck, he pulls me in to kiss me harder. I part my lips and feel his warm soft tongue enter my mouth, exploring every inch of it. I slide mine into his and savor his delicious taste. Running my tongue around his mouth, I graze his lower teeth. I moan and his hold on me tightens in response. I feel his fingers move into my hair. Swiftly breaking our kiss, he pulls my hair gently so that my head falls back and to the side. I feel his soft lips on my neck and behind my ear. His kisses trail across my neck as he guides my head to the other side.

I want more. I can't seem to get close enough. I pull him tighter with my legs. He removes his hand from my hair and once again wraps an arm around my waist. Pulling me greedily off the counter, he holds me tightly and carries me out of the kitchen, across the living room towards the bedroom. His mouth is on mine the entire time. I suck his bottom lip as he opens the door and when he lets out a sexy groan, I almost come undone. I force his head back as I nip and lick his neck.

Finally reaching the bed, he gently lowers me down. I release my arms from around him and let my head fall to the pillow below. He pauses, letting his eyes wander up and down my body. He brings his hand to my face and strokes my cheek with his thumb. He flattens his hand and runs it down the side of my neck, moving it slowly to the front of my body. With his palm flat, he lays his hand on the top of my chest and moves his eyes to meet mine. Our rapid breathing is the only sound in the room.

"Alex, you have no idea how long I have waited for this moment."

I reach up and touch his cheek with my fingers. I place my hand on the back of his neck, and pull him down so that his lips once again meet mine.

And in that moment, with absolutely no hesitation, I give myself completely to Blake Morgan.

After three years of not being intimate with a man, I find that I'm pretty insatiable. I give myself completely to Blake Morgan...three times. Three times! *Not too shabby.* But as much as I would love to spend all day being so giving, I cannot. We have a party to get ready for!

With goofy grins plastered on our faces, Blake and I take care of everything together. We blow up all of the balloons, laughing at each other when we can't tie them, making them shoot all over the room. Then, we make out on the couch for a while.

We finish wrapping the remainder of Rylie's gifts...the

whole time I poke fun at him for how well he wraps. Then, we make out on the living room floor.

I finally finish making her cake, slapping Blake's hand every time he tries to stick his hand in the batter. Then, we make out, leaning against the kitchen counter. Which, by the way, has officially graduated to being my favorite spot in the house.

Now we find ourselves rushing to set up her party in the backyard. We hang the banner on the porch and set up her presents on the table. Her theme this year is *Teenage Mutant Ninja Turtles*. Leonardo, Donatello, Michelangelo, and Raphael are everywhere. Even Splinter makes a guest appearance or two. Stepping back to look at our hard work, I clasp my hands together. "Blake! It's perfect! She's going to love it!" I pat the four little stuffed turtles on the head. They're positioned all around her double layer yellow cake with chocolate frosting. The frosting actually earned Blake the most slaps on the hand. "Seriously, we did a great job!"

Blake walks up behind me, putting his arms around my waist. Moving my hair aside, he sets his chin down on my shoulder. "We make a great team, Alex. I'm glad you've finally figured that out." I turn around to smack him on the arm, but his handsome face distracts me. I run my fingers through his hair and stand up on my tiptoes to give him a peck on the lips. "Better late than never." He grins against my mouth. "True."

I hear the girls yelling in the front yard and grab Blake's hand. "Hurry! They're here!" Making a mad dash into the house, we close the blinds as quickly as humanly possible. Both on the windows and the back door. Both of us jump onto the couch and position ourselves as though we've been sitting there all day. Which makes absolutely *no* sense, because once Rylie rings the doorbell twenty times in a row, I remember that I locked the door earlier. Blake and I grin at each other when we both come to this realization at the same time and get up off the couch.

I open the door and the girls completely bypass me and bum rush Blake. I lean against the wall and watch their interaction. Looking back at me with a content smile on his face, Blake gives me a quick wink as he embraces the girls.

"Hello! A little help here!" I turn around to see Harlow hauling two backpacks, two lunch boxes, and a huge Hello Kitty pillow, about to drop them all. I giggle while watching her struggle for her balance and grab the backpacks and pillows. "I gotcha girl!"

She shoots me a relieved smile and exhales a breath of air blowing the hair out of her face. Shutting the door, I hear the girls squeal loudly. "It smells like cake in here! Yay!" *Damn it.* Another reason why I meant to make the cake first. I roll my eyes at myself. *Dumb.*

The girls run into the living room and immediately peek through the blinds. "Girls! Get away from there! Go to your rooms for a second, please." Rylie hasn't caught onto this yet and I intend to keep it that way as long as possible. Nycole and Kyndall giggle loudly and run out of the room. Rylie follows them for absolutely no reason, giggling just as loudly.

Blake takes a seat on the couch and I move to sit by him. I look into his beautiful green eyes. I lean forward to give him a quick kiss because I just can't help myself. But I'm stopped abruptly by someone clearing their throat.

"Is there something I need to know?" The look on

Harlow's face is not what I expected. She looks…pissed. That is actually the last look I would have expected to see on her face. Wasn't it just a month ago that she was practically forcing me to interact with this man?

My defenses go up immediately. Clearing my *own* throat, I bite back at her, "No, there isn't anything you need to know. When there is, I'll be sure to tell you." I snap my body up off the couch. We stare each other down for a minute, until the tension in the room builds enough to where Blake decides to clear *his* own throat. "Um, I'm going to go grab something to drink. Harlow? Alex?" Neither one of us answers him as we continue eying each other. Taking the hint, Blake wisely exits the room.

"What the hell is *wrong* with you?" I ask her, my voice just above a whisper. "Were you or were you not in favor of Blake just a week ago? What the hell has happened since then? I thought you'd be happy. This is the *last* reaction I would've expected from you."

She watches me closely as she walks across the room. When she's directly in front of me, she puts her face right in front of mine and narrows her eyes, like she is trying to figure something out. "Well, aren't you defensive all of a sudden? Interesting." She turns and walks out of the room making her way to the girls' rooms.

What? I'm getting really tired of her and these freakin' obscure messages. What the hell does that even mean? I make my move to follow her when I hear a gentle knock at the door. Knowing who it is, I put a fake smile on my face before I answer the door.

Hello fake smile. I wasn't planning on using you ever again…

"Hey John! Hey Nancy! Come on in!" I give them both a quick hug. I can't help but smile when a couple of Rylie's friends from down the street also make their way to my door. I usher everyone into the living room after closing the door behind them. I hold my finger in front of my lips, silencing the hyperactive children. "Listen – Rylie's in her room. She has *no* idea about the party so we need to be *super* quiet. Okay?" They all put their fingers to their lips, following my lead. "Good. Now, go ahead and head out back. I'll get everyone else out there and then I'll bring her out." Nodding their heads, Nancy and John lead the pack, tiptoeing with huge grins on their faces. I don't know who finds these parties more exciting... the girls or John and Nancy.

Once they're safely outside, I dart into the kitchen to get Blake. He's standing by the refrigerator, glass in hand, staring at the floor. I think Harlow's reaction really upset him.

"Blake – its fine. I'll take care of Harlow." I try to sound as sympathetic as I can while grabbing his arm. "Listen, don't let her ruin all of our hard work." I open the door and force him outside. "Oh yeah, you know Mrs. Meyer, right? Go say hi!"

I shut the door and pick up the pace to the girls' rooms, where I hear clinking tea cups in Rylie's room. I slow down as I approach the room, taking in a deep breath before I open the door. I immediately have to suppress a giggle. If I wasn't so upset with Harlow and her dumb undecipherable code, I would've laughed at seeing her with the pink boa wrapped around her neck and huge tea hat on her head. She twists her body around in the kiddie sized chair and I jerk my head toward the party. She nods in response.

"Whew! Alright girls, it's too hot for tea in here." Standing up and taking off her boa, she fans herself dramatically. "Let's go out back for some fresh air." Nycole and Kyndall jump up and shriek loudly, running out of the room. Rylie attempts to go as well, but Harlow reaches out and catches her before she can escape. Maintaining her hold, she takes off her hat and puts it on the table. Before passing me, she pauses. "I'm sorry Alex. I need to talk to you. Come see me when things settle down." I nod my head and let her move by me. Rylie lets go of Harlow's hand and gives me a quick hug before skipping down the hall after her.

When they reach the door, Harlow stalls Rylie until I meet up with them. I look at Harlow and we both nod to each other, signaling "party time". I open the door and guide Rylie outside.

"Surprise!" Everyone yells together. Rylie looks at the set up and turns to hug my leg. "Oh – thank you Mommy!" Holding her fist in the air she adds, "Turtle Power!"

There's a collective laugh among everyone and we watch as she runs to her cake. She grabs the stuffed turtles and holds them in her arms. "Thank you all for coming to my party!" She giggles, eyeing her presents. "Are all of these for *me*?" My little actress. I shake my head at her theatrics and look to Blake as he does the same. When our eyes meet, I melt.

An hour into the party and it's an absolute success. The best part? Presents, of course.

Harlow gives Rylie a make-up kit. I attempt my first use of "mommy death glare 2.0" on Harlow when I watch her open it. She just laughs. Seriously... this glare needs a lot of work.

John and Nancy give her this annoying mini-ATV that has an obnoxious police siren.

Note to Self: Conveniently lose the ATV. It hurts my ears.

I give her useful and educational things like clothes and books. She always hates my presents. It's nothing new.

But Blake's present? His present takes the cake, of course. When she opens it, her eyes double in size and she claps her hands together excitedly. It's the perfect present for her…a trunk full of Disney dress-up clothes. Every Princess outfit is accounted for. From Cinderella to Ariel to Rapunzel…they're all there with all the accessories. She runs to him and jumps in his arms. He holds her tightly and then places her on the ground.

He crouches down to speak to her. "Okay Rylie, there are enough Sunday Breakfast Date clothes in there to last a while. I want to see you in all of them, okay?" She nods her head and gives him another huge hug. He watches her as she runs to John and Nancy to show them the Snow White tiara. When he glances my way, I mouth a small, *thank you.* He gives me a slight smile and a nod, and then goes back to watching her as she starts to pull everything out of the trunk.

After presents, we sing the usual birthday song and Rylie blows out her candles, in her new and improved Sleeping Beauty dress I might add. I make her take it off before she eats cake. It's funny how you can get kids to do anything for cake with no temper tantrums.

Afterwards, we all mingle outside for a while, well... everyone except Blake and Harlow who seem to be going out of their way to avoid each other. After a couple of hours, Rylie's friends leave and John and Nancy decide to head out. I walk them to the door and give them both an embrace before they leave, thanking them for coming. Closing the door, I turn to head back to the living room, when I hear voices coming from my bedroom. Switching to stealth mode, I quietly tip toe with the voices getting louder as I approach the room. I press my ear to the door.

"Blake, this is ridiculous. When I called you here, it was to help her, as her friend. Not to sleep with her!"

"She's a grown woman capable of making her own decisions. This isn't your call to make, Harlow. It's hers."

"She can't make any decisions in the state she's in, not clear-headed ones. The woman you see is not the woman I helped through the tragedy of losing Derek. She isn't ready yet. Not for this. You're completely taking advantage of her vulnerability."

"Bullshit! She's perfectly fine. She's grieved enough. For God's sakes...let her move on. You know, if I didn't know better, I would almost say that you want her to need you. I would almost even say that you want her to remain miserable so that you have a reason for existence."

"Fuck you, Blake! You don't know shit. You've been here for like, what, two seconds? You don't know her. You know what she wants you to know. I called you because she wasn't getting any better and I thought maybe you could get through to her. But if I knew this was going to happen, I would have dropped all communication with you a long time ago. Bastard!"

Stepping back from the door, I feel the blood drain from my face. My hands are shaking. A lump starts forming in my throat and the tears start to flow from my eyes. But these tears are different from my usual ones. These tears are tears of anger. I can feel the walls building up around my heart, suffocating any emotion I previously felt for Blake. I'm completely void of anything but rage now. I keep running parts of what I just heard through my mind.

"When I called you here, it was to help her."

"She can't make any decisions in the state she is in."

"You're completely taking advantage of her vulnerability."

"When I called you here."

"When I called you here."

"When I called you here."

I can't believe it. He lied.

Everything that Blake has said to me was a lie. Everything I thought I felt was a lie. Everything is a lie.

Hand shaking, I reach out and throw the door open. I look right at Blake. He stares back at me, guilt radiating from his eyes. It makes me want to vomit.

"Harlow, take the girls please." My eyes don't leave his.

"Alex–"

"Now Harlow!" I break my glare from Blake to look at her. "Take them. They don't need to hear this. Take them anywhere but here. We'll talk later."

She bows her head in defeat and closes the door as she leaves the room. Blake and I continue to watch each other. I drum my fingertips anxiously against my armoire. Not a word is spoken until we hear the front door shut.

"Alex –"

My hand shoots straight up to his face, signaling him to be quiet. "I don't want to hear anything but the answers to my questions right now." Once I'm confident that he isn't going to start rambling like a bumbling fool, I lower my hand.

"Is your dad even retiring?" I watch him shift back and forth, apparently looking for an acceptable explanation. No answer.

"Blake, is your dad even retiring?" I glare at him until I get an answer.

"Eventually," he finally manages.

Is he *serious* with this shit?

"Like now? Is that why you came back?" My heart is pounding in my chest. I'm about two seconds away from having a full blown heart attack. There's no way my heart can beat any faster.

"No. That's not why I came back." Blake takes a step toward me and I automatically take a step back. "Stay right there. I don't want you near me."

He stops. "You've got to hear me out Alex. This isn't fair."

"*Fair*? Are you *serious*? You've *got* to be freakin' kidding me." I laugh at his audacity.

"Really, Blake, you're right. It's *not* fair. How *fair* do you think it is that I let you into my life, into my *heart*, only to find out nothing you've said has been the truth? How fair do you think it is to give yourself *completely* to someone who was just using you to get laid? That doesn't sound *fair* to me. But hey, at least you conquered your conquest. Right? Congratulations by the way. Would you like me to make you a t-shirt?"

254

Blake slams his hand on the side of my armoire. I move back until I hit the wall.

"You've *got* to be kidding me! You believe that? After all we've been through, after all we've shared, you honestly believe that shit?" He narrows his eyes and shakes his head. "No, I don't think you do."

I angrily throw my hands up in the air. "I know that I don't believe a goddamn word that comes out of your mouth! You've been lying to me since the day you got here. Our whole relationship has been rebuilt on lies!"

"You want the God's honest truth, Alex? I'll give it to you. *I* contacted Harlow when I found out about Derek. I wanted to check on you, because no matter how upset I was, I still loved you and I wanted to make sure you were okay. From that day forward, Harlow and I stayed in touch. She would give me updates about how you were handling things. She made it sound like you were struggling, but you were getting through it. When you told me how bad it was, I had *no* idea. That's why I was so pissed that night we discussed Derek's death. I should have been there for you, and I wasn't. I wasn't ready to face you and I'll never be able to take that back. That kills me."

His eyes hold mine as he continues.

"Yes, Harlow asked me to come back. She was worried about you, Alex. She thought that if I came back here, somehow I might be able to get through to you. That you might be able to move forward in your life, learn to let go and live your life again. And even though I was obviously still upset at you... at myself, I came back. For you. To help you."

I shake my head. "*Nope.* Not good enough, Blake.

Listen, I get that you were worried about me...which makes you no different than anyone else in my life. I get that you didn't want to come here because you didn't want to deal with my grief. I also get that you feel some ridiculous need to *help* me. Yes, I get all of that. But know this. I'm *not* your charity case. I don't *want* you here and I don't *need* you here. I've been doing it on my own, *without* you, for a while now. So, if you don't mind, just get the hell out of my house!"

Blake stalks toward me and, finding I have no route for escape, I stand my ground and throw my shoulders back. We both stare fiercely at each other, refusing to be the first to break. He finally lets out a defeated laugh. "So this is it, huh? This is where you push me away? This is where you just give up because you're scared? This isn't about the lies, is it, Alex? You want to yell at me, to *hurt* me by saying things you don't even believe, in order to keep from getting hurt yourself. I get it. I do. But I'm not a punching bag, Alex. I love you, but I refuse to be treated like this. I've lived my entire life being hurt as a result of your thoughtless actions and I'm not going to do it anymore. I didn't come back here for this."

His statement only fuels my anger. I hit that wall behind me with the palms of my hands.

"I never asked for you to come back! *You* wanted to march in here and save me from my miserable life! Well, guess what? I can't be saved! Get. It. Through. Your. Head." I press my finger against my temple with each word.

Blake watches me closely, then exhales a long breath. He rakes his hand through his hair in obvious frustration. He steps closer to me and leans down to look me directly in the eyes.

"Well done, Alex. You've just managed to push me out of your life. I'm gone. But let me tell *you* something before I go. You want to live your life safe. You don't want to feel anything for anyone. You don't want to get hurt again...I understand all of that. But you can't continue to live that way. Stop punishing yourself for something that was completely out of your control. Stop punishing your *girls* for God's sake."

As soon as the statement leaves his mouth, I can't control myself. The anger finally consumes my body. I feel nothing but adrenaline as I deliver the blow to his face with my open hand.

Blake takes a step back and cups his jaw with his hand. His eyes reveal a flash of pain before they go vacant. His face is now completely void of any emotion...his walls rebuilding just as quickly as mine. After a second or two, he lets out a long breath and shakes his head in disbelief as he steps towards my door.

"Well, it's clear you've made your decision. There's nothing left for me here now. Nothing I want anyway. I'm letting you go, Alex, but for *your* sake, I really do hope you find your way back to the Alex I once knew. Because what you're doing now, just seems like such a lonely way to live the rest of your life."

With that said, Blake Morgan walks out of my bedroom, out of my house, and out of my life.

And I remain alone in my room.

Knowing deep down that *I just made the biggest mistake of my life.*

CHAPTER EIGHTEEN

It's been three weeks.

I miss Blake. I miss everything about him. I miss the way he makes me laugh, the way he holds me when I cry, the way I don't have to pretend with him. I know the girls miss him too, especially Rylie, but they haven't asked me about anything yet. And honestly, they've seen me cry enough this lifetime, so I prefer to avoid the conversation until they decide they want to have it.

Missing him definitely isn't easy...by any means. But missing him without Harlow to make me laugh, well, that just sucks.

I've been attempting to avoid Harlow, which is pretty much impossible. I mean, we do work together, so for now my work days consist of walking through the front door of Prestige, mumbling a hello, darting into my office, and shutting my door. I stay in there until we have an appointment. I get into professional mode, conduct interviews with Harlow by my side, then walk back into my office and shut the door again. I'm not sure I can handle another dramatic exit from my life, so at this point I might as well be the first to cut the proverbial cord.

At least that's my plan until one day in the early afternoon Harlow storms into my office, dramatically throwing my door open and slamming it closed. Mouth wide open, my eyes follow her as she grabs one of my office chairs, moves it in front of the door, and parks herself in it. Crossing both her arms and legs, she doesn't say a word. She just continues to bore her eyes into mine, waiting for me to ask her what's going on. I refuse to give her the satisfaction, so I begin to whistle as I doodle on my paper trying to look busy. When I have run out of room on my paper, I start straightening my desk. I open my drawer, still feigning a cleaning routine, only to see the note Blake left on my desk after our wonderful first exchange. My heart aches as memories play out in my mind. I shut the drawer pretending nothing's wrong.

Like a lion to the gazelle, Harlow evidently senses my weakened defenses when I opened that damn drawer, because as it shuts, she clears her throat. "So, how long is this going to continue? How long are we ignoring Harlow? Huh? It's been *three* weeks, Alex. Would you mind sharing with me when you're planning on ending this stupid ass tantrum!" She uncrosses her arms and leans forward. "I'm just asking because I would *really* like to put it on my calendar. Maybe even put together a celebration." She pauses. "With a lot of alcohol." After another brief pause she adds, "And strippers."

The stripper comment catches me by surprise, as I'm sure she intended, and a slight smile breaks across my face. I continue looking down, hoping she doesn't notice. My pens are now in groups based on color.

"Alex, seriously. This is ridiculous. Talk to me." I look at her and tilt my head as I raise my left eyebrow at her. I'm so tired of being mad. Knowing I'm about to cave, I attempt to keep my mouth in as straight of a line as possible while speaking. "What would you like to talk about? My celebration? If so, I would like to go on the record as saying that if you're going to have strippers... get that guy Tony... remember? The one from Australia. He was hot!"

I watch her face as relief floods her features. She leans back in the chair. "Alex, I'm really sorry."

Note to Self: Harlow Reed just said she's sorry. Waiting for hell to freeze over.

"You should've told me, Harlow," I say, placing my elbows on my desk and folding my hands underneath my chin.

"I was going to tell you, remember? But I didn't want to upset you before Rylie's big surprise, so I was waiting until after the party. Then I ran into *dickhead* and I decided to go off on him first. In retrospect, I should've probably discussed it with you first." Her mouth moves to the side and looks down at her fingernails as she contemplates. "Yeah, that would've definitely been more advantageous for me in the long run." She nods and continues her murmuring.

"Harlow! Focus!" I shout at her. I have watched her do this before; I could literally be sitting here for *days* watching her go back and forth with herself.

"Oops! Sorry. Anyway...Yes, I should've told you. Honestly, I didn't know there was anything going on. I asked him here to help you as a *friend*. That's all. I was worried about you and nothing I was doing was helping. So I figured maybe there was something *he* could do since you two were so close, for so many years. I never really expected anything to happen romantically. I just said all that stuff early on to aggravate you. Because I happen to find it very entertaining... as if you didn't already know that. I had no idea either one of you had actual *feelings*. Hence my slightly overdramatic reaction to all of this at Rylie's party." She pauses to straighten her skirt.

Her voice softens. "That being said...Trace told me he left. Went back to Colorado." She looks up to eye me closely.

"What?" I clear my throat to try to prevent the Mack Truck from lodging in my throat. I wasn't expecting that. I mean, it's so permanent.

"Yeah. Trace said he left the day after the party." She continues to watch my reaction. I feel moisture starting to gather in my eyes. I have no idea why I'm reacting this way. I know it's over. Maybe I just wasn't expecting him to completely pick up and leave.

I shrug my shoulders. "Well, I hope he made it back safely." I move on to organizing the files on my desk.

"Does that bother you? That he left? Without telling you?" Harlow takes her shoes off and slides both feet up into the chair underneath her bottom, something she does when she is settling in for a long conversation...or a lecture. I would rather the former.

"No... I mean, yeah," I sigh loudly and smack my forehead in frustration. "I don't know. Does it matter?" I open my file drawer to deposit the now alphabetized files.

"I think it does, yes." She shifts a little in her chair. "Do you care about him? *Really* care about him?"

"I don't know. I thought I did. But, he lied to me Harlow. How can I ever trust anything that he says after

261

that?" I close the drawer and slide back in my chair. I watch her twirling the ends of her hair around her finger.

"Alex. You two have a long history together. He knows you. Even better than I do, which is saying something considering you hadn't spoken to him in years before recent events. He knew what your reaction would be to him showing up here to check on you. He also knew he would have absolutely no chance of any type of relationship with you if he stormed in here expecting to carry you away on a white horse. I really don't see that he had any other choice." She hesitates, but continues.

"Look. He said some things to me that will put him on my shit list for a while, but I have to be honest with you. I don't really think he lied to you in order to deceive you. I think he did it to protect you...from yourself. Alex, the man loves you. There's no doubt about it. And whether or not you choose to admit it to yourself, you love him. I see that now." I open my mouth to speak but she holds her finger up in the air, signaling for me to shut it.

"But since we're playing the 'Lying is Unacceptable' game, why don't we both just admit that this has absolutely nothing to do with the lies themselves. I've had time to think about this. And I'm not going to let you do this to yourself. I love you *too* much, so you're going to listen to what I have to say." She moves her feet back to the ground and repositions herself in the chair. I can feel the lecture coming but I have no words to distract her after she called my bluff with her made up lying game. *Damn it.*

"*You* know, deep down, you pushed that man away before he even had a chance. You pounced on the first opportunity you had to do it. And you did it successfully.

Congratulations. Now you're miserable. Are we seeing a correlation here?" I really need to come up with some words...*any second now*...

"I've watched you spiral downward from being the happiest I have seen you in years to absolutely heart-broken. The light in your eyes is gone. I haven't seen you smile in weeks. I know you're sad, Alex, but you don't *have* to be. You're not proving anything to anyone by doing this to yourself, yet you still do it. Is this about Derek? Do you think this is the life Derek wants for you? Do you think he would prefer to see you sad than to see you happy? I don't."

Memories from the day at the park race through my mind. "You're right, Harlow. I've had time to think about what I did to Blake, and you're absolutely right. And you're also right about Derek. He wouldn't want this for me. I know he wouldn't. Like, I *know* he wouldn't." I'm pretty sure that if I tell her about Derek the butterfly, Harlow will have me committed.

"But that doesn't make it easier to take that leap of faith. I know I pushed Blake away, but, the thought of losing him, like I lost Derek...I can't go through that again. Just the thought..." My eyes start to well up with tears. "Harlow, it's too much. I guess I would rather push him away and lose him now, when I'm in control, than later, when I'm not. I'm *scared*, Harlow."

Harlow gives me a sympathetic smile as she delivers a bag of salt to my already exposed wound.

"It's okay to be scared, Alex. There's nothing wrong with that. I was scared to take that jump too. But, someone I love very much once told me something that changed my life. She said, 'You'll never have your happy ending unless you're brave enough to open the book and start your story.'"

She pauses for dramatic effect.

"Are you *brave* enough to start your new story, Alex?" She raises her eyebrows in question.

I continue to hold her stare until I drop my eyes to glance at the drawer containing the note from Blake. When I still say nothing, she continues to use my silence to her advantage and drives her point home.

"That's what I thought." She slaps her hands down on her thighs and sighs loudly. "Well girl...you better put your big girl panties on. Because *your* book is in Colorado."

Jeez – I really hate when Harlow's right.

With no appointments scheduled for the rest of the day, Harlow and I decide to close shop and begin to work on the master plan to get Blake back. I have a feeling getting Blake to forgive me won't be as easy this time around. Let's just hope he hasn't "moved on" in the last three weeks.

Our first stop is her apartment. After a half hour of both of us searching, we find Blake's address that she wrote down on what has to be the smallest piece of paper in the world.

"See, I told you it was in the drawer. You just didn't look hard enough."

"Harlow. Seriously. How do you expect to find anything in here?" I look down at the 'junk drawer' that she keeps. It's ridiculous. Batteries, electrical tape, pens, phone chargers from 3 phones ago, screwdriver, and of course multiple Pez dispensers. *Why not?* I really need to get Nycole over here to help her organize it. There's no telling what hazards are hidden in that drawer. It's a freakin' deathtrap.

"It's a junk drawer. That's its purpose. Come on, let's get going. We need to devise a plan." She throws in an evil laugh and I roll my eyes at her. I'm glad my current situation is providing my best friend with the utmost of entertainment.

On our way, we throw some ideas around before we land on something that actually shows a little promise. After fine tuning the main points of 'Operation: Major Damage Control', we decide we're definitely going to need the girls' help. I call Nancy, letting her know that we'll be picking them up from school today and we race to get them.

The girls make a mad dash to the car when they see Harlow hanging out the window waving.

"What's up, my beauties?" Harlow yells as she opens the door and hops out of the car while it's still moving.

"Harlow! We missed you!" They run straight to her. Lots of hugs and kisses are exchanged. You would think the woman had been gone for *years* the way they were acting.

Once everyone is loaded and all the seatbelts are buckled – including Harlow who always tries to get out of it, we turn the music up in the car and jam out to the radio. Singing songs that might be deemed somewhat inappropriate for younger ears, we all laugh and scream the words as loud as we can in the car.

Finally, we make the turn into the parking lot of Rylie's day care to pick her up.

"Aww! Do we *have* to get her? Can't she just stay at

school?" I watch both of them roll their eyes and let out very dramatic sighs. "You know, she *is* your baby sister. You should be nicer to her. She loves you so much."

Nycole looks at me in the rearview mirror, not pleased. "I know mom, but she only wants to play with what we play with and then whines until she gets her way and we have to give it to her."

I look at Harlow in the passenger seat. "You do realize that's completely *our* fault, right?" I mutter under my breath. She laughs quietly and starts to open the door as I put the car in park. "Yeah, but she's the baby. Isn't that like a rite of passage or something?"

I nod my head. "Exactly. Yes, let's go with that." She laughs out loud and exits the car. I let Harlow go in to get her by herself. I figure it would be a nice surprise for Rylie. Plus, I need the time to discuss things with the older two.

I lower the volume on the radio and turn to face Nycole and Kyndall sitting in their seats. "Girls, we need to talk for a second."

They both look up at me with huge eyes. I know those looks all too well. "No, it's fine. You aren't in trouble." Although now I'm wondering why they automatically assume they were in trouble.

"Listen, I'm sure both of you have noticed that Blake hasn't been around in a while?"

Kyndall raises her hand to speak. My sweet girl. "Yes, Kyndall?" I give Nycole a smirk before turning my attention to her sister.

"Is he coming back, Mama?" I can see hope in her beautiful eyes.

"Well Kyndall, I don't know. I really hope so. But, that's

why Harlow and I picked you up today. We have an idea that we need you to help us with."

"To get Blake back?" Nycole asks sarcastically. "Like that's going to happen. I'm sure you chased him away for good." She turns her head and puts it against the window, watching people pass by.

"Nycole." She doesn't move a muscle. "Nycole!" She continues zoning out. I soften my voice, trying a different tactic. "Nycole. Please look at me, baby."

She glares in my direction. I feel like crawling over the seat to strangle her... but I don't... *obviously.* "Nycole. I know you're upset. Listen to me," I say as she starts to look away. "Nycole." I stay quiet until she turns in my direction. For once, so does Kyndall.

"Listen baby, Blake and I are adults and sometimes adults have bigger problems than you can understand right now. Blake and I have been friends for a long time. Friends sometimes get into fights, just like you do with your sisters. Sometimes things are said that you don't mean and when that happens, you have to apologize and make it right, just like with your sisters. Regardless if Blake accepts my apology or not, I need to tell him I'm sorry because it's the right thing to do. It's just a little more difficult when you're adults, that's all." I watch her to see if anything I just said absorbs into that thick head of hers.

I don't think it does. Why would it? She's had the lecture a million times and still hasn't grasped the concept of a true apology.

She looks me dead in the eyes. "I just don't see why it has to be so difficult. It's not a big secret, even though you think we don't know. It's simple. You love him. He loves

267

you. What's difficult about that? Just fix it and move on. Isn't that what people do when they love each other? Like with my sisters?"

The honesty and simplicity of her statement knock the breath out of me. I have to inhale deeply before I can continue.

"Well, that's what I'm trying to do. To fix it. Which is why I need your help. And that, my dear, is the mission for today...if you choose to accept it." I watch a slight smile appear on her face.

"I accept it, Mama!" Kyndall claps her hands in excitement. I shoot her a huge grin. I fix my eyes back on Nycole.

I soften my tone. "I really need your expertise on my mission. Would you like to help me?" After a few deciding seconds, she accepts with a gentle dip of her head.

"Okay," I answer her turning around just in time to see Harlow exiting the doors with Rylie on her back. Nycole's words are still buzzing in my head. "Then let 'Operation: Alex Was an Idiot' commence," I mutter to myself.

I hear a soft snicker from behind me. I look at Nycole in the mirror. She gives me the thumbs up sign. I smile back at her, but honestly, I'm not sure if she is telling me I'm an idiot or simply saying she's on board.

Harlow opens the door, places Rylie in her seat in the far back – since girls called "seat check" on the captain's seats, and sits down beside her after finally buckling her in. Going through her art folder, they both giggle at her work.

"That is *not* a cow, Rylie!" Harlow laughs. "That looks like a pancake with mold on it!"

"Yes it is, Hah-low! I'm not playing with you anymore.

You cheat!" I can tell Rylie isn't really mad because she's smiling as she turns her face opposite Harlow's.

"Okay – You're right Rylie, it's a cow." She looks at Kyndall who's been watching their exchange and slowly shakes her head, indicating otherwise. Kyndall puts her hand over her mouth and turns back towards the window.

Rylie holds the picture in front of Harlow's face. "You know what this is Hah-low?"

"A cow?"

Rylie giggles. "No silly, it's a pancake with mold!"

"You're impossible!" Harlow tickles Rylie in the tummy. "It's a good thing you're so darn cute or I would throw you out the window!"

"Haaaah-low… no you wouldn't."

With everyone laughing, I shift the car into drive. I find myself tuning them out as I think about Blake leaving. I know he had every right to leave. He waited so long to be honest with me about his feelings, and the first chance I had, I said things I honestly didn't even believe, just to push him away. He told me once how he respected my strength, but in that moment, I was nothing but a coward. I wouldn't blame him if he didn't forgive me. But… I have to try. I have to know that I did everything I could to get him back. And, just like he did with me, I'll lay it all out there for *him* to make the decision.

It seems the tables have officially been turned.

CHAPTER NINETEEN

Using her voucher, Harlow books the red eye from Dallas/Fort Worth International to Denver International Airport, which doesn't leave us a whole lot of time since Dallas is only about an hour and a half from Waco. Denver is the best option because Blake lives in Aurora, which is only twenty minutes away. I plan on taking a cab to his house, and I pray things go well...because that's about as far as I've planned in advance. With my knack of thinking things to death, I figure it's better to leave this one to chance. I can always spend the night in the airport if I need to. The key will be finding a cab that late at night.

Ahhh... Stop thinking Alex!

While Nycole is putting the final touches on our plan, I throw some extra clothes in a bag. I pack the essentials...toothbrush. Yep, that's it. I throw a little makeup on so I don't look like the walking dead when I make my psychotic stalker grand entrance at his house around midnight.

What if he has someone there? Taking a seat on the bed, I suddenly feel like I'm going to throw up beef and broccoli all over my comforter. Oh.My.God. What if he does?

Note to Self: No more beef and broccoli take-out during possible life changing ploys.

"Stop thinking, Alex." Harlow whips into the room, grabs my bag off the floor, and chunks it in my lap. *Not helping with the nausea.* "You need to go, you're barely gonna make it as is. You have almost a two hour drive and check in. Get off your ass and in your truck now!"

"Harlow – what if he has someone there... you know... like *there*, there." The nausea is slowly creeping into my throat.

"Stop it! Not going to happen. He loves you, Alex. Stop trying to talk yourself out of it. Check in with Nycole, make sure it's done, and get going. You're going to miss your chance and I'm gonna be pissed if I lose my voucher because of this. It isn't often that I find myself being charitable... don't make me regret it! Now go!"

She is kind of starting to scare me with her yelling, so I snatch the bag and throw it over my shoulder. "Alright! I'm going!"

I walk into the living room and Nycole shows me the finished product. I clasp my hands together, "Nycole, it's perfect!" I place it in my bag and give her a hug. "I love you, Nycole. I couldn't have done this without you. But remember, if it doesn't go well, this is about doing the right thing. Not about bringing him back, okay?"

She unwraps her arms from my around my neck and puts her hands on her hips. "It's going to be fine, mom. Like I said, he loves you and you love him. Everything will be fine.

And if not, it wasn't meant to be." *Jeez* – this kid and her infinite wisdom. *She totally gets it from me.*

I give her a quick kiss on the forehead. "Thank you. I love you, baby."

"Love you too, Mom. You better get going or Harlow is *really* going to start yelling. Or have a heart attack." I can't help but laugh. She's completely right.

"Kyndall! Rylie! Mommy's leaving and I need some hugs!"

I hear a bedroom door slam then their loud footsteps as they run down the hall. I watch Rylie's eyes light up with excitement as she enters the room.

"Do you think he'll like his present, Mommy?" I bend down and scoop her into my arms. "Of course he will baby. You helped make it. He'll love it!"

She gives me a big grin and all I can see are the divots in her cheeks where her dimples are. I push her curly hair away from her face. Strands of it stick to her mouth from the ice cream she ate earlier. Licking my thumb, I wipe the remainder of the chocolate off her face. "I love you, you messy little thing!"

Giggling she shouts, "Love you too, Mommy!" I set her down and watch her and her hair run wildly around the living room. Turning to Kyndall, I pull her close to my side.

"I'm going to miss you, Mama." I can tell she's a little worried about me leaving. I crouch down and stroke her cheek. "I'm gonna miss you too, sweetheart. But, I'll be back before you know it. I promise." I kiss her forehead and put my hand on her shoulder. "I need you to help Harlow with Rylie tonight. She's acting like a crazy person. Just look at her."

We both watch Rylie take her shirt off and swing it around over her head. Kyndall looks at me, eyes wide. "See, Kyndall. She's nuts." Kyndall giggles and I give her another quick squeeze. "Can you help with her, because Harlow's kinda going crazy tonight and I don't think she can handle much more of naked Rylie." Right on cue, Harlow yells from my bedroom, "Go! You're going to be late!" I roll my eyes and turn back to Kyndall. "I love you, baby. I'll be back soon." I get up and kiss the top of her head.

"Alright, Harlow! I'm out!" Harlow comes out of the bedroom. She hooks her arm in mine and walks with me to the door with all three girls following closely behind. I turn to her and give her a tight hug.

"I've got this, Alex. Don't worry. Nancy already told me she would swing by in the morning. We'll take the kids and she'll drop me off at work. We've got everything covered. Just go to him, sweetie. This is your second chance; don't waste it."

I pull back from our embrace. "I love you, Harlow. Thank you. For everything. I owe you so much, more than you can possibly imagine." Harlow gives me a quick wink. "Don't worry, I'm keeping a tab."

I give her another quick hug and whisper in her ear, "Oh – and no sleepovers with Trace... *whore*." She laughs and then releases her arms from around my shoulders.

Looking down at the girls, she instructs, "Tell Mommy goodbye and good luck."

"Goodbye!"

"Good luck!"

"We'll miss you!"

I lift my bag up onto my shoulder. "I love you *all*. I'll

see you soon, okay?"

I turn and walk to my car; the door shuts softly behind me. I hear the girls giggle loudly, scream, and then run. Yeah, I don't think they'll miss me *too* much.

Throwing my bag in the passenger's seat, I exhale a cleansing breath. I can do this. I have to do this. I *will* do this.

I've already lost one good man during my lifetime. I'll be damned if I'm going to lose another one.

After the two hour flight that seemed to land way too quickly, I find myself hailing a cab in the front of the airport. My nerves are at an all time high. While waiting for the cab, and holding the world's smallest, now crumpled up, piece of paper with Blake's address, I can't stop tapping my foot. The same damn foot that started tapping when I boarded the plane and the realization hit me that I passed the point of no return.

I think my shin is cramping.

A cab finally decides to stop for me and I climb in, handing him the paper. I close the door and rehearse the speech in my head. I decide to stop going over it when the cabbie looks at me in the mirror like I'm crazy. I guess mouthing it while rehearsing isn't such a good idea. I remain quiet the rest of the ride.

Soon after, the cab begins to slow, and I take my first look at Blake Morgan's home. It's actually really cute. It's in a nice suburban neighborhood and has red brick with white siding. There's a big oak tree in the front and I notice the lawn's well kept...he must have a regular crew considering how long he was in Texas.

Looking down at my watch, I cringe.

12:37 AM. Alex Meyer. *Psycho Stalker.*

Oh well...here goes nothing.

I tip toe as I walk onto the porch. I'm not really sure why, since I'm about to wake him. I guess it's a habit I developed from toilet papering Ashley Thompson's house with Harlow. I wipe the sweat from my palms on my pants and raise my fist to knock on the door. Taking in a final deep breath, I say a little prayer and knock quickly. *This whole situation seems very familiar.*

I wait for a couple of seconds. Nothing. I knock again and wait. Still nothing. I lean over to look in his driveway. His bike is parked by the garage. Getting frustrated, and cold – I dressed for Texas weather, *dumb* – I ring the doorbell the same way Rylie would, at least twenty times in a row.

I cover my mouth in nervous excitement when I hear Blake stomping down what sounds like stairs and approaching the door. The porch light comes on momentarily blinding me. I think quick and cover the peep hole with my finger. Which is pointless, because I soon see Blake move the curtains aside on his front window. I give him a hesitant wave.

"Alex?" I can hear the aggravation in the tone of his voice. *I guess this is a bad time to start having second thoughts?* "What in the hell are you doing here?"

Here we go.

"Freezing my ass off. Let me in, Blake. I need to talk to

you." I start jumping around in place to keep warm. I hear the locks turning and then he cracks open the door.

"Go back home, Alex. I'm done. I can't do this anymore. I'm sorry you came all the way here for nothing. But I have nothing else to say to you. I've moved on…just like I said I would. You've made your decision. Now please, go."

Ouch. That was a little rougher than what I expected.

"Really, Blake? Where am I going to go? Seriously, let me in." Before he can refuse, I push my body up against the door, once again placing my foot in the doorjamb to keep him from being able to close it. I take both hands and push them through the crack of the door, making sure to keep one set of my fingers extended while the other wraps around the side. "My fingers are in the door, Blake! Just letting you know so we can avoid any unnecessary injuries! It would be really shitty for you to break my hand again!" Even pushing with all my strength the door doesn't budge. "Just open the damn door!" I give it one last push and the door flies open.

I immediately fall forward and almost land on the floor when I feel Blake's arms wrap around my waist from behind to keep me from falling. As he pulls me up, I can feel the current flowing between our bodies. I sink into him without realizing it. The only reason I know is because as soon as he sets me back on my feet, he steps away and the weight I was putting on him causes me to stumble back a bit. I correct my balance and turn to look at him.

"*Necessary?* Do we have to do this *every* time? All I'm asking for is five minutes of your time then I'm gone. That's it." I watch as he shuts the door. He turns back to me. "Clock's ticking, Alex."

Oh, the pressure.

"Well, I was planning on longer than five minutes actually, so I'll have to give you the shortened version I guess. It's not the one I rehearsed on the way over here so bear with me." Nervous rambling. *Nice.*

Obviously annoyed, he crosses his arms over his chest and shifts his weight to his other leg.

"Okay, so, I came here to tell you I'm sorry. For everything. I never really gave you an honest chance. I know that now. I think in the back of my mind, I was waiting for something to happen so I could push you away. It just happened sooner than later. And I'm sorry for that."

He doesn't say anything so I continue.

"Blake, you deserve so much better than me. The way I treated you in the past, up until how I treated you a couple of weeks ago...I'll understand if you choose to *move on* after this conversation, but I need you to know something before you do. I need you to know that you make me feel whole. Before you came back, I was empty. Completely empty. I thought I could live like that but I was wrong. You have given me hope that I can be happy again. That I can love again. That I can feel again. The warmth I feel when I'm around you...it soothes my soul. You have given me life again. Your love fills my heart with such joy; I can't even put it into words."

I take a step forward to gauge his reaction. He steps back. *Okay – more convincing needed.*

"I love you, Blake. I love you and I don't want to lose you. So I had to come here and fight for what I love. I want you. I want you in my life every day. I want to kiss you every day. I want to fall in love with you, over and over, every day. I want to live the rest of my life showing you how grateful I am that you saved me. You saved me from allowing myself to live a life with no emotion. No happiness. And I'll live everyday in debt to you for that. So if you don't choose me, I get it. I understand. But I had to come here and tell you face to face that I love you. And that I don't mind *needing your help* for the rest of my life." I say the last sentence with a smile.

When I finish my speech, I take a step backwards. I take off my jacket to show him the last ditch effort to get him back. I chuckle to myself, watching the glitter as it falls onto the floor. Nycole loves her glitter.

"The girls and I made you something and I would like you to see it before you make your decision. It's no G.I. Joe replacement, but hopefully it will do." With my back to the door, I let him read the front of the t-shirt we crafted.

Top 10 Reasons We Need Blake Morgan:

"I'm going to turn around and let you read why we need you in our lives. If you still feel that you want to move on, I'll understand. I'll walk out this door and you won't see me ever again. I'll go willingly, knowing that I gave everything I had to get you back. So when you've finished reading, I need you to tell me whether to stay or go. I won't be looking at you so it will be easier for you if you need me to leave."

I let my eyes graze his handsome face for a few seconds. Once I've burned his image into my brain, I turn slowly and allow him to read.

10. He pushes me high like a collar roaster. – Rylie
9. He's super tall. He can get candy off the candy shelf. –

Nycole, Kyndall, Rylie
8. He has big muscles like Superman. He can protect us forever. – Kyndall
7. He makes Mom smile. – Nycole, Alex
6. He gives really good hugs. – Alex, Nycole, Kyndall, Rylie
5. He gives really good presents. – Alex, Rylie
4. He's willing to watch Barney so I don't have to. –Nycole
3. He takes really good care of Mom when she's hurt. – Nycole, Alex
2. Sunday Breakfast Dates!!!! – Alex, Nycole, Kyndall, Rylie
and
1. He reminds me every day that when you're running on empty, you won't ever get where you need to be. Both in Life and Love. (And sometimes Suburbans...) – Alex

I remain facing forward for a few minutes letting him take his time to read all the work that the girls and I put into this t-shirt. My heart's pounding so hard I'm worried I might actually pass out.

I wait.

And wait.

And wait.

Finally, when he doesn't say anything, all hope leaves my heart. *I've lost him.*

I wait a little longer... nothing.

Still facing the door, I ask him, "Well...what do you think?"

He says nothing, but I can hear his bare feet crossing the floor. Then, I feel him standing directly behind me. The warmth of his body behind mine.

"What do I think?" I wait for another couple of seconds. I almost start to take a step towards the door, when his hand runs all the way up the words on my back. Then he slowly makes his way to my hair and moves it aside.

"I think…"

He slowly places feather light kisses all the way up my neck. My body reacts instantly.

"I think you look good, wearing my future."

I smile to myself, immediately recognizing the quote. I half expect my children to show up, disappointed that they didn't keep me from hearing it, but I must say that nothing will ever compare to hearing it come out of Blake Morgan's mouth. I think he might have actually ruined all of my future viewings of that movie, or just guaranteed that it will forever be my favorite part of any movie.

Ever.

I let out a relieved sigh. I turn to him with tears in my eyes and put my arms around his neck. It might not be the best time, but I take a few seconds to gloat.

"I *told* you that's the best line ever and that you might need it one day!" I giggle upon my realization. "I guess that makes me the woman of your dreams." He nods at me. I watch the corners of his mouth turn up into a sexy smile and I notice the small crinkles around the sides of his eyes. God, I love his eyes.

His words start to settle in my head. "Blake, are you *sure* you want this future?"

He leans and barely touches my lips with his. "I've *always* wanted this future. I was just waiting on *you* to catch up." I wrap my arms around his neck and squeeze him tight.

I now understand how truly empty my heart had become.

Because right now, in this very moment, my heart is completely filled with my love for this man.

And with that knowledge, I find the courage to open my book and start my second story.

Knowing that I've finally found my happy ending.

ACKNOWLEDGMENTS

This book exists because of some pretty great people. I would like to take some time to say a much needed "Thank You" to those who were involved in helping me get my story onto paper.

First and foremost, my husband Dustin – Thank you for believing in me. You have been there every step of the way and I owe you everything. Without you, I wouldn't have had the courage to keep writing. Your support, your opinions, your advice…well, I couldn't have done it without you by my side. Thank you from the bottom of my heart. I love you.

Megan, Janie, Alison, and Jena – You have all been *my* Harlow at some point in my life. Thank you for being there for me no matter what craziness was going on in my life. Girls' nights out, "Danceparty" at my house, shoulders to cry on, and lots and lots of laughing. These are all things I think about when I think out you. I love each of you dearly. Thank you for showing me the meaning of *true* friendship.

Jena – A special thank you is needed just for you. Thank you for listening to me talk, and talk, and plan, and talk, and deliberate, and talk about this book. You're support amazes me. You are my rock. I owe you more than you could possibly imagine.

Amy Burt, Deana Wolstenholme, Jonda Liles, and Jillian Dodd – Thank you for reading my baby and giving it such high praise. I would not have taken the steps to publish if it hadn't been your belief in my story. Thank you for taking the time to read it and giving me your feedback. Your suggestions helped make my story even better.

Sarah Hansen – Thank you for creating such a beautiful cover. It's absolutely perfect. You looked at each of my million ideas, found the perfect one, and just ran with it. You're a freaking genius. I can't thank you enough for giving me something that represents my book perfectly. You are so talented my friend, in more ways than one. And I am so lucky to have met you.

Jennifer Roberts-Hall – Wow. There is so much I have to say to you, it would be a completely separate book on its own. Thank you. Thank you for not only doing a beautiful job editing my book, but also for taking the time to love my characters as much as I do. Thank you for your never ending patience…You are a saint. Regardless of how many times I wrote you with random questions, told you to stop editing because I made revisions…again, called you when I needed guidance – you were always there for me. Always. And I love you so much for that. I am so glad we met and I am so lucky to have you in my life.

Gail Marino-McHugh – There are just some people you meet in your lifetime that you know you are destined to meet. Those people that you know as soon as you meet them, you have created a lifelong friend. You are one of those people for me. Thank you so much for making me laugh, believing in me, the continuous support, and just being my friend. I love you.

And to my readers – Thank you for taking your time to read my story. I hope you love their journey as much as I loved writing it. And I hope each of you can take something from it. Thank you from the bottom of my heart for your support and believing in this book.

ABOUT THE AUTHOR

L.B. Simmons is a graduate of Texas A&M University and holds a degree in Biomedical Science. She has been a practicing Chemist for the last 11 years. She lives with her husband and three daughters in Texas and writes every chance she gets.

Learn more about L.B. Simmons and her books at:

Facebook – www.facebook.com/lbsimmonsauthor

Blog – www.lbsimmons.wordpress.com

Twitter – www.twitter.com/lbsimmons33

Email – lbsimmons33@gmail.com

3896870R00162

Printed in Great Britain
by Amazon.co.uk, Ltd.,
Marston Gate.